BRINDLE

BOOKS

http://www.brindlebooks.co.uk

WELLINGTON'S DRAGOON 3:

BEHIND THE LINES

BY

DAVID J. BLACKMORE

Brindle Books Ltd

Copyright © 2023 by David J Blackmore

This edition published by
Brindle Books Ltd
Unit 3, Grange House
Grange Street
Wakefield
United Kingdom
WF2 8TF
Copyright © Brindle Books Ltd 2023

Acknowledgements

The ongoing encouragement, enthusiasm and support of friends has been invaluable in keeping me going. It is surprisingly hard work at times, producing 83,000 words or so that are both entertaining and avoid any historical anachronisms. Gillian Caldicott has hung in there as my primary proof reader and spotter of inconsistencies. Janet McKay continues to make useful suggestions and keep my feet on the ground. The local writing group continues to stimulate and challenge. Others who have helped me include Neil Hinchliffe, Mark Atkinson, the owner of the incomparable Johnny, B Troop, 16th Light Dragoons and Gabby Monet who provided the image on the back cover.

Michael Crumplin FRCS, has been of great help on the matter of wounds, their treatment and recovery times. I have also found very helpful his books on medical matters during the Napoleonic Wars. Any medical related errors are mine.

A number of historians have helped me to get events in the correct order and to describe them. These include Sir Charles Oman, whose monumental work A History of the Peninsular War has been constantly referred to. Even more vital have been the diary of William Tomkinson and the published selection of material written by Charles Cocks, both of the 16th Light Dragoons.

Finally, once more, my thanks are due to my publisher, Richard Hinchliffe of Brindle Books and Emma Garbett for her work on photos and covers. .

Introduction

"Behind the Lines" is the third book in the "Wellington's Dragoon" series. It continues the adventures of Michael Roberts of the Sixteenth Light Dragoons during the war against Napoleon. It brings to a close what I have found myself referring to as the Portuguese Trilogy, as the first three books of the series ends cover the campaigns that led to the final expulsion of the French from Portugal. This one deals with events occurring when the Anglo-Portuguese army retreated to safety behind the Lines of Torres Vedras, the long hard winter suffered by the French outside the lines and the subsequent retreat of the French into Spain pursued by the allied army. It takes the reader from the Battle of Buçaco to the Battle of Fuentes d'Onoro. Michael's part in all of that is both with the Regiment in action, but also, once again, dealing with espionage matters for Viscount Wellington.

Oh, and there's a young Portuguese woman as well.

Michael's part is, of course, fictional, but the events surrounding his adventures are very much the history of the war, including Wellington's unhappiness with the communications that went on between individuals in Lisbon and the French. The actions the Sixteenth takes part in are also real events, as are many of the characters in the Regiment and the army.

Michael's Welsh batman, Emyr Lloyd is a fictional character, the Welsh phrases that pepper his speech are not. To help, 'chwarae teg' means fair play, 'diolch yn fawr' is thank you very much, frequently shortened to just 'diolch'. Other phrases you can guess at from the context.

Chapter 1

Lieutenant Michael Roberts, of His Majesty's 16th Light Dragoons, rode listlessly along the dusty road from Lisbon to Belem, where the Royal Palace now housed the main depot of the British army in Portugal. He was not a happy man. The last few days had been one, long, tedious anti-climax. A week ago he had killed a man, Jean Paul Renard, a French spy, but also so much more than that. By killing him, Michael had kept the secret of the massive lines of fortification being built from the Tagus to the Atlantic. Lines that Viscount Wellington intended to use to stop the French seizing Lisbon and thus taking control of Portugal. It was a vital part of the plan that the French should know nothing of them until they ran into them.

Just as important, at least to Michael, was that by killing Renard he had avenged the murder of the woman he loved, Lady Elaine Travers. They had met in London, when Michael had foiled an assassination attempt on the Duke of York, the Commander-in-Chief of the army. At the same time Michael had become embroiled in the secret counter-intelligence war against the French, recruited by Thomas Musgrave of the Aliens Office. Elaine had been one of Musgrave's agents. They had fallen deeply in love, a love they had kept from each other until Elaine lay dying, shot down by Renard. She had left him a letter, telling him of her love, telling him that, as she had discovered, love could come more than once, and that she freed him from any bonds he might feel, so that he might find love again. But he still loved her, still felt bound to her, to her memory. At times, far away in Portugal, Michael could almost believe she was waiting for him in her little house in Covent Garden.

For a week now, Michael had been left in a state of limbo, his job of keeping the secret of the lines was done, Renard was dead, and Elaine was avenged, but, to his bewilderment, he took little satisfaction from that. She was still dead, lost to him. That had not changed, and he felt dissatisfied, strangely empty, flat. His birthday passed, almost unremarked. Senhora Santiago, his Baba, remembered, of course, and gave him a splendid dinner. Roberta, his long time friend, lover, and Portuguese agent, had joined him, and stayed with him that night. It lifted his spirits for a day or two, but there seemed to be nothing left for him to do. He wanted to get back to his Regiment, back to his friends, van Hagen, Alexander, and all the others, but without orders he was trapped in Lisbon while the Regiment fought the French. He was not a happy man.

At Belem Michael sought out General Peacocke, in command of the depot. Peacocke had never been quite sure what to make of Michael and his rather vague orders from Murray, the Quartermaster General. There was something about the young man that he found slightly disturbing, particularly this last week. If pressed, the best he would have been able to say was that "He's a pleasant enough fellow, but there's a hardness about him, and, well, I wouldn't care to cross him." Today, he had news for Michael.

"Ah, Lieutenant Roberts, we have orders for you, came in yesterday. From Colonel Murray himself, no less."

Eagerly, Michael read his new orders, and almost cheered out loud. He was to rejoin the army at once, and report directly to Colonel Murray on his arrival. Thanking a startled General Peacocke profusely, Michael rushed out and rode hard back to Lisbon and his home, the splendid house where he had been born. Within an hour all was hustle and bustle as preparations got under way to travel north. His Portuguese groom, Parra, prepared the horses and baggage mules. Emyr Lloyd, his dragoon servant, packed his trunks and canteen, and put an edge on Michael's sabre. He sent Francisco, his young Portuguese servant, to Roberta, with a note, giving her the news and inviting her to dinner that evening. Senhora Santiago flapped about in the kitchen preparing a meal that she considered worthy, her husband helping Parra. Everyone knew what needed to be done, they had done it many times, and in many different places, grand palaces, peasant hovels, and open fields. Then, all at the same time, the preparations were finished, dinner was ready, and Roberta arrived.

After dinner, Michael and Roberta sat companionably, the dining room lit by two candelabra and the flickering fire. Roberta was feeling relieved. She had been worried about Michael, he had been strangely detached since he had killed Renard, but now his old enthusiasm had returned with the prospect of getting back to his regiment and proper soldiering as he called it. When he had said as much, teasingly, she had teased him back.

"Oh, so what we have done together against the French counts for nothing?"

He laughed. "Touché! You know very well that I am happy to do whatever helps to beat Buonaparte, even out of uniform and in the back streets of Lisbon. It's all part of the war."

Roberta smiled, Michel hadn't laughed much this last week, and said, "And it was her war as well." She didn't need a name.

"It was," Michael replied, "and it is yours," he smiled, "and that makes it good enough for me."

Michael's smile disappeared, and he stared thoughtfully into the firelight. Roberta waited. "I suppose that with Renard dead, I have to remember why I joined the army in the first place. To fight the French, to avenge my parents, to do something useful with my life." He gave a little, ironic laugh. "That should be enough for any man, don't you think?" Roberta reached out and took his hand.

Michael gave hers a gentle squeeze and looked into her eyes. "But, somehow, I don't think I have finished with the intelligence war. I seem to have a knack for it, and there are those who will use me for that."

For a moment Roberta saw what Peacocke had seen. A cold, hard resolve. Then it was gone as he laughed himself back into the warmth of the room and Roberta's company. "Enough of that!" He stood, still holding her hand, took her other hand, and raised her from her chair. "Tomorrow I return to the Regiment, to the beck and call of duty, but, tonight, I am all yours."

They breakfasted together before dawn. Michael in his old dolman, with its yards of silver braid and dozens of buttons, and overalls, ready for the road, Roberta in a banyan that she now left at Michael's. Senhora Santiago fussed over them both, and then left them. There was little said, it had all been said. Then came the thud of boots on the stairs, and Lloyd appeared.

"Begging your pardon, sir, but everything's ready."

"Thank you, Lloyd, I shall be down immediately."

Lloyd disappeared, and they heard him thudding away down the stairs.

"Go, now, Michael," Roberta gave him a wan smile, and they both stood. For a moment Michael held her close, then turned and left. She watched from a window as Michael left the back of the house and walked briskly down to the stables. She hoped fervently for his safe return. She hoped he would finally be able to reconcile himself to the loss of Elaine, and open himself to the possibility of finding true love again. She knew it wouldn't be her, she didn't mind, their friendship was a different type of love. She sighed, and turned away.

Michael was eager to get back to the Regiment, but not so eager as to push the horses too hard, never mind Fred the pony, with his servant Francisco riding him, and the two baggage mules. Parra, his groom rode Harry while Michael alternated riding his two horses, Johnny and Duke. Lloyd alternated between his official troop horse, Edward, and his unofficial mount Rodrigo, taken from a French officer when they had broken out of the besieged Ciudad Rodrigo with Don Julian Sanchez and his lancers.

Three days steady riding took them to Coimbra. It occurred to Michael that he could go and see if there was any news of Sofia, but he decided against it. It was nine months ago that they had parted, amicably, knowing they were merely passers-by giving each other a little love and comfort while they could. The last couple of times he had been in Coimbra he had gone looking for her, in vain. He smiled ruefully to himself, and consigned her to his past. He wondered if he would ever be able to do that with Elaine.

In Coimbra he learned that the army was somewhere to the north, falling back before Massena's French Army. At first light they pushed on, and a passing commissary officer told him that Anson's Brigade, made up of the Sixteenth and the 1st King's German Legion Hussars, were north of Mealhada somewhere, but that the Regiment's baggage should be in Mealhada itself.

Arriving in the small village, Michael found the baggage and Harrison, the Quartermaster. He was the only officer there, assisted by a couple of mounted sergeants and the dismounted men of the regiment. With the regimental mules, officer's baggage animals, spare horses, numerous servants and the thirty or so wives following their men, it all made for a scene of confusion.

"Roberts, it's good to see you!" Harrison looked harassed.

"And you, Harrison, what's going on?"

"Wellington has the army up on that ridge," he pointed away to the east and a distant, long crest running north south. "But there's no room on it for cavalry, so we are all down here. Are you here to rejoin the regiment?"

"No, I'm afraid not," Harrison's face fell, "not yet, anyway, I have to report to Colonel Murray. Do you know where I might find him?"

"Wellington's headquarters, I expect. He's set up in a convent towards the north end of the ridge. If you ride due east, the road will bring you straight to it."

"Thank you, and where's the Regiment?"

"Anson has the whole brigade together, somewhere between here and the ridge. All the cavalry brigades are there, all together. By the bye, Roberts, I see you and Lloyd have new tarletons? That would account for the shortage in the shipment."

"Ah, yes," Michael grinned, "sorry about that." Harrison merely gave a thin smile that belied the smile in his eyes. "If it's alright," Michael went on, "I think I'll leave my baggage here, with you. I hope that Murray will send me back to the regiment, and Lloyd and I can manage for a few days."

"Yes, by all means." Harrison glanced at Lloyd. "Err, that's not Lloyd's troop horse, is it?" Lloyd, sitting comfortably on Rodrigo, looked away.

"No," Michael confessed, "it's mine, I put Lloyd on it to spare his horse," Michael lied. "And if I am on staff duties it means he can keep up with me better," he said, honestly.

"Hmph, it's a good thing Stanhope isn't here anymore, he would have a fit. I doubt Archer will care, just be glad to see two more sabres. You had best get along now, and I hope to see you back with us soon."

Michael and Lloyd set off, riding east, leaving Parra and Francisco, who were happy to get reacquainted with their friends amongst the servants. Michael thought that it was indeed a good thing that Major Stanhope had gone home. He had definite ideas on the background that made a suitable officer, and Michael's didn't qualify. He didn't like the way Michael was repeatedly called upon to act in intelligence matters. There had been friction, but now, to relief of everyone, he was gone. Stanhope might have been an excellent field officer, but Major Archer, who now commanded the regiment, was much more sympathetic.

Not far beyond Mealhada they found the Regiment, the brigade, and the other two cavalry brigades. It was an impressive sight. The six regiments in all, some two and a half thousand men and horses, were formed in three successive lines, each over a quarter of a mile long, and facing east. They were all dismounted, the men sitting at ease on the ground, reins in hand. Michael and Lloyd passed by De Grey's brigade of heavy cavalry, and then Slade's mixed brigade of heavy and light dragoons. Forming the front line they found Anson's brigade, the Hussars closest to the road, the Sixteenth further away. Michael turned Duke off the road towards the brigade.

"We had better pay our compliments, Lloyd. Let Major Archer know what we are doing."

In front of the brigade Michael could see General Anson, accompanied by Major Archer, Colonel Arenschildt of the German Hussars, and Captain Pelly of the Sixteenth, who was Anson's aide de camp. Michael rode across to them, Lloyd trying to hang back, and saluted. Archer returned his salute, and spoke.

"Mister Roberts, good to see you, rejoining us, I hope?"

"I'm afraid not, sir." Michael saw Anson turn to watch the exchange. "I wish I was, but I have orders to report to Colonel Murray."

"Damn it, we could do with you, Roberts, officers are getting a little thin on the ground. Ashworth is very short, Captain Lygon has gone home to recover from his wound, and Keating was wounded yesterday, nothing too serious, but he's struggling."

"I'm sorry, sir, but I will try to get back as soon as I can."

"Aye, well, can't be helped, I suppose." He looked past Michael. "We could do with Lloyd's sabre as well." He paused. "What is Lloyd riding?"

"One of my horses, sir, his was struggling a little with the long ride here."

"Hmm. Very generous of you. Now get along, and find Murray."

Leaving the brigade behind Michael and Lloyd carried on riding east, and before long the heights of a great long ridge began to appear above the trees, and the road began to climb, gently at first, and then more steeply. They were frequently forced off the road by commissary carts and ammunition wagons moving in both directions, there were wounded men heading for the rear and treatment, some walking, some in carts, crying out as the carts jolted down the slope. As they neared the top of the ridge they came across a brigade of Portuguese infantry in their dark blue uniforms, formed on the road in column. They passed along the left flank of the infantry, on the right was a high stone wall with a thick looking wood behind it. In front of the Portuguese were units of Crauford's Light Division, who they recognised from their time together around Gallegos. The wall continued, turning away from the road to run along the crest of the ridge. Outside the wall, the ground was open, bare, scrubby and rocky. They turned off the road to follow the wall along, passing behind the line of the Light Division.

An outbreak of musketry and cannon fire caused both men to jerk their heads round to look eastwards.

"Duw, will you look at that." Lloyd exclaimed, softly.

Michael had been looking ahead, keeping an eye out for Murray, now he uttered a heartfelt "Damn me!" Both men reined in and stared. Below and across the valley were the massed ranks of the French army, infantry, cavalry, artillery, stretching into the distance, where the dark mass of a huge baggage train could just be seen, The French spread out to either side of the road towards the ridge. Small clouds of smoke showed where skirmishers were already in action. Intermittently an artillery piece roared, a sudden billowing of smoke followed seconds later by the distant thunder clap of the discharge.

Turning back to look along the ridge, Michael caught sight of a group of horsemen some two hundred yards away, some with telescopes trained in the direction of the French. "Come on, Lloyd, that looks like a covey of staff officers if ever I saw one."

The group were just outside a gateway in the wall, which, presumably, gave access to the convent. As Michael approached he could see that it was Wellington and a group of senior officers and staff, including Murray, and Michael halted Duke a few yards away, waiting his chance to speak to Murray. To his consternation Wellington caught sight of him, spoke to the group around him, and with only Murray for company, rode across to Michael. The abandoned group looked at Michael with considerable curiosity as he gave Wellington his best salute.

"So, Roberts, I gather you accounted for your fox?"

"Yes, my Lord, I did."

"And did he get word out about the lines?"

"Only those about Lisbon, my Lord, and the fort at Sao Juliao, he was looking at the lines when I, err, accounted for him."

"Excellent. Good work, Mister Roberts. I'm grateful to you, sir, again. And, now, I have a battle to fight. Murray, if you have no further use for Mister Roberts, I expect his regiment will be glad to have him back."

"No, my Lord, there is nothing to detain him here."

"Very good, off you go, Roberts." And with that Wellington turned and rode back to the group of officers, followed by Murray. Michael turned his eyes across to the east, across the valley at the French army. He sensed Lloyd ride up alongside him.

"Lloyd, I think it's time to find the regiment."

As they turned to ride back the way they had come, they heard sporadic musketry fire break out as the French light infantry continued to probe the position on the ridge.

The brigade was still standing quietly in fields south of the road from Buçaco to Mealhada. The only change was that Anson, Archer, and the others were now dismounted as well, and were sitting on the ground making the most of cold rations. Michael dismounted short of the group and led Duke the rest of the way. Trying to address both Anson and Archer, he saluted and said, "Reporting for duty, sir."

Anson merely nodded, but Archer replied with, "Excellent news, Mister Roberts, I am sure Captain Ashworth will be delighted to have you back, get along now, but come and see me once we bivouac for the night."

"Yes, sir."

Ashworth was sitting alone on the ground at the head of his squadron, but got to his feet to return Michael's salute. "Damn glad to see you, Mister Roberts, damn glad. Captain Lygon has gone home while you have been in Lisbon, van Hagen and Alexander are managing his troop. You can take command of my troop; I have been trying to run the troop and the squadron. You've only got Sawyer, and young Keating, and Keating is carrying a nasty cut to his thigh, and another across his arm, I'm afraid. Should have kept his arm straight. Fortunately, Sar'nt Major Flynn has managed things well."

"Thank you ,sir, but what about Sawyer?"

"You're the senior."

"Yes, sir, but only by two months."

"Roberts, one day would be sufficient." An irritated tone crept into Ashworth's voice, then he looked away from Michael towards the distant ridge, and dropped his voice a little. "I trust your business in Lisbon was satisfactorily concluded?"

"Yes, sir."

Ashworth glanced at him. "Glad to hear it, and I am glad to have you back. You will do a good job with the troop. Now, tell me, what is Lloyd riding, and where is his troop horse?"

Throughout the rest of the day the sound of sporadic musketry interspersed with cannon fire reached Michael where he sat on the ground, Duke's reins in his hand. George Keating lay nearby, snoring gently. Sawyer had seemed frankly relieved to see responsibility for the troop descend on Michael, and was a little way off, talking to Will Alexander and Henry van Hagen. He looked briefly over the troop, saw Sergeant Taylor looking at Lloyd and Rodrigo, and shaking his head. The whole brigade had been dismounted and were resting quietly in the fading heat of the day. No orders had come. The sounds of fighting were not those of a pitched battle.

Late in the afternoon the sounds of firing had largely stopped, and a staff officer appeared from the direction of the ridge. As he got closer there was a general stirring in the brigade as men rose to their feet in expectation of orders. Michael realised that it was Sam Dudley, a lieutenant in the Sixteenth, but serving on the staff of Sir Stapleton Cotton, who commanded all of Wellington's cavalry. Dudley rode to speak to Anson, and then rode on towards the brigades behind. It soon transpired that they had received orders to look for forage in the area.

Anson quickly issued orders, and before the other two brigades could move, the Sixteenth and the Hussars were riding away to the north west. Ashworth grinned at Michael. "Anson's taking us to the north side of Mealhada, we should be able to get access to our baggage."

By the time night fell the Regiment had managed to find forage for the horses, not as much as they might have liked, but it would have to do. The commissary had also managed to distribute three days of rations, mostly ships biscuit and cheese, and a little stringy, but fresh, beef. They bivouacked amongst groves of olive trees, running lines between the trees, briefly untacking, grooming the horses, and then tacking up again. The horses would remain saddled, with their bridles hanging from their saddles. They could be mounted again in a matter of a few minutes. The men stayed near their horses, small fires here and there heating water for tea, cooking up rations, a few bottles passing around. Michael found himself slipping easily back into the routine of managing the troop. With Sawyer and Sar'nt Major Flynn, it was all fairly straightforward. Keating did what he could, but while the sword cut to his thigh didn't stop him riding, it left him hobbling around painfully. Lloyd rode off with some other batmen, towards Mealhada and the baggage, returning later with some welcome food. He had also exchanged Rodrigo for Edward.

The squadron's officers all gathered together by a small fire, pooling their supplies to make a passable meal. There was little conversation. Michael got to his feet, and addressed Ashworth.

"If you'll forgive me, sir, Major Archer wanted a word once we were settled."

Ashworth grunted, "Best get along then."

Leading Duke, Michael set off towards where Archer was, passing through the rows of tethered horses and their dragoons. Here and there small fires illuminated dragoons seeking a little warmth, many huddled in their cloaks against the falling temperature.

Archer was at the centre of the bivouac with the Adjutant and the Regimental Sergeant Major. "Good evening, sir." Michael saluted.

"Ah, Roberts, I'm glad to have you back." He turned to Lieutenant Barra and RSM Williams. "Would you be good enough to give me a few minutes with Mister Roberts." The two men drifted away into the dark. "Sit yourself down, Mister Roberts,"

"Thank you, sir."

"I saw Colonel Murray a few days ago." Archer coughed, and cleared his throat. "He told me that what you were doing in Lisbon, what you did, was very important. He didn't give me any details, of course, and I don't want any. He also intimated that Viscount Wellington approves of your actions. That being the case, I approve as well."

"Thank you, sir, that's good to know."

"That was all, Roberts. I believe Captain Ashworth is leaving his troop to you to manage?"

"Yes, sir."

"Good, a chance for you to show what you can do. Carry on, Roberts."

Michael returned to the troop, his troop, even if only temporarily. Strangely, he didn't feel at all daunted by the prospect. No, he felt very much at home. He hoped he would be able to stay a while. It was time he made his mark with some proper soldiering.

Chapter 2

Someone was shaking Michael's shoulder. "Bore da, sir, time to be stirring."

Michael grunted, rolled over, and struggled to his feet. He was cold. With the horses left saddled up there had been no blankets to sleep under, and every man had got what sleep he could wrapped in his cloak.

"I've got you a mug of coffee, sir, with a drop of brandy in it."

It was still night, but Michael could see the mug Lloyd was offering. "Thank you, Lloyd, what time is it?"

"Just after three o'clock, sir."

Michael took a swig of the lukewarm coffee, and felt the welcome jolt of the brandy followed by a warm glow. Michael looked around, and saw Ashworth standing by a small, feebly flickering fire. He finished the coffee and passed the mug back to Lloyd. "Diolch, Lloyd, that was very welcome. Have you had anything?"

"Yes, sir, thank you, and I've some bread and a bit of cold beef for breakfast, sir, when you're ready."

"Splendid. Where have they dug the trench?"

Lloyd pointed out into the dark. "About thirty yards that way, sir."

Fifteen minutes later Michael had finished chewing his way through some stale bread and tough beef, and joined Ashworth in his attempt to get some warmth from the fire. "Good morning, sir."

"Morning Roberts," Ashworth rubbed his hands together briskly, "I want the squadron ready to mount in half an hour, Anson wants the brigade back where we were yesterday before first light."

Moving at night was always difficult, and fraught with danger, but the Sixteenth was now no stranger to night work, and moved off in column threes, back towards the ridge of Buçaco. They were not helped as a fog developed before dawn, slowing everything down, and hiding squadron from squadron as they tried to form their line. Archer rode about incessantly, helped by Barra and the Regimental Sergeant Major. Eventually Anson appeared out of the fog, spoke to Archer, and they all came to a halt where they stood. Slowly, the early morning light grew, and the fog began to lift. revealing all three brigades back together, just as they had been the day before. Ten minutes of manoeuvring sufficed to straighten out the faults in their deployment.

Once Anson was satisfied, the word came to dismount. The squadrons opened their ranks, and the men dismounted, to stand quietly by their horses' heads. No one wanted to sit on the cold, damp ground, but the sun was beginning to show and warm things up as the fog dispersed.

The top of the ridge to their front was still shrouded in patches of mist, when the crash of musketry came from immediately ahead. It rose in intensity, the sounds of volley after volley reaching them out of the mist. It faded for a few minutes, then returned with equal ferocity, and still the waiting cavalry could see nothing of the battle raging only a couple of miles away. Michael stood with Sawyer and Keating, all three silent, straining to catch a glimpse of anything that might tell them what was happening, but the distance and intervening trees made it impossible.

Gradually the sound of cannon fire and musketry diminished, became intermittent, and then broke out again with renewed violence, but this time further to the north, towards where they knew the Convent stood that was

Wellington's headquarters. Heads turned as one to look in the new direction.

"Damn it," said Keating, dropping to the ground. "I can't see anything, I don't care if the ground is damp, I need to sit down." He carefully stretched out his wounded leg. "This aches like the very devil."

The sound of artillery fire and musketry continued, growing in intensity, rolling down from the ridge.

"That's coming from where I saw the Light Division yesterday," offered Michael.

"What's the ground like up there?" asked Sawyer.

"Steep, open, rocky, scrubby vegetation. Slow climbing up."

"Good," replied Sawyer, "give the Lights plenty of time to deal with the French."

The sounds of fighting in the direction of the Convent went on, while the noise of battle from the immediate front gradually faded away to nothing.

Keating spoke from the ground where he was now lying full length. "It sounds like that first little fracas is over. One can only assume that our infantry did the business. I suspect that we would know by now if they hadn't."

No one replied, and in a moment Keating gave every indication of having dozed off. Gradually the sounds of firing decreased, and faded away, until only intermittent musketry was heard.

"Whatever that was all about," observed Michael, "it sounds like it has deteriorated to skirmishers bickering." He pulled his watch out. "But it's barely midday, plenty of time yet."

The Sixteenth spent the rest of the day sitting by their horses, reins in hand, waiting for orders and listening for sounds of battle. Periodically sections of the Regiment were sent away to feed and water their horses. Remarkably their commissary appeared with a few mules carrying bread and wine. Michael was able to assuage both thirst and hunger, and then followed Keating's example, stretching out and dozing off and on, Duke's reins wrapped loosely around his wrist. It was surprisingly quiet and peaceful, and the warmth of the sun was welcome after the chill of the night.

Early in the afternoon he heard a dragoon say, "Ere comes Mister Tomkinson and 'is patrol."

Michael sat up. He hadn't even been aware that a patrol had been sent out, and guessed that he had missed it in the early morning fog. As he watched he saw Tomkinson report to General Anson, who was sitting with Major Archer and Colonel Arenschildt of the Hussars. A few moments later Archer turned to the Regiment, and, in his best parade ground voice, shouted "Squadron commanders!" Arenschildt likewise called out to his regiment. Ashworth, Cocks, Hay and Murray walked across, leading their horses, joined by four German officers. When Ashworth returned to the squadron he gathered his officers and senior NCOs together.

"Tomkinson saw a French attack on the left of the ridge, he thinks it was against the Light Division. It seems that the Lights gave the French a bloody nose and sent them packing. When he reported that his patrol had seen no sign of any French movement to the north, he gathered that there had been another attack, on the 3rd Division, that was also repulsed." He smiled. "Let the men know."

The sounds of firing continued to drift across to the brigade, but it did not again reach the intensity of the morning. So, the brigade sat in the heat of the sun and waited. The routine of watering the horses and foraging for feed for them continued, half a squadron at a time. As night came on, the brigades retired, the Sixteenth returning to the olive groves they had occupied the previous night.

In the rapidly fading light orders were given for the horses to be briefly unsaddled, and quickly groomed. Dragoons busied themselves with picket lines, Lloyd took Duke from Michael, leaving him free to supervise the troop. As the very last of the light faded the work was done. All the horses stood, tied to the picket lines, saddles in place, bridles hanging off the saddles. Accompanied by Lieutenant Sawyer and Sar'nt Major Flynn, Michael made his rounds, checking all the tack and accoutrements, asking after the condition of each horse. When they had finished, Michael addressed the two men. "I have to say that I have seen the troop in better condition, but, all things considered, it will do, it will do nicely. Well, done Sawyer, Flynn. I shall inform Captain Ashworth. Now, in the meantime, can you see if you can get a few fires going? It will cheer the men if they get a warm drink, even if there's little in the way of food."

Sawyer and Flynn saluted and disappeared into the dark. Michael went in search of Ashworth, and found him exactly where he had expected to, between the lines of the two troops.

"The troop is settled, sir, although there's no forage for the horses."

"I know, Roberts. Major Archer has sent the RSM and a few men off towards Mealhada to see what they can find. Whatever they come up with isn't going to go far between the four hundred and some horses we have. Hopefully we will move tomorrow, and pick up food and forage as we go."

If the RSM had any success, Michael's troop didn't see any of it. They passed the night as they had the previous one, huddled in their cloaks, or walking about trying to keep warm. Once again Michael was woken by Lloyd, who offered him a mug.

"Bore da, sir, mind the mug, there's no coffee this morning." The mug contained a tot of neat brandy, and Michael felt it sear its way down his throat.

"Damn, that's rough stuff, Lloyd. No, don't tell me where it came from, but thank you." He handed the mug back as Sergeant Major Flynn appeared.

"Good Morning, sir, we have fifty three men and horses fit this morning, sir. I'm afraid we have two horses that are in bad shape. One got badly kicked, the other is showing signs of colic."

"Damn. Very well, Sar'nt Major. Lloyd, go and have a look will you, I doubt the Vetenry's around at the moment. Flynn, show Lloyd the horse, and then give my compliments to Mister Sawyer and Mister Keating, tell them I want the troop ready to move in half an hour. I'm going to find Captain Ashworth."

Michael found Ashworth, and the other squadron commanders, in conversation with Major Archer. He waited quietly until the group broke up, then stepped forward, saluting Ashworth. "Good morning, sir."

"Morning Roberts," came Ashworth's reply with his return salute. "Same as yesterday, it seems. Are you all ready?"

"Your troop will be ready to move within the half hour, sir. I haven't seen van Hagen or Alexander, so I don't know about their troop, sir."

"Very good, you carry on, I'll seek out Mister van Hagen."

When he returned to the troop, he found Flynn and Lloyd with two fed up looking dragoons holding two equally unhappy horses. "What have you got?" Michael asked.

Flynn gestured at Lloyd, who explained, "Owen's horse is lame, sir, it's got a very nasty gash on its offside, rear. It will be alright in time, sir, but it won't be carrying anyone for a week. Mitchel's does have a touch of the colic, sir, but I think it's quite mild, and he might walk it off. It would probably be best if they joined the baggage, sir."

Michael looked at Flynn who nodded in agreement. "Right, then, they had best do that, thank you Lloyd, bring me my horse will you? Sar'nt Major, I'll scribble a note for Mr Harrison, in the meantime, get the troop formed and ready to mount." Michael opened his sabretache, pulled out his notebook and a pencil, and started to write. "Owen, Mitchel, walk your horses to Mealhada, you know where it is?" They both nodded. "Report to Mr Harrison, and the Vetenry if you see him. Stay with the baggage until the Vetenry says your horses are fit. Here." He handed Owen a note. "Now, get along sharpish, and don't ride them."

That morning there was no fog, and the three cavalry brigades were quickly reassembled where they had spent the last two days. The morning passed quietly, and still nothing happened, no orders came. Their commissary did, with his mule train and much needed rations and piles of forage. It wasn't possible to fall out to cook, but the men hungrily ate the biscuits that were doled out, and a small amount of forage was dropped in front of every horse. The mood of the regiment perked up, chatter broke out, interspersed with the occasional burst of laughter. At midday they heard firing again, but it was faint and sporadic, skirmishing from the sound of it.

Finally, in the early afternoon an order came for the brigade to move. The two regiments wheeled by threes to the left, and headed north, walking steadily at first, but then increasing the pace to a trot for a few miles. An easy ride brought them into and through the small village of Moita. Anson halted the brigade, on open ground east of the village, and there they bivouacked. It was new ground, and with plenty of daylight left, dragoons and hussars were soon busy collecting forage, much of it maize almost ready for harvesting. Michael was sent into the little village to see what supplies he could obtain. The regiment's own commissary was still six or seven miles away, in Mealhada with the baggage. The village was almost deserted, and those few villagers left were nervous. He learnt that most of the village had fled northwards to Oporto, leaving only the elderly, too frail to make the journey. There was little food or anything else left, and certainly not enough for over nine hundred hungry dragoons and hussars. They would have to make do with what was left of the rations issued two days ago. Although they were supposed to last three days, with everything in short supply they were barely adequate for two.

That night the hussars provided the pickets, and all the regiment's officers were able to gather together. Anson, who was an officer in the Sixteenth, joined them. After they had eaten a frugal supper, he addressed them. "Gentlemen, it seems that the French are marching north to find another road out of the mountains, quite possibly this one we are watching. De Grey's brigade has gone further north to another likely road. Tonight, the army will be starting to march south, first to Coimbra, and then on towards Lisbon. At some point, we will turn and fight. The cavalry will form the rear guard, the Light Division will be the last infantry, and just ahead of us. And that is all I can tell you."

Michael knew exactly where the army would turn, behind the massive line of fortifications that ran from the river Tagus to the Atlantic, running along the hills north of Lisbon, from Alhandra, past Sobral, and Torres Vedras to the sea. Fortifications that the French were unaware of. All they had to do was carry out a retreat of some hundred and twenty miles in the face of a larger French army.

At three in the morning the same routine as the previous days began again. This time they were sent back towards the ridge of Buçaco, and the ground they had occupied during the battle. The army had gone, marching south for

Coimbra, leaving only the Light Division on the ridge. At about midday the Light Division marched down from the ridge and headed towards Mealhada and the main road south. Anson's brigade followed them, and then halted in Mealhada.

The regimental baggage was still there, but ready for departure. Michael sought out Francisco and Parra.

"Parra, I want to change horses, quickly now. Francisco, get me a bag with three or four days cold rations." He turned round to Lloyd. "Lloyd, do you want to change onto Rodrigo, I don't think anyone is going to complain."

"Yes, sir, diolch yn fawr, sir, but there's nothing wrong with Edward, he's as fit as any other troop horse, sir, one of the dismounted lads could have him, sir."

"Good idea, I think we are going to need every sabre. Go and pick someone."

"Yes, sir."

The regimental commissary was busy issuing rations, this time as much as the men could carry, anything left was to be destroyed so the French wouldn't get it. With a few hours of daylight left the brigade was ready, and the baggage sent on its way south. The mule train was now very lightly loaded, and carried some of the regiment's women. Michael noticed that Parra had Mrs Taylor up on one of his baggage mules. He shouted to him. "Parra, you ride Duke, put Mrs Taylor on Harry. If any of the ladies struggle, take one up on the mule." Parra waved his acknowledgement, and Michael turned his attention to the troop.

With Sawyer, Keating and Sergeant Major Flynn shouting and swearing the troop was soon assembled and ready to march. Michael saw Mitchel back in the ranks and rode over to him.

"How's your horse, Mitchel?"

"Sir, he's fine now, Lloyd was right about the colic, sir."

"Good." A few yards from Mitchel, Michael saw Owen, now sitting on Edward.

Michael called out to him. "Nice horse you have there, Owen, better take good care of it." There was laughter at that, and Owen grinned and replied, "Yes, sir, Lloyd has already had a word with me, sir."

Michael laughed, wheeled Johnny away and rode across to Captain Ashworth.

"The troop is ready, sir," he reported, saluting at the same time.

"Excellent," Ashworth replied with his return salute. "Van Hagen looks to have his troop ready, let's form the squadron."

The other three squadrons were also forming and the regiment was soon ready to move.

Word reached them that the heavy brigade to the north was being driven towards them by a larger force of French cavalry. Anson took the brigade out of Mealhada to ground just outside the village on its north side, where the French would be coming from. Michael was in his usual post, on the extreme left of the squadron, which itself was on the right of the regiment. Twenty five yards away was Captain Cock's squadron, and on its extreme right sat Lieutenant Bishop. Bishop looked across at Michael, grinned, shrugged, and turned his attention back to the front. Quite, thought Michael, hurry up and wait, again. Fifteen minutes later the brigade was ordered to dismount. Then, with night fast approaching, orders came to collect forage. Clearly they were not going anywhere, just yet.

It was another night in the open, the regiment in its ranks, every dragoon by his horse, wrapped tight in his cloak. Each dragoon held his horses lead rein, the bridles were off and hanging on the saddles so the horses could more easily eat what little forage there was. Lloyd had taken his place in the front rank, next to Michael, but as the ranks had opened to allow everyone to dismount, he was now a horses length back. Michael led Johnny forward, turned him around, and walked back towards the troop. Michael peered into the dark where he could just make out his covering sergeant, who was on the end of the second rank.

"Sar'nt Taylor?"

"Yes, sir?"

"Take my post, I am going the rounds."

With a "Yes, sir," Taylor lead his horse forward to take Michael's position, just as he would if anything should happen to Michael in action.

Michael walked along the front of the troop, leading Johnny, speaking to each dragoon as he went. Even in the dark he knew every one of them. At the centre of the squadron he found Keating at his post. "All well, Mister Keating?"

"All well, Mister Roberts."

"How is the leg holding up?"

"The cold and damp are not helping, but the wound seems to be clean, it's more an ache now."

At that moment another figure appeared, Henry van Hagen, checking on his troop, the other half of the squadron.

"Glad to hear that, Mister Keating. All well, Mister Roberts?"

"Good evening, gentlemen," Ashworth's voice broke in on them. "I think we can stand the men down, let them get some sleep, if they can. Captain Hay has pickets out. And get some sleep yourselves. It's a long way back south, and if the French stay on our heels it will be a very long way.

We've to slow them so that the infantry divisions can get to wherever Viscount Wellington chooses to halt."

Chapter 3

It was yet another early start, rousing the regiment at three in the morning, feeble fires heating a little water for tea or coffee, brandy passing around, stale bread dipped in both and chewed. By first light the brigade was mounted and assembled facing the road to the north. As the light grew and the pickets reported no enemy in sight, Anson ordered the brigade to dismount and everyone prepared themselves for another long day of waiting. Then came the sound of firing from the north, it sounded like skirmishing, and Anson readied the brigade for action. Michael was in his usual post on the left flank of the front rank of the squadron, Lloyd next to him, Sergeant Taylor behind.

The firing died out, and De Grey's heavy brigade came in sight, riding briskly down the road towards them. The six hundred and more horsemen came on, six abreast, and passed through Anson's disappearing into Mealhada. Once they were through there was a rise in tension, as everyone expected the French to appear, hard on their heels. Nothing happened. Gradually, as gossip does, it spread around that in the early morning gloom the heavies' pickets had mistaken some bushes for French cavalry, and skirmished with them for half an hour. There was an outbreak if chatter and laughter at this, and Michael let it go for a moment before he turned, and bellowed "Silence", before turning back to his front with a grin.

Anson's brigade followed de Grey's through Mealhada, and on the other side of the village they formed again, with Slade's brigade, and waited some more. In the afternoon they marched an easy ten miles or so through a rolling, wooded countryside and along the main road to Lisbon. Just short of the town of Fornos they were halted, and preparations made to bivouac in a nearby wood. Slade's and De Grey's marched on through Fornos. Pickets were sent back up the road towards Mealhada. No one was happy with the situation.

Ashworth called Michael and van Hagen to him. "I am afraid that we are stuck here for the night. I can't say I like, and neither does Major Archer. We will have to stay saddled up again. If the French come on there will be very little warning. We will have to try to feed and water the horses a half squadron at a time. The Hussars are providing the pickets tonight."

Around midnight a patrol by Captain Cocks returned, with the news that the French advanced guard was only five or six miles away. With the French so close, the brigade did not dare to unbridle, making feeding and watering even more difficult. The precarious, isolated nature of their position made everyone nervous, and, like most of the Regiment, Michael got little sleep, dozing in his cloak, laying in front of Johnny, his reins around his wrist.

With the dawn came General Sir Stapleton Cotton, who gave orders to Anson, and rode away through Fornos. The brigade was formed in line, with Michael, this time, as the extreme right hand man of his squadron, the regiment, and the brigade. The gently rolling countryside all around was enclosed, perfect for infantry, but dreadful for cavalry, and there was only one road they could retreat on, the one through Fornos. The Hussar picket, a mile or two towards the French, was commanded by Captain Krauchenburg. Just after dawn the sound of firing reached the brigade as the pickets were attacked. They were quickly driven back and on to the brigade. For a while the brigade skirmishers held up the advance of the French cavalry, but then infantry started to work their way forward through small enclosures, safe from attack by cavalry and their muskets more effective than the light cavalry's short Paget carbines. The Hussars did their best, but in the face of French infantry steadily working their way forward from enclosure to enclosure there was little they could do, and they started to take casualties. Two or three men were killed, Krauchenburg was struck on the hip by a musket ball, but managed to stay in his saddle and continue.

Eventually, Sir Stapleton reappeared, and ordered the brigade to retire through Fornos. The Sixteenth moved off first, at the walk, left in front, and Michael was in the rear of the regiment. The firing behind them intensified, and the order came to advance at the trot. Then the gallop, and the regiment tore through a deserted Fornos, heading for the plain of Coimbra beyond. Looking behind him, Michael could see the Hussars following close behind. The regiment galloped out of Fornos, and then thundered over a narrow bridge across a large drainage ditch. The pace dropped to a trot, the regiment swung right, and formed in line to the left of the road from Fornos. Michael had barely halted when the Hussars came up, and swung to the other side of the road. Beyond the ditch, French cavalry appeared, green coated dragoons, and then British horse artillery opened fire, sending them scuttling back into Fornos for cover. Michael looked around. Behind him were the other two brigades. He glanced across the narrow road at the hussars. The squadron nearest him had been the rear guard, under Krauchenburg, and Michael could see him receiving attention from their surgeon.

Michael took out his watch, it was not yet ten o'clock, and he had a feeling it was going to be a long day. Just then he heard orders being called out, and the two other brigades began to march away towards the Mondego river to the rear. Then the hussars moved off, followed by the Sixteenth, save for Ashworth's squadron, which was left as a rear guard. Michael could see several squadrons of French dragoons coming down the road from Fornos towards the bridge, and it was with considerable relief that he heard Ashworth's orders. "Threes right! Left shoulders forward, trot!" and they were off after the rest of the regiment, Michael now at the head of the squadron. The distance to the Mondego was quickly covered, and they splashed across a ford through the wide river, and onto the plain on the other side. Then it was "Right shoulders forward", followed by "Halt! Threes left!" The squadron was facing the ford, a mere two hundred yards from it. The most advanced squadron of the French dragoons was just approaching the edge of the ford, under fire from the Sixteenth's own skirmishers who had covered the crossing of Ashworth's squadron.

Ashworth's commands came, clear and loud. "Draw", pause, "swords!" another brief pause, and in quick succession, "Walk, trot, gallop, charge!" and the squadron hurled itself across the short distance at the French dragoons, who were just splashing into the ford. Into the river they crashed, throwing up waves of water, one horse stumbled, fell, and sent its dragoon headlong into the water. The squadron forged through the water, overlapped the French dragoons on both flanks and swept around them, sabres flashing. Michael saw a French dragoon Colonel, and rode at him. Another Frenchman, a young officer, rode his horse between Michael and the Colonel, and thrust his long sword at Michael's face. Michael ducked, and brought his sabre round to catch the Frenchman's, riding past him. Michael urged Johnny forward, towards the French Colonel.

He heard Lloyd shout, "On your right, sir!"

He turned to his right to see the young officer coming at him again, and Lloyd and Taylor pushing forward through the spray as well. Michael parried a vicious back hand cut at his head and, as the man pulled his sword to make a fore hand cut, he thrust with his sabre over the head of his opponents horse. He failed to reach the man's face, but with his arm out straight he cut left and felt his sabre bite into the man's sword arm as he tried to make his cut.

Taylor was pushing past as Michael was vaguely aware of French dragoons protectively gathering around their Colonel. Then the man closed to Michael, right side to right, he tried to make a cut, Michael parried it, pushing the blade past him, then he cut left and caught the man across the throat. The end of the blade, honed razor sharp by Lloyd, sliced through, a fountain of blood following. The man threw back his head, and fell into the river.

Michael looked around, Lloyd and Taylor had reined in just beyond, watching carefully as party of French escorted their Colonel to the bank and safety. All around there seemed to be only British dragoons and empty French horses. Ashworth was now shouting, "Retire, retire!" and the squadron turned back and pushed quickly out of the river, riding back to where the rest of the regiment was waiting. As he cleared the ford, Michael looked back across at the French. On the far bank he could see the French Colonel, looking straight at him, staring at him. Next to him another officer had an arm on his shoulder, and seemed to be urging him to something.

Michael turned away, saw his spot, rode there, faced about and began to shout at the dragoons to form on him. He was panting, flushed with the excitement, rather wet, but, at last, he had charged with the regiment, and he had done his job. He was elated, and grinning.

The French appeared content to abandon the chase, and turn away to loot the nearby, abandoned town of Coimbra, leaving the cavalry to continue their march towards Lisbon unmolested. Tomkinson was left with a troop to cover the ford in case the French changed their minds. To everyone's surprise, in the next village they came to, only a mile or so further on, they found the regimental baggage. Archer was furious, it should have been long gone, but Harrison had received no orders to move. Michael could not help but think it was a mistake Stanhope wouldn't have made.

The baggage we swiftly sent on its way, and the regiment followed. They joined the main road from Coimbra to Lisbon, and Michael saw the full impact of Wellington's strategy to evacuate the countryside. Hundreds of people were still making their way southwards, panicking at the thought of French cavalry on their heels. The side of the road was strewn with abandoned baggage, and the cavalry were forced off the road by the sheer number of people fleeing Coimbra. Families of all classes were streaming south, carrying away with them what they could of their possessions and valuables. Houses on the road side were abandoned with all their contents waiting for the French. Occasionally they passed by the body of a civilian, left at the road side.

The next town on the road, Soure was already abandoned by its population. They passed through in silence. An hour's march further on they bivouacked. Since Coimbra and the fight on the Mondego there had been no sign of a French pursuit. They made the most of the respite to care for the horses, and find what feed they could. There was little for the men to eat, the commissary didn't appear, and the baggage was now long gone, carried along in the tide of refugees.

As Michael made his rounds of the troop, Regimental Sergeant Major Williams approached him. "Begging your pardon, sir."

"Yes, Sar'nt Major?"

"Sir, I was talking to one of the French dragoons we took at the ford, sir."

Michael thought Williams looked a little uncomfortable. "Yes, Mister Williams?"

"Well, sir, that young French officer you sabred, sir, seems it was that Colonel's son, sir."

"Oh!" Michael thought for a brief moment. "Thank you for letting me know, Sar'nt Major."

The RSM saluted and marched away and Michael thought no more of it.

The next day's march was a short one, to a few miles north of Leiria, on the bank of a small river. There they caught up with the Light Division, the rear guard of the infantry, who only moved away as evening fell. So far, the retreat had been well executed and, since the Mondego, almost leisurely, it was if the French were content just to follow along behind the British and Portuguese army.

The leisurely calm continued the next day, as the brigade stayed where it was. The calm lasted until the evening, when a false alarm resulted in the whole regiment turning out. It transpired the French were still some fifteen miles away. They didn't stay that far away.

In the morning the French drove in the brigade's pickets and advanced rapidly. Captain Murray's squadron, with Ashworth's squadron in support, moved to support the regiment's skirmishers who had become engaged in a lively exchange with the French dragoons. Michael watched from his position on the right of Ashworth's as Murray charged home against a French body of dragoons pressing too hard. Murray's men drove the French off, capturing two officers and ten men in the process.

Then two small cannon appeared and opened up on the Sixteenth. At once two dragoons went down, killed by the same ball. Archer wheeled the regiment about by threes and moved closer to the river behind them before wheeling it back to face the French. As more French appeared the brigade withdrew across the small river, Swetenham's squadron bringing up the rear. He managed to bring his squadron off, but took a cut in his thigh in the process as the French dragoons pressed home their advance. Once across, the horse artillery were able to open fire and the French stopped their advance.

The whole brigade with the artillery passed through Leiria. It too was completely deserted, and for once the men were allowed to pillage the houses for much needed food and forage, better than leaving it for the French. Once through the town the brigade halted again, but was forced to retire further when the French pushed infantry towards them through enclosures. Another fraught night passed by with no alarms, at daylight the pickets retired, and the brigade marched quietly to just short of Rio Maior, but that evening there was yet another clash between the Sixteenth's pickets and the advanced pickets of the French.

As the next day dawned, the pickets retired and the regiment marched some ten miles before bivouacking. With no sign of the French it gave an opportunity to feed the horses and men, but there was nothing hot. There was no sign of the regiment's baggage, and that meant Michael was still riding Johnny. The French finally made an appearance in the evening, and there was a sharp skirmish, with two of the Sixteenth being wounded. With the French so close, the regiment spent the night formed up in its squadrons, the men huddled around numerous small fires, the horses bridled and ready to mount. Relief came in the morning when Slade's brigade took over as the rear guard and Anson's were able to pass Rio Maior with the chance of a rest and a cooked meal.

It was a welcome break. The baggage arrived, fires were lit, the commissary distributed rations. Michael was able to change Johnny for Duke, and looked forward to whatever food Francisco could provide for him. Michael settled down on the ground with Ashworth and the other squadron officers. Coffee was being served out and he was looking forward to a hot meal. Suddenly there was a shout from the gloom of the evening, "Stand to!"

At once the bivouac became a scene of frenzied activity. Ashworth leapt to his feet, "Roberts, van Hagen, get the squadron formed, Mister Alexander, get the baggage away, I'll find out what's happening."

All around the dragoons were emptying camp kettles out on to the fires, gathering them up and getting them on the mules. Michael left Francisco to sort out his baggage, and went to find his horse. Lloyd was already at hand with Duke and Rodrigo. They both mounted and Michael took his position as the right flank marker, Lloyd to his side, and started to bellow, "Squadron, form on me."

Dragoons came running up, some mounted, some still leading their horses. NCOs were shouting and cursing, getting the men into their places, he heard Regimental Sergeant Major Williams shouting at the baggage to "Get the hell out of here". Slowly order prevailed and within fifteen minutes the squadron was ready. From where he was Michael couldn't make out what the other squadrons were doing. Then Troop Sergeant Major Flynn appeared at his side, "Sir, you best take the squadron until Captain Ashworth returns."

Michael rode forward to the front and centre of the Squadron while Flynn took his place. He took a deep breath, and called out, "Squadron, attention!" Silence fell behind him. He realised that it was quiet everywhere. Then Ashworth rode up out of the dark and halted next to Michael.

"It was a false alarm." He sounded very, very tired. "A bloody, God damned, false alarm!"

Michael thought that he had never heard him swear like that, or sound so very angry.

"Take post, Mister Roberts."

Michael rode back to the right flank, Flynn rode to the rear of the squadron, Ashworth faced the men. "Squadron!" In the gloom Michael couldn't see the expression on his face. "It was a false alarm."

A groan went up from the ranks, they had just thrown away the first cooked food for two days. Flynn bellowed out, "Silence!"

In the quiet that followed Michael felt the first few drops or rain.

It rained all night as the men sat, cold and hungry, huddled around the few fires they managed to relight and keep going. Michael wrapped himself in his cloak and shivered. The dawn brough no respite from the rain, rather it became heavier, a lot heavier. Cold, wet and miserable the regiment moved on in the morning, heading for Alcoentre, and leaving Murray's squadron as a rear guard. The regiment passed across a long causeway and bridge, over a deep and wide stream, that was the only access to the town. Like other towns, Alcoentre had been abandoned by its civilian populace, and stood eerily silent save for the clatter of the regiment's hooves echoing off the buildings on either side of the narrow streets. In the town centre they rode through a small square overlooked by a church. The square was occupied by the horse artillery battery that had been with them all through the retreat. Five or six miles beyond the town the regiment halted and bivouacked in a wood. It gave some shelter, but large drops of water were continuously dropping from the leaves. The baggage and the commissary arrived, and at last the men got some rations issued, but only biscuit and cheese. The Hussars and Slade's brigade of heavy dragoons were nearby.

Michael stood with Ashworth, chewing on a biscuit, their squadron was saddled and bridled ready to support Murray if needed. In the early afternoon the sound of firing came from the direction of the town. At once all the dragoons started to gather up their kit and get mounted even before Ashworth could call out, "Squadron, prepare to mount". Moments later they were trotting back the way they had come, as the sound of firing increased. Ahead of them five guns with their teams straining at the harness suddenly burst from the town and down the road towards them. Ashworth ordered "Left shoulders forward", and took the squadron off the road to clear the way for the guns. The squadron was advancing right in front, so Michael was only just behind Ashworth as he took the squadron into the town by a side road. Just short of the junction with the main road through the town, Ashworth halted the squadron, and went forward to see what was happening, saying to Michael as he went, "Best draw swords, if you please, Mister Roberts."

Michael gave the orders, "Squadron, draw, swords! Carry, swords." He glanced back and saw every man with his sabre rested on his shoulder, the squadron, six wide, filling the street as far back as he could see. Ashworth returned, "There's a gun and some wagons still in the square, and Murray is falling back towards them. With luck we shall catch the French in the flank."

Suddenly there was deafening clatter of hooves, and Murray's squadron rode across the end of the street. Seconds later the head of a column of French dragoons followed, and Ashworth shouted at the top of his voice, "Squadron, charge!" He clapped his spurs on and his horse shot forward toward the junction where the French dragoons were still passing. Michael urged Johnny after him, followed by the rest of the squadron. Some of the French dragons saw them, and tried to halt and turn to face them, but their comrades behind them pushed on and into them, throwing all into confusion, then Ashworth and his squadron struck like a battering ram of men and horses. There was no room for fine sword play, everyone was jammed to tightly together, Michael parried a cut, and drove the knuckle guard of his sabre into a French dragoon's face. Then the French gave way, and were careering back down the street towards the bridge, pursued by cheering British dragoons. Clear over the bridge they went, everyone hacking and slashing furiously, but also fighting to manage their horses.

Ashworth reined in, Michael with him. "I think that is quite far enough, let's get the men back through the town." The two officers started to shout, "Retire, retire!" Then Ashworth instructed Michael, "Roberts, lead them back, form outside the town, I shall bring up the rear."

Shouting out, "Retire, follow me!" Michael led the way back along the causeway, across the bridge and through the town. The square was now empty, the gun and wagons gone. Murray was waiting outside the town with his squadron reformed, ready to cover Ashworth's retreat. Once past Murray, Michel turned to face the town and started shouting to the arriving dragoons to reform on him. A few minutes later all were present, along with a handful of French dragoon prisoners, Ashworth among the last to arrive, chivvying along a few stragglers with Sergeant Major Flynn for company. Ashworth rode up to Michael and looked past him to the captured French dragoons.

"What are those fellows staring at?"

Michael turned in his saddle and realised that the eyes of every French dragoon were on him. Ashworth rode to them, and in broken French asked them what the devil they were staring at. One, a sergeant replied, and Ashworth rode back to where Michael and Flynn were sorting out the squadron.

"Ah, Roberts, you should know, that French officer you sabred at the Mondego…"

"Yes, sir, their Colonel's son, sir, the RSM told me,"

"Yes, well, apparently the Colonel has sworn to see you in Hell, and promised promotion and a large sum of money to any man who kills the British dragoon officer with the scar on his face."

"Oh."

"Yes, but there's nothing we can do about it, just bear it in mind, eh?"

At that moment Murray rode over. "Thank you, Ashworth, that was nicely done. If you would care to lead off, we will follow."

Covered by Captain Cocks' squadron the cavalry retreated to Quinta de Toro, a tiny hamlet with a bridge over a small stream. The rain continued unabated, and the ground became a sodden quagmire. Michael and the rest of the regiment not on picket duty tried to get what sleep they could lying on the road.

The following afternoon there was yet another skirmish, as the French drove the outlying picket of Captain Linsingen's Hussar squadron back onto Cock's squadron that was supporting them. Faced with two French regiments, the Hussars were hard pressed and lost almost a score of men. Michael could only sit and watch from his position across the bridge where Anson had formed the brigade, supported by the horse artillery. Once Linsingen and Cocks had got their squadrons across the bridge and re-joined the brigade, the guns opened up on the following French cavalry. It wasn't long, however, before French infantry worked their way across a bog where the cavalry couldn't get at them, and opened a long range fire on the brigade. It was enough, and Sir Stapleton ordered Anson to march the brigade away.

That night the Sixteenth found itself in an olive grove, and knee deep in mud. At least the Hussars were between them and the French. Nearby there was a wine vault, and most of the Sixteenth's officers took shelter there. Michael was walking that way with Tomkinson, when they spotted a shed at the back of the vault. Investigating it they found it occupied by some Portuguese infantry who had no business being there.

Michael addressed an officer with them. "Senhor, it is very brave and noble of you and your men to make a stand with us against the French."

The officer and his men looked worried, and the officer asked Michael, "What do you mean? Are the French nearby?"

"Certainly," answered Michael, "my comrade here," he pointed at Tomkinson, "was engaged with them not half an hour ago."

Ten minutes later the shed was briefly empty, before Michael, Lloyd, Tomkinson and his dragoon, Robinson, along with their horses, moved in. Michael and Tomkinson went to see their separate troops, and on their return, found that Robinson had produced a turkey from somewhere. Helped by Lloyd, he was roasting it over a small fire of broken furniture. The two dragons took it in turns, holding the bird by its wings and feet as they held it in the flames. Smoke blackened and burnt, it was delicious, and the four men companionably shared it.

The rain continued to fall, but at last the regiment reached Carregado and shelter, uninterrupted by the French who once again seemed content to follow along at their own pace. The respite didn't last long, orders came to march to Povoa, on the bank of the Tagus. They passed through the fortifications at Alhandra, familiar to Michael, but a considerable surprise to the officers and men of the Sixteenth, indeed, to all the army, who had no idea of the existence of the lines. In Povoa billets were issued and men and horses were got under cover. More than that, the regimental baggage was waiting for them, along with their commissary and a mule train of supplies. Here, at last, was a chance to get dry, change clothes, get warm, and get something hot to eat. Michael found Parra and told him he would ride Duke the following day, giving a very tired Johnny a break. Francisco provided Michael with a clean shirt and linen, making him feel disproportionately refreshed.

The realisation spread quickly through the regiment that they were now safe from the pursuing French cavalry, safe behind the first line of fortifications that ran from the Tagus at Alhandra to the Atlantic Ocean at the mouth of the Rio Sizandro. That evening all the officers and senior

NCOs not on duty gathered together, and Michael told them about the lines. They listened in amazement at his description, and when he had finished there was silence for a moment.

Then Major Archer spoke, "I had no idea, no idea at all." He looked around the gathering. "And you, Mister Roberts, err, it was in connection with this that you were away from us for so long?"

"Yes, sir, it was."

"Good Lord. I had no idea, no idea at all. Well, well done Mister Roberts, well done indeed."

Word of the lines soon spread around the regiment, and from there to the German Hussars. As it did, Michael felt the brigade relaxing, the imminent threat of combat lifted. The relief was palpable, and everyone who could took advantage to sleep.

The regiment was roused at dawn. Orders came for a fifteen mile or so march to Mafra. It was a comfortable distance, and Anson didn't want to push the brigade after the rigours of the retreat. The brigades horses were almost exhausted after the days of hard marching, short rations and repeated fighting. A few more days of that and they would have started to lose horses. The men were also in bad shape, tired and hungry, but the slow and steady start meant that there was time for shaving and a warm breakfast before the regiment mounted and set off. It was still raining.

The horses were nursed along, some had lost shoes, others struggled to keep up, and some dragoons were forced to dismount and lead their horses. It finally stopped raining, but everyone was wet, and a miasma of wet wool and wet horses hung around them. A slow day's march saw them ride, and walk, into Mafra in the mid-afternoon. They hadn't ridden far into the town when they were ordered to halt and form in a large square in front of a massive, long building with twin bell towers on either side of a tall portico. Michael saw Anson ride across to Archer, and speak to him. Archer suddenly jerked around and looked at the building. Anson rode off, and, with the German Hussars, marched further into Mafra. Archer turned his horse to face the regiment.

"Sixteenth!" Archer called out in his best parade ground voice. "The building behind me is the Palace and Convent of Mafra." He paused and looked across the regiment. "It is also our billet!" A broad smile appeared on his face, as a surprised buzz ran through the dragoons. "Silence," he roared. "I will remind you that we are guests here. You will behave accordingly. You will respect the building and everything in it. Do I make myself clear? Quartermaster Harrison, troop commanders, let us go and allocate, err, rooms and stables."

There followed a busy few hours, settling horses in courtyards and cloisters, and allocating large rooms to twenty or more dragoons each. The Palace boasted a huge kitchen, and organising the cooking for the whole regiment together was a challenge met by the women of the regiment under the stern eye of Mrs Taylor. Archer made no demands that evening, beyond a few sentries, letting everyone rest and relax. Michael found he had the luxury of a small room to himself, with another adjacent for Lloyd, Parra and Francisco.

As Lloyd commented, "Well, sir, I thought the Palace at Vila Vicosa was something, but, Duw, this is something to remember, sir."

Chapter 4

Several days of hard work followed. Every horse was reshod, the farriers working at the forges of their wagons from dawn to dusk. Dragoons were sent out to find forage, the commissary mule trains came in with supplies. The Regiment quickly began to recover from the demands of the summer campaigning and the retreat. The quarters were spacious, if not entirely comfortable, marble and stone floors made for hard beds. The cloisters and sheltered courtyards provided plenty of stabling for all the Regiment's horses, and space for the farriers to work. The officers established a mess, and enjoyed the rare opportunity to all be together. Good humour abounded, aided by good rations and warmth.

Michael was strolling around the interior when he discovered the library. It was breath-taking. It was early evening and the library seemed to disappear into the gloom as it ran away from him. He started to walk, counting his paces. On either side shelves ran up to the underside of a balcony that ran along both sides, and which in turn had book shelves climbing up to meet the ceiling that curved majestically over the width of the library. The Baroque decoration was stunning and ornate, but most surprising of all were the books. They were still there despite the passage of the French army three years before.

He reached one hundred and fifty paces, and found himself in the centre, under a dome, with a shallow transept to either side. He walked slowly on, his boots sharp on the red, black and grey marble floor. He had barely counted another twenty paces when a cough from a window recess startled him. He spun towards the sound, hand flying to his sword hilt, and saw a priest sitting at a small desk, an open book before him.

The priest, a thin man who looked to be in his sixties, lifted his hands, palms towards Michael, and spoke in halting English. "Forgive me, my son, I did not mean to startle you."

Michael relaxed and replied in Portuguese, "It's no matter, Father, I thought I was alone in here." He gestured around. "It is stunning, and the books!"

"Ah, you speak Portuguese, and very well too." He rose from his seat and stepped out of the recess towards Michael. "Yes, we were fortunate. General Loison placed the whole Palace under his personal protection."

"Is that so!" Michael was frankly surprised.

"Indeed, perhaps his conscience troubled him? Who knows, but he preserved my job here."

"Oh?"

"Yes, I am the Librarian."

At that moment a black shape hurtled past Michael, who ducked as it disappeared into the dark.

The priest laughed. "Do not be alarmed. It is just one of the bats. They live behind the books, and protect them from insects. But tell me, my son, how does a British officer come to speak such good Portuguese?"

They walked companionably down the length of the library while Michael gave the priest an edited version of his history, and marvelled at the bats as they flew about. The priest, who introduced himself as Father Nascimento, was intrigued to hear about Michael's grandfather, the Reverend Isles, and asked him a lot of liturgical questions that Michael was unable to answer.

The priest laughed. "Well, my son, I suppose I must forgive your Godless nature as you drove the French away, even if they are now at our threshold again."

Over the next few days Michael was a frequent visitor to the library. Save for Father Nascimento it was usually deserted, having little or no appeal for his fellow soldiers. He found the quiet and tranquillity soothing, and the good Father left him in peace as he went about his duties.

Michael also had his duties, and he kept busy. Looking after the horses of his troop was no hardship, and the troop's NCOs, with Lloyd, knew their business. He wasn't so keen on all the paperwork, accounting for losses of men and horses, mercifully few, and equipment losses. Updating service records was a chore. The situation wasn't helped by the shortage of troop commanders. Of the Regiment's eight captains that should have been present, there were only three, the others being wounded, or sick, or, in one case, away on staff duties. It put a lot of work onto the shoulders of the lieutenants.

Under the cover of the stables and cloisters of the convent, the horses rapidly began to recover their condition. There was, for once, plenty of forage, and the exercise was light, just enough to keep them fit. The state of the men also improved with warm quarters and regular rations. While Lloyd was busy with the troop's horses, Parra was dealing with all of Michael's horses, and Francisco was pleased to be able join in with all the other servants in running the officers' mess. Michael finally completed all the paperwork for the troop, and went through it all with Ashworth.

"Good work, Mister Roberts, we will make an adjutant of you yet." Ashworth grinned as he teased Michael.

"Oh, God, no sir, anything but that," he replied, laughing, "I really don't know how Barra does it."

"Ah, the ways of the Adjutant are a mystery to all." Ashworth replied. "However, given the way things are, I think I might spare you for a few days, if you want to ride down to Lisbon, that is? I think Keating and Sawyer can manage affairs for a while. It will do Sawyer good."

"Thank you, sir, that will be very acceptable."

"Very well, you can leave in the morning. But I'm afraid I need to keep Lloyd here, he's far too useful with the horses just now. Your own servants can go, of course. I've told Bence he can take a few days as well, and I think Cocks has given Tomkinson the same, you can make a party of it." Ashworth pulled out his watch and flipped it open. "Nearly time for dinner, let's take ourselves along and you can speak to the pair of them." He returned his watch. "I have to say it is a real pleasure having regular meal times, and everyone together."

Tomkinson was already in the mess, and Bence came in just behind Michael and Ashworth, who walked over to talk to Major Archer. The three lieutenants were soon gathered together, and arrangements made. Tomkinson and Bence had also been told to go without their dragoon servants, and neither had their own private servant, relying on their dragoons and the shared grooms, like Pedro and Rafael who looked after the horses of the officers of Ashworth's troop. It meant that would have to rely on themselves, and Michael took pity on them.

"Why don't you come and stay with me?" he asked. "I have plenty of room, and stabling, and my servants can look after all three of us as well as just me."

Tomkinson had dined at Michael's, but not stayed there. "Thank, you, Michael, that's very kind of you, and your cook is certainly very good."

"And I shall be more than happy to sample Senhora Santiago's cooking again, thank you," added Bence. He had been Michael's guest for a couple of weeks earlier in the year.

After dinner Michael strolled down to the stables, and as he expected he found Lloyd there. They exchanged salutes and Michael asked, "How are they doing, Lloyd?"

"Very well, very well, sir. They've all recovered nicely."

"And how is Edward?"

"Ah, well, now, sir, Mitchel is looking after him just fine, thank you ,sir."

"Good, good. Now, I've been given a few days leave, but I'm afraid Captain Ashworth wants you here, to help with getting the horses up to scratch."

Lloyd shrugged. "Chwarae teg, sir, they do come first. Who will you be taking?"

"Duke, I think, give Johnny a few more days rest."

"Right you are, sir."

"And Parra and Francisco are coming as well, so they will need their mounts. I'll speak to them; I want to be ready to leave at first light."

"Very good, sir."

The morning was overcast and dull, with a chill in the air, but at least it wasn't raining. The three officers were in good spirits with the prospect of a few days in Lisbon ahead of them, Tomkinson and Bence were particularly looking forward to enjoying the hospitality of Michael's home. Michael was only too happy to put them up, but planned to escape to see his friend and lover Roberta. While he was fully aware that there was speculation about their relationship in the Regiment, he had no intention of making it public. He had too much respect for his friend.

They arrived in the mid-afternoon and all was soon hustle and bustle as Senhora Santiago rushed around preparing rooms. Senhor Santiago helped Parra with all the horses, and Francisco quickly and efficiently dealt with the small amount of baggage. Once he was finished Michael sent him off to see his sister for an hour or two, and at the same time let Roberta know he was in Lisbon. He hoped Francisco would return with an invitation.

Francisco did return with an invitation, for all three officers to join her and her guests for supper. He found them enjoying a glass of wine in one of the reception rooms, with a cheerful fire warming them.

"What guests?", asked a slightly disgruntled Michael.

"Senhor, she has a family from Coimbra staying with her, they are old friends of her family. They have left the city like everyone else, and had nowhere to stay, so the Senhorita took them in, and their servants, Senhor."

"So how many are there?"

"There is the mother and father and four children and five servants, Senhor."

"Good God, well, another three for supper will not be noticed."

"It sounds rather good to me," Tomkinson broke in, "it will be a pleasure to meet the Senhorita again."

"And I will be delighted to make her acquaintance," added Bence.

The family staying with Roberta were Senhor and Senhora Marcelino, and their three children, two very well behaved girls, and a boy of twelve or so who was fascinated by the uniforms and swords of the three officers. The Marcelinos' servants along with Roberta's maid, Constanca, ensured that supper was a delightful affair, and the evening was most convivial.

After supper, Michael managed to get a few words with Roberta in the quiet of her courtyard. He even managed a wry smile. "Not quite the reunion I had hoped for."

Roberta punched him playfully on the arm. "And how was I to know you would be at home with two of your comrades? Tell me that?"

"At least I have been able to see my friend, and that's the most important thing."

"And there is more you can do, tomorrow the General is having a soiree, you can escort me."

"Of course, my pleasure, and it will be good to see him again." General de Silva, head of the Lisbon Police, was a relation by marriage of Roberta, for whom she also worked as one of his secret agents. Michael's counter-intelligence activities were well known to both Roberta and the General. "Will it be a large gathering?"

"I believe it will, he is entertaining some of the better families from Coimbra, the more politically interesting ones."

"Ah, so not just pleasure for you?"

"Not entirely." She smiled. "People's reaction to a British officer might be interesting."

"Just as long as it's not too interesting. And I shall let Tomkinson and Bence loose on Lisbon on their own."

"Good, now we had better return to my guests before they wonder where we are."

The following morning, Michael dressed in his civilian clothes, explaining to his friends that he had some private business to conduct, and that he would see them for dinner later that afternoon. Together the three of them strolled towards the centre of the city, until they reached the Palacio Quintela. There they parted company, with a promise from Michael to give Tomkinson's regards to Senhor Rodrigues.

Inside the Palacio Michael was quickly taken to Rodrigues' office.

"Michael! How good it is to see you, and very timely as well."

"It is?"

"Oh, yes, but first, let me get some coffee sent in."

They were soon settled with some excellent coffee, but then Michael would expect nothing less from the chief clerk of one of Portugal's most successful and wealthy merchants. While they exchanged pleasantries, Michael passed on Tomkinson's regards and told Rodrigues that the baggage pony he had helped Tomkinson acquire was doing very well. Then the conversation took a serious turn.

"Now, tell me Michael," Rodrigues began, "will Lisbon be safe, will the army hold the French? Are these fortifications that we hear about strong enough?"

"Ah, you've heard about them?"

Rodrigues nodded, "Yes, but only in the last few days. It is as if they have sprung from the ground overnight."

Michael laughed, "Not quite, Senhor, but they were a very well kept secret. And I have seen them, and I believe they will hold."

"That is a great relief, Michael, the idea of fleeing Lisbon again is not a welcome one."

"But you said my visit was timely, why is that?"

Rodrigues smiled mysteriously. "Because, my dear Michael, I have had a letter from Baron Quintela that concerns you."

"Me?" Michael exclaimed in surprise.

"Oh, yes." Rodrigues was delighted at Michael's surprise. "Now, as you know he held your father in high esteem, and had hoped that they would be able to work together, more as partners than employer and employee. The idea was to increase trade with England."

"Yes, you spoke to me about it before."

"Well," Rodrigues paused dramatically, "the Baron has instructed me to make you an offer."

"What!"

"Oh, yes. He has written to me to say that if, and it is an important if, Michael, if you can recover the missing portion of your father's wealth, and will set yourself up as a merchant in Falmouth, the Baron will trade with you, and you only."

Michael was astounded at Rodrigues' words. Rodrigues smiled and went on. "You see, Michael, your father was someone the Baron trusted completely, and he is confident that he can also trust you. However, you must have the necessary capital for such an undertaking, which the missing diamonds will give you. He says he can wait a year for your decision, but, of course, if you have not got the diamonds by then." He shrugged apologetically.

"But, but," stammered Michael, "I have no idea where they are!"

"Come, come," Rodrigues replied, "twenty five thousand pounds worth of diamonds don't just vanish! What about this Augusto your father said he had entrusted them to?"

"Senhor, these diamonds have just vanished, and I still have absolutely no idea who Augusto is!"

Rodrigues shrugged. "Well, there you have it, Michael. Find them, take up the Baron's offer, and you will become a wealthy man."

"I don't know what to say!"

"Michael, there is no need to say anything. I realise this would be a big thing for you, even if, or when you do recover the diamonds. But tell me that you will think about it, I must tell the Baron something."

Michael hesitated; he was completely taken aback. It was too much to take on board. He would have to think about it. "Yes, of course. Tell the Baron that I will consider his, his most generous offer, and if, or when I find the diamonds, he will have an answer."

"A year, Michael, you have just a year."

Michael was in a daze when he left the Palacio. He paused at the foot of the steps and glanced across the road. Old Priscila, the flower seller was in her usual place. He walked across to her.

"Hello, young man, back again, eh?"

"You remembered?"

"Of course I did," she laughed, "I remember all the handsome young men." She slapped her thigh as she laughed. "But you look as if you have had a shock?"

"You could say that," replied Michael.

"A good one?"

"Yes, I suppose so."

"Then you should buy flowers for your love."

Michael smiled at her. "Senhora," he pointed to the biggest bunch, "I shall take those."

Priscila took his money and handed the flowers to him. "She is a lucky lady."

He just smiled, and walked away.

Back home he asked Senhora Santiago for a vase for the flowers, and placed them in his bedroom, next to the picture of Elaine.

Walking through Lisbon, Michael became aware of the effect the huge influx of refugees was having. Many, he knew, had crossed the Tagus into the Alentejo region of Portugal. It was clear however, that Lisbon was doing what it could for the poorer refugees, providing food and shelter. Curiously, at the same time, Michael could detect an unusual level of gaiety and excitement, as if people were determined to make the best of circumstances.

His next call was on his lawyer, Senhor Furtado. His business was straightforward, financial. He asked Furtado about making some banking arrangements for him in Lisbon. Preferably with a bank that could transfer funds between Lisbon and his London bank, or the Regimental agent. Furtado said that could easily be managed. He would make arrangements on Michael's behalf at the bank he used and that Michael's father had used. That settled, there was just the matter of making sure the Santiagos were able to look after his home and themselves, and arranging some ready money for himself.

Their business concluded, Michael was about to leave when Furtado said, "There is one thing more, senhor." He searched his desk, and produced a letter. "I have heard from Mister Rutherford," this was Michael's London lawyer, "there is nothing serious, routine matters concerning your investments. However, he did include an interesting piece of news, that may be of interest to you." Michael raised his eyebrows in question. Furtado scanned the letter. "Ah, here we are. It seems that your uncle is retiring, selling his legal practice. Of course, it is of no direct consequence to you, but..."

"No, Senhor, it is not, but, still, it is curious, I never thought he would do that."

"No? Mister Rutherford hints at ill health. Perhaps that is behind the decision?"

"Perhaps it is, but while it is curious, it is no business of mine. But thank Mister Rutherford me, if you would be so kind?"

"Of course."

The mention of his uncle had brought back to Michael's mind his conflict with him, and their parting, which had not been a good one. In fact Michael had told his uncle exactly what he thought of him and his attempts to force him out of the Regiment and into a career in the law. That in turn brought his parents to mind, and the mystery of Augusto.

"One last thing, Senhor, I wonder, have you any thoughts on the identity of Augusto?" He didn't need to explain to Furtado.

"No, senhor, none at all."

"Ah, well, no matter."

Back home Michael was sitting in a contemplative mood, enjoying a cup of coffee, and wondering about the day's events. The idea of a partnership with Baron Quintela was staggering. He was well aware of what it could mean, he had his father's wealth as evidence of that, and he had worked for Quintela, not with, although he knew that difference was sometimes stretched. On the other hand he rather liked life as it was, the comradeship of the Regiment above all. At which moment he heard noises from downstairs and realised Tomkinson and Bence had returned.

"Hello, Michael!" Bence burst cheerfully into the room. "May we join you, the Senhora is bringing more coffee."

"Hello, Henry, William. Have you had a good day?"

"Very pleasant, wandered around, visited a few churches, oh, went to that shirt maker, got to pick up half a dozen each tomorrow afternoon."

"Don't forget that tavern!" Tomkinson added. "Wonderful place down in Black Horse square, good wine and very pretty girls."

Michael laughed. "And might you be going back there tonight?"

"Err, well, possibly," replied Bence. "What are you doing?"

"I shall be escorting Senhorita Roberta to a deadly dull soiree at General de Silva's."

"Ha," cried Bence, "I can't imagine anything with the Senhorita being dull!"

"No? Well you will just have to. Now, shall we go and see if dinner is ready? Then I must change, full dress tonight, not like you two."

At Roberta's Michael discovered that the family friends were also going to de Silva's. Senhor and Senhorita Marcelino were pleasant enough, but it meant that conversation with Roberta was limited. The Marcelinos were a little unsure of what to make of Michael. Roberta had simply told them that he was an old friend, born in Lisbon. She had said more about Michael's parents, and their loss fleeing from the French. She wanted no close examination of their relationship. It was, she would be the first to admit, unusual. They were the closest of close friends, lovers, and both involved in the dirty war, as Michael called it, of counter intelligence against the French. She did not disagree with his description. But both of them knew, and acknowledged, that they would never be more than the closest of close friends, their relationship was just not like that. What they had was special to them, and beyond description.

Chapter 5

At de Silva's there was already quite a crowd, and they escaped notice for a moment, then the General saw them. "Lieutenant Roberts, Roberta! How lovely to see you both! Come, come, get yourselves a drink." He waved a servant over. "Take the Lieutenant's sword and helmet for him. Senhor and Senhora Marcelino, you as well, come, come, don't stand on ceremony."

They were soon swept into the midst of the very cheerful gathering. As Michael had noticed around Lisbon, the near proximity of a French army seemed to be making people more than ever determined to enjoy themselves while they could. Leaving Roberta talking to the Marcelinos and various other couples, all strangers to him, Michael worked his way to the side of the large reception room. It was warm, and the ladies were working their fans vigorously, and some looked quite flushed. It was good wine, and there seemed to be plenty of it. He wondered if the General was hoping to loosen tongues. He certainly caught one or two glances that hinted at hostility before they became blank with the realisation that he had noticed. He worked his way further around, and through some doors to where food was laid out for the guests to help themselves. There were far too many for anything more formal.

As he stood at the table he glanced to his left, and saw a young woman sitting on her own in the corner. She was without doubt attractive, but looked far from happy, with a far away look on her face, as if she was somewhere else in her mind. She caught his eye, and looked quickly away, her fan raised to cover her lower face, but her eyes flickered back briefly to Michael, and he though he saw the hint of a smile in them. He was wondering who she was when he became aware of someone standing next to him, it was de Silva.

"Lieutenant Roberts, admiring the ladies, I see."

Michael felt his face reddening. "Err..." he stammered.

The General chuckled. "Come along, now, I shall introduce you." He strode across the room, leaving Michael no choice but to follow.

The young woman looked a little startled as General de Silva bore down on her, Michael trailing in his wake. The General beamed at her, and gestured at Michael.

"Senhorita Cardoso, may I present Lieutenant Roberts of the 16th Light Dragoons. Lieutenant Roberts," the General turned to Michael as he caught up, "Senhorita Cardoso, from Coimbra. A town I believe you know a little, Lieutenant? Senhorita, you will find the Lieutenant speaks the most perfect Portuguese. And now I shall leave you to get acquainted, I believe my wife is trying to attract my attention." Michael glanced round, but could see no sign of Senhora de Silva. "Senhorita, Lieutenant." With a nod to each of them, the General left them.

For a moment Michael and the Senhorita stared at each other, then she laughed, delightfully, and smiled. "I think the General is worried at seeing me sitting alone, but I have only been here for a few moments, resting my poor feet." She indicated the chair next to her. "Please, do sit down, it will be easier to talk."

"Thank you, Senhorita," Michael sank into the chair, "I am quite glad of the opportunity to rest myself."

"Are you not a cavalry officer?"

"Yes, I am."

"Then do you not spend most of your time sitting down?" Her look was serious.

Michael floundered slightly. "Err, no, not at all, Senhorita, you see, well, the thing is..."

Senhorita Cardoso suddenly burst out laughing. "Oh, forgive me, Lieutenant, I am being cruel and teasing you, and on such a short acquaintance. I had ponies and then horses myself, so I know very well what hard work it can be, riding or looking after a horse."

"Indeed, it can, but I seem to have walked over most of Lisbon today."

She smiled sympathetically. "So tell me, Lieutenant, how is that that speak such good Portuguese?"

"I was born and grew up here. My father worked for Baron Quintela, but I was sent to live in England. Then my parents left for England in '08, but their ship was lost at sea. Then I joined the army, and here I am."

"Oh!" Senhorita Cardoso's eyes opened wide in surprise at Michael's story. "I am so sorry, that is a tragedy to lose your parents like that."

Michael shrugged. "Indeed, Senhorita, but many people have lost loved ones because of Buonaparte." He gave her a small smile of encouragement. "But tell me about your horses?"

They fell into an easy conversation about horses, and she told him about her first pony, and riding in the hills above Coimbra, or in the plains along the Mondego. Michael for his part, told her about Johnny and Duke, and about hunting in Cornwall. Michael found that he was enjoying her company. Then she looked over Michael's shoulder, and her face dropped.

"It seems I am needed."

Michael turned, in the doorway stood a tall, thin man, with a look of arrogance on his face, he seemed to sneer as he glanced at Michael. He raised his eyebrows at Senhorita Cardoso, who immediately stood, and muttered "Please, excuse me." before walking towards the man.

Michael was annoyed and irritated to have such pleasant company abruptly, and rudely, snatched from him. He caught up with the Senhorita as she reached the man. "Good evening, Senhor," he spoke in his clearest Portuguese, "may I introduce myself, I am Lieutenant Roberts, here at the personal invitation of General de Silva."

The man looked visibly taken aback at being so addressed. "Senhor Venâncio, at your service," he gave Michael a miniscule nod. "I trust that Catarina was not bothering you?"

So that's her name, thought Michael. "No, Senhor, not at all. We were having a most enjoyable conversation about horses."

Roberta suddenly appeared at Venâncio's side. "Ah, Senhor Venâncio, I see you have met my very good friend, Lieutenant Roberts." Venâncio turned to her and was rewarded with one of her most brilliant smiles. "Surely you are not leaving already?"

Venâncio gave a little, apologetic smile. "I fear so, Senhorita de Silva, my wife has developed a nasty headache."

Out of the corner of his eye Michael saw Catarina, as he now thought of her, roll her eyes. He decided he liked her, as he supressed a grin. The man really was the most awful prig. Roberta, however, had not finished with him, and was blocking his exit.

"Oh, such a shame, and you have all only just met." She paused, looking thoughtful, and then gave Venâncio another brilliant smile. Damn, she's good, thought Michael. "I know," she declared, "we shall all have to visit the Lieutenant at his home tomorrow!"

"His home?" questioned Venâncio, confused.

"Oh, yes," Roberta gushed enthusiastically, "he has a most delightful house right here in Lisbon. He was born here, you know, his father was connected with Baron Quintela." Venâncio's face showed his surprise. Roberta went on, "The ballroom has a splendid view across the Tagus. I am quite sure that he would be delighted to give us coffee tomorrow, would you not, Lieutenant Roberts?"

Michael bowed his head in acquiescence, "Of course, Senhorita, I would be very happy."

"Ah, yes, of course," Venâncio replied, "if Senhor Roberts does not mind? Would it not be an imposition at such short notice?"

Roberta did not give Michael a chance. "No, not in the slightest. I promise you, Senhor, his servants are quite used to sudden arrivals. Now, that's settled, shall we say one o'clock, Lieutenant Roberts? We shall. Good. Now, lets us find Senhora Venâncio and get you on your way. The poor woman, headaches are the most dreadful bore..."

As Roberta swept Venâncio away, Catarina followed, and as she did she turned back, and gave Michael a smile full of amusement.

Michael walked Roberta home in company with the Marcelinos, who pressed ahead, eager to get back to their children, and chatting away to each other about the evening. Michael and Roberta followed on, a little behind.

"So, Michael, Senhorita Cardoso! Does she interest you?" Her smile was broad, her amusement genuine.

"No," protested Michael, "not at all. Is that why you contrived that invitation to my home tomorrow? That was quite shameless of you."

"Yes, it was, wasn't it?"

They walked on in silence for a moment. Roberta spoke first. "I could understand if you were interested. She is a very attractive young lady, your age, I believe, well educated, rides very well too, I hear. I enjoy her company, for what that is worth. Did the General tell you about the Venâncios and the Senhorita?"

"No, is there a story?"

"Oh, yes, a very sad one. The Senhorita was born in Coimbra, her family was wealthy, her father was a successful landowner, but her parents both died when she was quite young, and she grew up in the care of her older brother, a sensible and pleasant man, by all accounts. Unfortunately he did not marry well, which might not have mattered if he, too, had not died."

"Damn, but that's a lot of bad luck. So what happened then."

"The Senhorita was the responsibility of her brother's widow, who remarried, to Senhor Venâncio. He is a boring, pompous man, a lecturer in something or other at the University in Coimbra. One of the intellectuals that my cousin is always so suspicious of. Naturally, with the advance of the French, they came to Lisbon."

"Ah, is that why they were at the General's soiree, so he could have a look at them?"

"Yes, and so you see, I had two reasons for arranging our little get together tomorrow." She smiled. "I will investigate the Senhor and Senhora and you can investigate the Senhorita."

Michael laughed. "You really are the most shameless woman, and I love you for it."

"As a friend Michael, as a friend, and friends always help each other out."

"Of course Roberta, and for you, my friend, anything."

"Then consider the Senhorita, she would be good for you."

"Roberta…"

"Yes, Michael, I know, Elaine."

When he arrived home he found Francisco and the Santiagos waiting for him and Tomkinson and Bence, who were still out somewhere. He asked Senhora Santiago to make him some coffee and that he would take it in the sitting room. He was surprised when he suddenly noticed that she wasn't moving with her usual bustle of activity.

"Baba, are you alright?" he asked.

"Yes, thank you, Senhor Michael, it's just a twinge in my back, don't you worry about it."

He caught Senhor Santiago's eye behind her. He shrugged and shook his head at Michael. Taking the hint, Michael took himself off to the sitting room and made himself comfortable in a deep armchair by the fire. A few minutes later Francisco appeared with the coffee.

"Thank you, Francisco" said Michael, "and is the Senhora really alright?"

"Oh, yes, Senhor, I think so, just a little tired." He paused thoughtfully. "But every time we come here, she seems a little slower, Senhor. Senhor Santiago as well. I think they are getting old, Senhor."

Michael thanked Francisco, and let him go. He sat staring into the fire, sipping his coffee, and considered the Santiagos. They had been with his family for a long time. The Senhora had been his Baba, or nanny, since the day he was born. She had been like a second mother to him as a boy, still was. He would have to see what he could do to make things easier for them. He would make sure that they were alright and looked after. He owed them that.

At that moment there was an outbreak of chatter and laughter from downstairs and Michael realised that Tomkinson and Bence were back. They soon came clattering in to the sitting room, and began to regale him with the tale of their night out in Lisbon. They certainly seemed to have taken full advantage of all the delights the city had to offer, although they had failed to get into the theatre, which was full.

The following day, Roberta arrived with the Venâncios and Senhorita Cardoso, or Catarina, as Michael thought of her. Roberta was in bubbling good humour, as she swept in past a bemused Senhor Santiago. Michael, now in his best civilian clothes, top boots polished and crisp white neckcloth frothing over his waistcoat, received them in the larger of the two drawing rooms. He had made sure that Tomkinson and Bence were out by the simple expedient of inviting them to join him for coffee with a University lecturer and his wife who spoke no English. They had positively fled the house.

"Senhor, Senhora, Senhorita, it is a pleasure to see you. Please, take a seat." Michael waved at the chairs gathered around a low table. Roberta moved quickly, to the sole single chair. Naturally, the Venâncios sat together, which meant he and Catarina were left to share a small settee. Roberta smiled at him.

As Senhora Santiago and Francisco served the coffee, Senhor Venâncio spoke. "Senhor Roberts, you have a very fine house. Senhorita de Silva has told us a little of your story, how you come to be here. Please, accept our condolences for the loss of your parents."

Michael gave him a nod. "Thank you, Senhor." The comment about the house brought Maria Barros to mind. Not again, he thought.

The same thought must have occurred to Roberta, who got in quickly with "Senhor Venâncio, I understand that you, too, have a nice house in Coimbra?"

"Indeed, Senhorita, and, of course, there is also the house on the quinta, which my wife brought to the marriage."

Michael saw Catarina stiffen, thought she was going to speak, saw the restraint she exercised. Like a dragoon in the face of Major Stanhope when he was being unfair, and knew protest would be pointless. Michael knew that emotionless expression all too well, after all, he had used it himself from time to time.

"Yes," Senhora Venâncio joined in, hurriedly, Michael thought, "we are so very lucky, and, of course, the quinta is Catarina's home, and where she has her horses."

Michael saw an opportunity to move the conversation on. He turned to look at Catarina. "Tell, me Senhorita, what horses do you have."

"Probably none at all, now the French have come."

Ouch, thought Michael. "Let us hope that is not the case." This was all getting a bit too difficult too quickly.

"Indeed, I hope that our groom managed to get them away. He was going to take them up into the mountains."

"Then, Senhorita, I think that there is every chance you will see them again."

Across the room Roberta had engaged the Venâncios in a conversation about their accommodation, leaving Michael and Catarina to continue.

Catarina's face showed some expression, some hope. "Do you think so, Senhor? Riding my horses is one of my greatest pleasures."

Their conversation turned to tales of her horses, Michael responding with more tales of hunting in Cornwall. It soon became clear to him that she was a real horsewoman, well versed in the care and management of horses as well as the art of riding.

"Michael!" Roberta cut through. "Perhaps you would be kind enough to give us a little tour of your house and the garden? And I believe your horses are stabled at the back?"

"Are they?" Catarina's face was alive with curiosity. "I should very much like to see them. If it is not too much trouble."

"Catarina, we must not impose too much, and they are only horses." Senhor Venâncio protested. Michael decided he did not like him very much.

"Senhor, it is no trouble. You can stroll in the garden, and I will have my groom bring the horses out. You can see the stables and paddock from the gardens." This last for the benefit of Senhora Venâncio, it would satisfy propriety, but put them out of ear shot.

Michael guided them around the main reception floor, and they admired the ball room, and the panoramic view across the Tagus. They could see clearly the ships of Admiral Berkeley's squadron of the Royal Navy, keeping the lower reaches and mouth of the Tagus free of the French.

Michael led the party downstairs, and out into the garden. Roberta took the Venâncios on a stroll around, while he escorted Catarina by a side path to the stables. Making sure that they stayed in view from the garden, he called to Parra, and asked him to bring out the horses for the Senhorita to see. She was delighted by them, and impressed Michael further with her knowledge, and the easy way she conversed with Parra.

He glanced back, towards the gardens and the house. He could clearly see Roberta and the Venâncios, they were admiring the Roman bust that stood towards the bottom of the garden. They were all sending occasional glances is his direction. No doubt, he thought, all for different reasons.

The visit came to an end, and Michael bid farewell to them all, with a promise to Roberta to call on her soon. She meant as soon as he could, that was clear from the look she gave him when she issued the invitation. The Venâncios expressed the hope that, one day, it might be possible for them to return his hospitality in Coimbra, or at their quinta. As she said goodbye, Catarina's eyes sparkled.

It was early evening when Michael walked across Lisbon to Roberta's home. He had dined with Tomkinson and Bence, who had then gone out to further sample the delights of Lisbon one last time. They were leaving for Mafra in the morning. The Marcelinos were at Roberta's, but busy with their children, and Michael was able to get a few minutes alone with Roberta. It had been a very warm day for October, and they were able to sit in her courtyard in the warmth of the evening.

"So, Michael, how did you get on with Senhorita Cardoso?"

"Well enough, thank you. And what about you and the Venâncios?"

"I don't know. They seem harmless enough, but they know who my cousin is. They were quite taken with you."

"What? Really? Oh!"

"Oh, yes. I don't think the Senhor is very worldly wise, perhaps it's those high University walls, but the Senhora, now. She did say to me, and I am not sure Senhor Venâncio heard her, and these are her exact words, 'don't they make a fine looking couple?'"

Michael groaned. "Oh, God, not again."

"Now, Michael, I don't think that you should immediately assume every young lady who might be interested in you is a treasure hunting Maria Barros. I admit she has no money of her own, but the Venâncios are very well to do. I think it might be more that they simply would like to get rid of their responsibility for her, rather than seeking any gain for themselves. After all, they are not blood relations.

I don't suppose they have particularly singled you out. However, she is a fine young lady."

"That's as may be, but it's not just that."

"Michael, I know very well what you are referring to, but, be honest, do you deny that you find her attractive?"

Michael sat in moody silence.

The following morning the small party were ready to set off at first light to return to Mafra. Now Michael was aware of it, he noticed clearly how Senhora Santiago was a little slow around the kitchen when he went to thank her for everything during the all too brief stay. He had noticed that it was the willing Francisco who had scuttled up and down stairs between the dining room and the kitchen with breakfast. He saw that it was Parra who got the horses ready, while Senhor Santiago held them, and led them out of the stable. He determined to do something for them.

Chapter 6

When Michael and his fellow officers rode up to the Convent in Mafra they found a hive of activity, and everything in the organised confusion that went with orders to move the Regiment. Archer greeted them briskly.

"Ah, glad you're back, gentlemen, you're just in time. We are moving at first light, twenty miles or so north. We are going to keep an eye on the French in case they move west and towards the coast. Now, get along, lots to do. And some good news. Colonel Trant has retaken Coimbra! Massena left it practically unguarded." And with that he was gone.

Not knowing how long they might be in the Convent, everyone had made the most of it, and made themselves very comfortable. There was a lot of grumbling at leaving such a grand billet, but the short stay with good rations and forage had worked wonders on the condition of men and horses alike, and they would be marching off nearly four hundred strong. A dozen or so men and horses were being left in Mafra for a week or two more, possibly longer in a few cases, as the men had not fully recovered from wounds, or the horses from various injuries and their poor condition. Michael confirmed who would be left behind from his troop, and gave a list to Harrison, the Adjutant. He made sure that Francisco was getting everything packed, talked to Lloyd and Parra about the horses, and decide to ride Duke. He went around the rooms occupied by the troop with Sergeant Major Flynn, and chivvied and chased to get everything and everyone ready for the morning. By the time he got to bed it was well after midnight.

The company of Tomkinson and Bence on the ride back to Mafra, and the immediate plunge into the work of preparing to move the Regiment had given Michael no time to think over the events of his short visit home, to Lisbon, and there was much to consider. The first chance came now, as he lay in his bed. Catarina, he thought, was undoubtedly an attractive woman, intelligent and mature, and, he guessed, only a little younger than himself. She shared his love of horses, and seemed to be a very competent horsewoman. She had a mischievous sense of humour. He had enjoyed her company. Roberta appeared to like her, and approve of her. On the surface she seemed to be a pleasant and genuine young woman, but so had Maria Barros. That had been a narrow escape from a treasure hunter. He shivered at the recollection. Catarina, it appeared, had little or no money of her own, but it wasn't a secret. And anyway, he thought, for the right woman, money wouldn't matter. The right woman? He had met her, and lost her, he couldn't help it, he was still in love with Elaine. And much of his money had come from her, how could he use it to live with another? And that was presupposing Catarina might be interested in him, rather than just going along with Roberta's suggestions out of a sense of good manners. Whether or not she thought anything of him, thought him in any way attractive, he had no idea. It was, in any case, irrelevant. While he was still tied to Elaine by the bonds of love, he could love no other. True, Elaine's letter to him, given to him by her lawyer after her death, had told him he was free to love again, that he might find love again, as she had with him, and his head told him it was so, but his heart was a different matter. It wasn't enough. He needed something more to show him the truth of it. What that might be was beyond him. He'd killed Renard, and that had brought some satisfaction, quite a lot to be honest, and he had been surprised at how easy he had found it, like putting down a rabid dog, but it hadn't set him free.

Of course, he might feel differently if he was financially independent in his own right, if he could find the rest of his father's diamonds. And that raised another question, what to do about Baron Quintela's offer? The offer of a lucrative trading arrangement, of potential wealth, against his life as a cavalry officer? His life as an officer was full of uncertainties, death was a constant threat. But the regiment was something he didn't feel he could walk away from. His fellow officers and men were important to him, he felt a responsibility to do his best for all of them, to do his duty by them. More, it was as an officer that he could, he felt, do most to fight and defeat the French, to defeat Buonaparte, to avenge himself for his parents' death. If he left the army it would be a betrayal. He found himself wondering what his father would want him to do, and then what his mother would prefer.

He thought about them, his memories of his childhood in Lisbon, the house in Lisbon, his Baba. Perhaps Musgrave had been right to ask him if he considered himself English or Portuguese. He hated what he saw every day, hated what the French had done to his country. Yes, there it was, his country. Was he Portuguese? He thought of his grandfather, and his country parish, and felt he was through and through English.

He felt himself beginning to go round in circles as each conflicting demand took its turn to become uppermost in his mind and tear him first one way, and then the other. Dammit! Why did everything have to be so complicated. He eventually fell asleep, but slept badly, and awoke with a sore head, and in a foul and irritable mood.

It was the usual early start, and Michael and the rest of the regiment rode away from the great convent just as the sun was rising. They hadn't gone far when Michael realised that he hadn't said goodbye to Father Nascimento. That further annoyed him, and he promised himself that he would get back if he could.

The Regiment passed through the Lines and headed north to the villages of Ameal and Ramalhal, some twenty miles away. The French army was away to the east, and they were to watch its eastern flank and try to confine its area of operations as far as they could. Between the brigade and the French was a long line of steep hills, almost impassable to artillery, and slow enough to cross to give plenty of warning. The two villages were only a half mile apart, and two squadrons took Ameal while Ashworth, Cocks and the Regiment's headquarters took Ramalhal. The Regiment soon settled into its billets, they were cramped, but the villages were largely deserted, which made things easier, and at least they had roofs. Three pickets were pushed out to watch various roads, and in particular the one over the hills.

On the second day in Ramalhal, Michael was sent out towards the mountains on picket duty, relieving his friend Alexander. He found him in the small village of Ermegeira, in the lee of a small hill that gave a clear view for his vedettes of the road across the hills. Alexander was pleased to see Michael and his dozen dragoons. He showed Michael around the village and the immediate area, pointing out the roads. He found Michael to be rather out of sorts, very quiet and a little terse.

"Is everything well with you, Michael," he asked his friend.

"What? Yes. Of course. Shouldn't it be?"

"Beg pardon, Michael, you just seem to have a touch of the black dog".

"No, no, not at all. I've just got a few things on my mind."

Alexander waited, but nothing more was forthcoming, so he mounted up his picket and set off back to Ramalhal. On his return he was talking with Henry van Hagen.

"Are you up next for the picket at Ermegeira?"

"Yes, off there tomorrow morning, why d'ye ask?"

"It's Michael, he seems terribly out of sorts, very quiet, but a bit snappy with it, best be careful."

"What's that?" Ashworth walked up to them, returning their salutes. "Is Roberts alright?"

Alexander repeated his story, and van Hagen added "He hasn't been himself since he got back from Lisbon, sir."

"D'ye mean before Buçaco ridge, or just before we moved here?"

Van Hagen thought for a moment. "Frankly, sir, both. He seems to have got worse."

"Very well." Ashworth thought for a moment. "I am sure he will get over whatever it is very quickly. I don't suppose there's anything to be concerned about. Best keep this to ourselves, eh?"

"Yes, sir," the two Lieutenants replied, but Ashworth thought he might just mention it to Archer. He didn't know what Michael had done before rejoining them at Buçaco, but he knew it was something of a different Michael who had returned to them.

When Michael returned from the picket duty, he found a letter from his grandfather waiting for him. They corresponded regularly, each writing to the other about once a month. Usually Michael's letters were full of the round of Regimental duties, and how his fellow officers were, with the occasional note of reassurance when there had been a fight. Michael's grandfather, the Reverend Isles, a former chaplain to the Sixteenth, took a great interest in what the Regiment was doing. Michael's last letter had been about the battle at Buçaco ridge and the long retreat afterwards. As it happened that letter and this one had crossed in the post, as his grandfather had written it on the same day Michael had penned his. It was unusual for his grandfather not to wait for Michael's letters, and he soon discovered why. Instead of the usual litany of Parish business he informed Michael that his uncle had paid him a visit.

Michael was surprised. He had lived with his uncle in Falmouth while his parents were in Lisbon. All had been very pleasant between them, until his parents had been lost at sea fleeing from a French invasion of Portugal. His uncle had tried to stop him joining the army, and it was only thanks to his grandfather that he had managed it. His uncle had then tried to force him out of the army, withholding money sent for Michael by his father, in order to force him to study law and join him in his legal practice in Falmouth. Elaine had taken him to the man who was now his London lawyer, Mister Rutherford, who had put paid to that. There had then been a last meeting in Falmouth, when Michael had lost his temper with his uncle over his actions, laid into him verbally, and then walked out, to join his ship for Portugal. Since that day he there had been no contact between them.

The Reverend Isles wrote that he had been surprised when Jocelyn Roberts had turned up on his doorstep a few days before he wrote. Michael had been completely open, and had told his grandfather about the row and subsequent estrangement. Jocelyn, it seemed, had confessed to Isles that he had been entirely in the wrong in his behaviour towards Michael. He came to ask the Reverend to help to bring about a reconciliation. Michael's immediate reaction to that suggestion was one of complete dismissal. Then his grandfather went on to say that Jocelyn had told him that he had decided to retire from his work as a solicitor, to sell his practice, and to live more easily and quietly. That matched what Michael had heard from Rutherford via Furtado. Then came the shock revelation. Jocelyn had named Michael as the sole beneficiary of his will, aside from a few small bequests to his servants. He was not, he had stressed to the Reverend, trying to buy Michael's forgiveness, the will was made, and would stand whatever Michael did.

The Reverend Isles wrote that he believed that Jocelyn was entirely sincere in his remorse, and that he would ask Michael, as a Christian, to seek in his heart to find it to forgive Jocelyn. He went on that he would be happy to intercede between Michael and his only other living relative. He asked him to consider how his father might feel about the estrangement from his brother. He admitted that it would not be easy for Michael to forgive such wrongs, but, if he could, and he prayed that he might find the strength to do so, he was sure that Michael would find peace and equanimity. Michael was astounded, his first reaction was to damn his uncle for his impertinence. He decided, however, to let the matter stew for a while, if only out of respect for his grandfather.

The following day, the brigade was ordered to send a troop from each regiment to Obidos, to reinforce the garrison. Michael was told to take the troop over to Obidos, with Captain Linsingen of the hussars, who would be in command of the detachment. Archer informed him that the shortage of captains meant Ashworth couldn't be spared. The prospect cheered Michael, it was a chance to show what he could do as a Regimental officer, and Linsingen was a highly respected officer, Michael looked forward to working with him. Driving everyone hard, not least himself, but always with a smile and a jest, he got the troop ready to move, and Ashworth was relieved to see the 'old' Michael again. They were on the road at first light and the two troops arrived at Obidos some four hours later.

Obidos is a long narrow town, sitting on a ridge, surrounded by a high mediaeval wall, and with a strong castle at its highest point. Michael and his troop followed the hussars into the town through a gateway so narrow they had to march in by twos. It had two offset gates forming a sharp dogleg, and, to his wonder, there was a high balcony on the left, covered with a vaulted and painted roof with walls covered in blue and white tiles depicting a religious scene. They followed the hussars along a narrow street until they emerged in a small square with a church.

Linsingen, was talking to a British infantry Major, and Michael quickly dismounted to join them. He introduced Michael to the garrison commander, Major Fenwick of the 3rd Buffs. Major Fenwick turned out to be a very friendly, energetic and enthusiastic man, and Michael could not help but be carried along by him. Within an hour, both troops had been installed in their billets and stables, and Fenwick invited Linsingen and Michael to join him for dinner in the castle.

The great advantage for the dragoons was that the garrison of two hundred and fifty Portuguese infantry meant that at night they did not need to find any sentries as the Portuguese guarded the walls. There was also a good supply of grain and fodder for the horses in the surrounding district, which was jealously guarded against any attempt by French foragers to seize it. Michael and his fellow officers of the Sixteenth, Sawyer and Keating, were billeted in a delightful house opposite the church, and to their great satisfaction they had a room each. The hussar officers were in the house next door.

Michael and Linsingen strolled together up to the castle where Fenwick greeted them, and insisted on showing them the view from the castle roof. They climbed up steep stone spiral stairs to finally emerge on the flat roof. There they found a sergeant and three men equipped with a large telescope on a tripod. The view was stunning. They could see for miles in all directions.

"We keep a permanent watch from here, through all the hours of the day and night," explained Fenwick. "In daylight it's allowed us to spot and intercept quite a few small parties of French foragers. In addition all our outlying pickets have alarm beacons, and we maintain the watch at night for those." He pointed out distant landmarks, and made suggestions about where the dragoons might patrol to cover areas of dead ground invisible from the castle roof. Then they went down for dinner, and further discussions about the role of the detachment.

Michael and Linsingen quickly established a routine of patrols, led by one of the officers or a sergeant, and these frequently returned with deserters, who reported that the French were suffering dreadfully from a lack of food for men and horses. They also, occasionally, came across small parties of French who had come over the hills looking for supplies. Michael took advantage of the relaxed evenings to write to his grandfather. As well as telling him he was well, and what he was doing, he addressed his uncle's desire for reconciliation,. He was brief. He wrote that he was reluctant, but that out of respect for his grandfather he would consider it, and that, after all, with him in Portugal for the foreseeable future, there was no hurry to come to a decision on something so important. He thanked his grandfather for his prayers.

Michael was leading a small patrol of half a dozen dragoons early one morning when they came across a small party of French infantry at an isolated farm. They had set out in a roughly north-east direction to have a look at the roads that came over the mountains from Rio Maior. The terrain became rugged and tree covered, interspersed with the occasional small farm, all abandoned in the face of the French. Riley was out in front, and spotted the French first. He rode back to Michael and reported.

"Sir, there's what looks to be a dozen or so French infantry at a small farm just ahead. I got within a hundred yards or so very easy, there's a bit of an orchard what gives some nice cover, sir."

"Could you see what they were doing?"

"They were milling around a bit, sir, looking for food, I think. And I think I might have seen some civilians, sir".

"Damn, they will be in trouble. Well done, Riley." He addressed the patrol who had been listening intently. "Draw swords. We will move in quietly at the walk until I say. Then, never mind your order, just charge in, and we will see if we can't take all of them. Watch out for any civilians." He gave a thin lipped smile. "And don't let any get away."

Sabres rasped as they were drawn, and Michael led the way cautiously forward, Riley next to him, pointing out the way. He was riding Johnny, and felt confident. They walked quietly through the orchard, and then, as they were coming up to the orchard's edge, an ear piercing scream rent the air. It was a woman's scream. Michael didn't hesitate, "Charge," he yelled, pressed his spurs onto Johnny, and they shot forward, weaving between the last of the trees.

They cleared the edge of the orchard at the gallop, and Michael took in the scene before him in a glance. Two Frenchmen had hold of a young woman, who was screaming and struggling, while one of the men, laughing, pawed at her, tearing her dress open. Lying on the ground nearby was a man, curled up in a ball, while another Frenchman kicked him savagely. Two screaming children were being held by two more of the French, while half a dozen more were standing around laughing. Michael and his men were half way to the small group before they were seen. The woman was released, and she immediately flew at the men holding the children. They let the children go, and started to unsling their muskets as she grabbed the children to her. Two or three of the French got their muskets to their shoulders, and shots rang out, the balls whistling harmlessly by. Then Michael was amongst them. He cut left, and right, feeling the jar as his sabre bit into flesh. He thrust at another who went down under Johnny's hooves. He was vaguely aware of his men, but he was cold with anger, and he went straight for the two had been holding the woman. Both men threw their muskets to the ground and raised their arms. Michael rode at them, hard and fast, and delivered a savage cut at each of them, hauling Johnny to a halt as he did. They went down screaming, and Michael leapt off Johnny. Running at the two men, he opened the throat of one with a back hand cut that almost decapitated the man. The other took the point of Michael's sabre in his heart.

Michael whirled round, panting, to see that the remaining French had thrown down their muskets, and were standing with hands raised, surrounded by his dragoons. Every one of them was staring at him.

They took eight prisoners.

On their return ride to Obidos, Michael rode apart a little, leaving his men to herd the French along. Back in Obidos the prisoners were handed over to the Portuguese infantry. He ordered Sergeant Evans to make sure the men cared for their horses properly, and then he reported to Captain Linsingen. That done, he went to his room without speaking to anyone, dropped his sabre and tarleton on the floor, and threw himself down on his bed. He lay there, waiting to feel something, some reaction, anything. After half an hour he gave up, and went in search of coffee.

Later, Riley spoke to Troop Sergeant Major Flynn. "I tell you, Sar'nt Major, I've never seen the like of it. The look on Mister Robert's face, I hope to God I never see it again."

"How many men?" asked Flynn, slightly incredulous.

"Five, and three of 'em dead."

"What about the Portuguese?" asked Flynn.

"We did what we could, Sar'nt Major. Mr Roberts, he went to the woman, she'd flung herself on the man, 'er 'usband, and he lifted her up, so gentle like." Riley shook his head. "Then he tells us to bring the man inside, and to shoot any French bastard that gave us any trouble.

Begging your pardon, Sar'nt Major, but that was what 'e said. I think he said it to them as well, well, he said something to 'em in French, and they was as quiet as anything. It looked like the man had just been badly bruised, cut lip, bleedin' a bit from his head he were. Anyway, the woman cleaned him up a bit, and Mr Roberts was talking away in Portuguese to her, and the children, like nothing had happened. It was too quick for me to follow all of it. I think he suggested they find somewhere to hide while the 'usband recovered." Riley shrugged. " But the way he killed them French, I've never seen the like."

Word ran around the troop like wild fire. Lloyd had been with Parra and the other horses when Michael returned, and hadn't seen him. One of the patrol had brought him Johnny, and told him the tale. When he heard what had happened he refused to comment, although pressed for an opinion. He had seen Michael angry, he remembered when he had bawled out that Maria Barros for following his patrol. Yet in all their time together he'd only seen him lose it completely the once, with that Musgrave, when Lady Travers was killed. Of course, no one in the Regiment knew about that. No wonder there was a sense of shock. But he knew his Lieutenant hadn't been himself. Not since he killed that Renard. Something else not known in the Regiment. No, there was more to it. He knew the Lieutenant had developed a bit of hardness, but then they all had. He could be ruthless, scary, like when he'd interrogated those two Portuguese traitors. But something else was going on, and he didn't much like what the Lieutenant might be turning into.

Reluctantly, he went to the officers' quarters, wondering what he would find. There he found Michael in the dining room, writing, coffee to hand. "Begging your pardon, sir, I've seen to Johnny. Is there anything else you're wanting just now?"

"Thank you, Lloyd, no. I'm dining at the castle later." Michael looked up, and smiled. "I suppose you've heard that we had a little run in with some French infantry?"

"Yes, sir."

"I'm afraid my sabre will need a bit of a clean and sharpening up a bit."

"Right you are, sir."

Lloyd left Michael, who put down his pen, and sipped at the steaming hot coffee. He knew Lloyd well, and had sensed his unease when he had come in. It must be all round the troop by now, thought Michael. And it won't be long before Linsingen and Fenwick hear, and it will get back to the Regiment. Damn! He thought about how he felt, and realised that he didn't particularly feel anything. He did recall a sense of visceral satisfaction as he had cut down the French attacking the woman. Much as he had when he had killed Renard, and he realised, much as he had in Abrantes, at the ball, when he had told that Portuguese officer that he was a killer, and seen the sudden fear in the man's eyes. He had thought that a brazen bluff, but, perhaps, it was the truth, and he just hadn't realised it back then?

His thinking was interrupted when Captain Linsingen came in. Michael stood up and saluted. Linsingen returned the salute, waved Michael back into his seat and sat down himself. "Is there some more of that coffee?" he asked.

Michael shouted out for the troop orderly, and more coffee was soon forthcoming. As the orderly left them Linsingen said to him, "Shut the door, will you." He took a sip of his coffee. "Lieutenant Roberts, I do not think that you told me everything about your patrol." He took another sip while Michael stayed silent, watching and wondering. "Word of what happened has reached me. It is all round both our troops, and no doubt Major Fenwick is also knowing the story by now." He looked at Michael over his coffee cup as he took another sip.

"Yes, sir," was all Michael felt able to say.

"Now, my men have no love for the French. Many do not know if they have homes or families to go back to in Prussia. They are happy to see French killed. But your English soldier does not think quite so. It is the British sense of, what do you call it, fair play? And they also expect their officers to behave like gentlemen." He gave a dismissive grunt. "For myself, I do not think war is a sport for gentlemen. However, Mister Roberts, I think you need to be careful. You are good with your men, they respect you, that you do not want to lose." He drained his coffee and got to his feet. "Thank you for the coffee, and now you must excuse me. I am not feeling very well." He went out closing the door behind him.

Indeed, Linsingen was not well, and the following day was confined to his bed. Michael sent a dispatch to General Anson, and was quickly informed a day later that the two troops were to be relieved by Captain Cocks' squadron and that they should prepare to return to Ramalhal. Michael wasn't sure how he felt about that. He wondered what the Regiment would make of his actions, because there was no doubt at all that word would go around like wildfire. He hoped Linsingen's reaction would be the norm.

As it happened, events conspired to overshadow Michael's actions, although he thought he detected a slight tendency for people to be a bit careful around him. Word reached the Regiment that Archer had finally got his promotion to Lieutenant Colonel to command the Regiment. Unusually, this gave the Sixteenth no less than four Lieutenant Colonels, three of whom also held rank as Generals in the army. Sir James Affleck was now too old for the rigours of campaigning, Sir Stapleton Cotton was in command of all the cavalry, and George Anson of the brigade. The officers of the Regiment determined to celebrate in style, and a fine dinner was produced. Ashworth's servant Brown, took the lead, and helped by all the other officers' servants, a long day's work resulted in as grand a feast as anyone could wish for. On a fine, frosty day they sat down to a dinner of mutton, beef, fowls, and turkey with potatoes, bread and butter, as well as figs and coffee. There was, of course, an excellent local wine, Collares. The Hussars had generously undertaken to provide all the pickets, and every officer of the Regiment was present, bar those of Cocks' squadron. Michael found it an occasion that managed to lift his spirits. He put aside his personal concerns, and enjoyed the celebration of a very popular promotion. Sitting between his friends Alexander and van Hagen, he recovered some of his old good humour. His friends were glad of it, and relaxed with Michael, enjoying his high spirits.

Sir Stapleton and Anson were both in attendance, and Archer took the opportunity after dinner to take them aside for a quiet word about Michael. He had, inevitably, heard something of the incident with Michael. He told the two Generals what he knew, and shared his concerns with them. They both listened carefully.

"Damn me, Archer," exclaimed Sir Stapleton, "young Roberts is too good to let go to wrack and ruin. He's a good troop officer, from what you say?" Archer nodded. "And Wellington speaks very highly of him. I can't say as I know what he's got up to, like his last jaunt in Lisbon, but it seems to have been some pretty tricky business." He paused. "Truth to tell, Archer, I don't know what we can do." He glanced at Anson who shook his head. Across the room he could see Michael in conversation with Alexander, van Hagen, and others. There was laughter, and he could see Michael joining in. "He seems bright enough at the moment. Look, make sure he's one of the officers that goes to this thing at Mafra for Beresford, and I will mention it to Wellington. Can't promise anything, but another jolly evening might help, and let's see if we can't keep him busy."

As it was, Michael had, for the moment, managed to shake off the black dog, and stop worrying about his personal conflicts. He was with his Regiment; he was doing what he loved. Unfortunately, well intentioned moves were about to make things worse.

Chapter 7

Marshal Beresford had been awarded the Order of the Bath, and the investiture was to be carried out by Viscount Wellington in the Convent of Mafra. Every regiment had been invited to send along as many officers as could be spared without compromising the security of the army. As it was, most were expected to return to their regiments before dawn the following day. That was not possible for the two regiments of Anson's brigade, so it was only a handful that made the trip. Anson was one, leaving colonel Arenschildt to command in his absence. Archer went, but had decided he couldn't spare either of Ashworth or Hay who, with Cocks in Obidos, were the only two captains currently fit and with the Regiment. Consequently, he chose to take along Michael, Bence, and Penrice. Another four officers from the German hussars completed the small party.

It was an easy twenty mile ride to Mafra, and they left at dawn. Like all the party, Michael was accompanied only by his batman, Lloyd, and they were riding Johnny and Rodrigo. For such a short trip, they should be away for only a single night, it wasn't worth taking Francisco, Parra, all the horses, mules, and the baggage.

The weather was fine for early November, and with good company the miles to Mafra passed easily and pleasantly. It was only the early afternoon when they arrived, and found that billets had been arranged in the Convent, which pleased everyone. Once the horses were happily stabled, Archer went off to check on the men and horses of the Sixteenth still there. Lloyd was sorting out the quarters, so Michael wandered off on his own to find the library.

As he had hoped, he found Father Nascimento in his usual place. "Hello, Father, how are you?"

Nascimento looked up at the sound of Michael's voice. "Lieutenant Roberts! This is a pleasant surprise. I didn't expect to see you again! I saw you ride off with your Regiment."

"My apologies, Father, I should have come to say goodbye." He gave an embarrassed shrug. "I'm afraid that I had, have a lot on my mind."

"That does not sound very good, my son? I think I detect a little weariness in your voice?" Nascimento looked at Michael, his head canted a little to one side, his brow furrowed.

Michael tried to rouse himself to be cheerful. "Really, Father? No, no, just a few things that I have to work out." He gave the priest an unconvincing smile.

"Hmm." Nascimento was clearly unconvinced. "You must remember, Lieutenant, that I see many people with many problems, some with a great weight on their shoulders. You remind me of them." He looked thoughtfully at Michael. "Of course, you are a heretic, and I cannot minister to you, but you are hazarding all to help Portugal, so, I can listen and, perhaps, advise, and I will, when you are ready. You know where to find me. Now," he put a fresh vigour into his voice, "tell me, how is your grandfather? Have you told him about your friend the papist?"

Michael was greatly relieved at the change of subject; the priest's perspicacity had taken him aback. He wondered how many others saw that he was troubled. Michael gladly gave him news of his grandfather, and said he had indeed mentioned the priest to him. Father Nascimento roared with laughter when Michael told him that his grandfather's response had been to ask Michael to give the priest his regards and to advise him that he would pray for his soul.

"Please," said the Father, "you must tell him that I shall do the same."

With the atmosphere lightened, the conversation turned to Obidos, which the father had never visited. An hour later, Michael excused himself, saying he better go and find his comrades and see what was happening about the investiture. He discovered several hundred officers, mainly army, but with a fair scattering of naval, and a number of prominent looking civilians, gathering in the Basilica of the Convent. It was a stunning venue, with its Baroque interior of pinkish marble walls, white marble columns, and gold leaf. It was a towering space, with an arched and soaring, vaulted ceiling with ornate decoration. The nave was lined with side chapels, and two larger chapels filled both sides of the transept. The scene was further coloured by the red infantry and blue cavalry uniforms of the army, and the blue and white of the navy.

Michael spotted the small group of officers of the Sixteenth and forced his way with many apologies to Captains, Majors and Colonels until he was able to ease himself alongside Bence.

"There you are, Michael, I was beginning to think we'd lost you."

"No, not at all, just a quick visit to the library."

"Really? There's a library?"

At that point a crowd of senior officers, including Sir Stapleton, and led by Viscount Wellington and Field Marshal Beresford entered from a doorway near the altar. The noise level dropped as Wellington and Beresford took centre stage. Wellington looked to be reading something out, but Michael couldn't make out a word of it. Then Beresford appeared to kneel as Wellington drew his sword, presumably to tap him on his shoulders, but it was all hidden from Michael's view by the crowd. He heard laughter, and it seemed that having dubbed Beresford, Wellington was having trouble returning his sword.

Word filtered through the crowd that dinner would be served at five o'clock in the long succession of rooms that ran across the front of the Convent upstairs. That was an hour away, and the crowd began to disperse as people looked to fill in the time. At that moment, an infantry sergeant touched him lightly on the arm, and when Michael turned he saluted and asked "Lieutenant Roberts, sir?"

"Yes?" Behind the sergeant he could see his comrades looking, including Archer.

"Begging you pardon, sir, but Colonel Murray wishes to see you, sir, if you be so good as to follow me?"

"Yes, of course." He stepped closer to Archer. "It seems Colonel Murray wants to speak to me, sir."

Archer smiled, and didn't look at all surprised. "Then you'd best get along, eh. Try not to miss dinner, or disappear."

Michael followed the sergeant along seemingly endless, and gloomy, picture lined corridors as dusk fell. One room they passed through was lined with marble busts, and Michael caught some of the names chiselled in the bases, Julius Caesar, Hadrian, Caesar Augustus, Tiberius, and many more. He shook his head at the sight of so much statuary on display. Another was hung with paintings of classical scenes. Finally they reached a door at which the sergeant knocked briefly, opened it, and stood aside for Michael to enter.

The room was large, furnished with a substantial table and a lot of chairs. A glance at one of the windows told Michael that it overlooked one of the cloisters. It had all the appearance of an office, and he was not entirely surprised to find not just Colonel Murray, but Viscount Wellington as well, both seated at the table amongst a sea of papers and maps. It was Wellington who spoke first. "Lieutenant Roberts, come in, come in." Michael walked forwards and heard the door click shut behind him. "Now," went on Wellington, "I have a little offer to make you."

Michael was taken aback at that, and feeling a little apprehensive, merely responded with "My Lord?"

"Yes, now, you have been extremely useful and very successful in your endeavours against the French intelligence services, and I am grateful. I also fully expect that I will need to call on you again from time to time, when circumstances arise that call for your, err, talents."

"Thank you, My Lord."

Wellington waved a hand dismissively. "That being the case, it would be advantageous if you were close at hand and more readily available. I also feel that you are deserving of some form of reward for your services." Michael wondered where this was all going. "Consequently, I am able to offer you a captaincy in the Corps of Guides under Major Scovell. It will serve both to keep you on hand for intelligence work, and give you the reward you deserve. What do you say?"

Michael was staggered, he had thought there might be some new task for him, but this was completely unexpected. He stood silently, his mind racing, considering the implications of the offer.

"Well? Come on man, all you have to do is say yes."

"I, I, err, that is, My Lord, forgive me, but I don't know."

"What!" Wellington barked. "What do you mean?"

Murray rolled his eyes and shook his head at Michael's hesitation.

"I am sorry, My Lord, but I just don't know if I want to leave my Regiment."

Wellington looked exasperated. "Murray, talk some sense into him." He turned away to stare out of a window, and the gathering gloom of the cloister.

"Mister Roberts," Murray spoke quietly in his soft, Scots brogue, "ye've done some excellent work for his Lordship, and ye must understand, it is his Lordship who manages all intelligence matters." Michael looked a little surprised at this. "Oh, aye, I know you have frequently had your orders and such like from me, but I can assure you that it is his Lordship who manages intelligence matters." He gave a little chuckle. "I simply help with some of the paperwork and the chores. So, ye see, if you will just accept this offer you will be working very much for his Lordship. Now, as Viscount Wellington has said, ye've done some good work, and you can do more. Ye've got a talent for it, and not every young subaltern has, so, Lieutenant, what do you say?"

Michael had hardly listened to Murray. Just as he was starting to feel like a real officer of the Sixteenth, charging with them, fighting with them, trusted with the independent command of a troop, it seemed that the world was doing its best to tear him away. First there was the offer from Quintela, and now this, from Wellington. But he also thought of the satisfaction of being part of and fighting with the Regiment. How he had felt at rescuing the Portuguese civilians from the French marauders. He conveniently forgot, for the moment, the cold fury as he had mercilessly killed.

"I beg your pardon, Colonel, My Lord, but I feel a great attachment to my Regiment, to the men in my troop, to my fellow officers. I…" He hesitated at the two very serious expressions observing him. "I…, I really am not sure that I want to leave the Regiment."

"Damn it, Roberts," snapped Wellington, "Then I suggest you take yourself off, have dinner, and think about this very carefully. I shall give you to the end of the month to decide, which is a damn sight more that you deserve. You can let Murray know. Good evening, sir!"

Michael came briskly to attention, snapped off a salute that was ignored, and got himself out of the room as quickly as he could. The orderly sergeant was nowhere to be seen, and Michael had to find his own way back to main rooms of the Convent.

His mind whirling at what had just happened, he followed the noise, and found himself in the midst of a scene of chaos as officers and civilians of all ranks fought for a place at the tables laid along the series of rooms over the front of the convent. It was clear that were many more people in attendance than there were places at the tables. It was now dark outside, and the rooms were well lit by large chandeliers. The tables laid with cut glass and silver cutlery.

Michael fought his way through several of the adjoining rooms, and to his great relief spotted his fellow officers. At the same time Bence saw him and waved and gesticulated to an empty chair next to him. He reached the chair, which was being manfully defended by Bence and Penrice against all comers.

"Everything alright?" asked Bence.

"Yes, yes, just an administrative matter, confidential, ye know." He winked. "Where are our esteemed Lieutenant Colonels?" he asked.

"Oh, they're off at the further end, with Wellington and all the other Generals, and that's fine by me," chipped in Penrice.

The food presented was good, various dishes of fish, game, fowl and other meats, the difficulty was in getting hold of any, such was the overcrowding. There was at least a plentiful supply of good wine, and Michael did not stint himself. Michael found the whole affair too crowded and noisy for him to relax and enjoy it as his fellow lieutenants were. He was far too distracted by Wellington's offer and everything else that was going on. He tried to be a convivial companion for his two friends, but not very successfully. Fortunately there was too much going on and too much wine for them to notice.

After the dinner was a rumour of a ball, and the three young men decided to seek it out and try their luck, although with very few ladies in evidence, and so many senior officers, they did not give much for their chances. They left their places, and were immediately replaced by less fortunate attendees. "I don't think we will be coming back here," observed Bence. They followed the sound of music, and found a nearby, largish room, that was packed around the walls with guests, leaving only a small space in the centre for dancing. Michael pushed forward, and bumped up against a brown coated officer of the Portuguese Caçadores. He turned to apologise to the man, and realised that it was the lieutenant he had faced down over Maria Barros at the ball in Abrantes.

There was an embarrassed silence for a moment, then they both spoke together, "Senhor."

Michael could not help but smile, and spoke, "I trust that you have been well since we last spoke?"

After a moment's hesitation the lieutenant replied, "I have, thank you, lieutenant, and yourself?"

"Passable, thank you."

They stood in silence, Michael wondering how he might enquire what had become of Senhorita Barros. The lieutenant saved him the trouble. "Err, you will recall, Senhor, the lady concerned when we met in Abrantes?"

"Of course, Senhor."

"I feel that I should tell you that I enjoyed a very pleasant evening with her, after you, err, asked me to, err, take over as her escort."

"For which Senhor, I am genuinely grateful."

The lieutenant nodded in acknowledgement. "Indeed, I was fortunate to spend some time in her company." He paused. "Unfortunately, she was later introduced to an officer in the Portuguese cavalry, a man of some means, and a prominent family."

"Oh!" was all Michael could say.

"Yes," the lieutenant went on, "I believe they are soon to be married, if they have not done so already." He shrugged philosophically, and then grinned. "I think he did me a favour, much as I did you."

Michael laughed. "You did, indeed, Senhor, and I am grateful."

The lieutenant gave Michael a slight bow. "Now I think I will see if I can get a dance with one of the ladies. Good luck, Senhor."

"And good luck to you, Senhor." The man disappeared into the crowd around the room.

Michael heaved a sigh of relief, that had been entirely unexpected. He turned to find Bence and Penrice at his shoulder.

"What was that about?" asked Bence.

"Oh, just a mutual friend from Abrantes."

Over Bence's shoulder he caught sight of Sir Stapleton, who beckoned to him. "Excuse me" he addressed his friends, "it seems that authority is not done with me yet." The two men turned and saw Sir Stapleton.

"We will wait here for you," said Bence.

Michael nodded his appreciation and walked through the crowd to Sir Stapleton, who turned and led the way out into the quieter corridor.

"I have just been talking to Viscount Wellington."

"Yes, sir." He seemed to be saying that a lot recently, he thought.

"Yes, well, I thought I would just say that it's quite a compliment that Wellington has paid you. And I also want to say, as an officer of the Sixteenth, that your loyalty to the Regiment is appreciated. That's all Roberts, now, get along back to your friends. It's up to you what you tell them, or anyone else. Good night to you."

Bence and Penrice were indeed agog to know what Sir Stapleton had wanted.

"Oh, just to remind us that we must make an early start in the morning. Anyway, if you will excuse me, I think I am going to take some air."

Outside the night was clear and sharp. Michael was glad they were not having to find their way home until the morning. On a whim he took himself to where the horses were. He was not terribly surprised to find Lloyd fussing over Rodrigo.

"Evening, Lloyd."

Lloyd came to attention and saluted. "Begging your pardon, sir, didn't hear you coming."

Michael returned the salute, "That's alright, stand easy. Is there anything wrong with Rodrigo?"

"Oh, no, sir. I just like his company, sir."

Michael had strolled over to where Johnny stood, and stroked his face. "I know what you mean, Lloyd. Well, if everything is in order, I am going to try to get some sleep, we've an early start."

"Don't you worry about that, sir, we will be ready."

On his way to his billet, Michael passed the entrance to the library, all was darkness. He would have liked a word with Father Nascimento. It looked as if he was going to be leaving without saying goodbye, again. And so it proved.

There were a few sore heads in the morning, and the ride back to Ramalhal passed off mostly in silence. Michael was glad of that. It gave him a few hours to contemplate his situation. He was still concerned about the consequences of his actions saving the Portuguese civilians, although nothing had been said to him, yet. His worry was how it might affect his position in the Regiment. And as if that wasn't enough to worry about, he had the offer from Quintela that would, if he recovered the missing diamonds, make him wealthy, but take him out of the Regiment he loved, out of the army, and out of the war against Buonaparte. To add to his difficulties, he now also had Wellington's offer. That would keep him in the army, with a very welcome promotion, but fighting the dirty, intelligence war. It would take him away from his Regiment and all his friends and comrades, away from proper soldiering. And then there was the whole business with Catarina and his continuing love for Elaine. He didn't know what to do about any of it. It was all distracting him, preying on his mind, he was becoming familiar with the black dog.

When they got back to Ramalhal Michael was able to throw himself back into the work of looking after Captain Ashworth's troop. The reaction to the incident at Obidos had passed, so far as he could tell, which came as a relief to him, but he still felt unable to completely relax with the men and his fellow officers. His time was taken up with paperwork, which he detested, taking out patrols, which he enjoyed, and generally ensuring the efficiency of the troop. It was only at night that his mind would inevitably turn to considering his situation, but not for long, he worked himself hard to ensure he slept.

A few evenings later, Colonel Archer, Captain Ashworth, and Captain Hay were absent, dining with General Anson. All the eleven subalterns who were not on picket duty had gathered together for dinner, and they were enjoying a relaxed evening together for the first time in a while. Dinner over, they were relaxing with a few of bottles of port.

There was a pause in the conversation, and Penrice asked, "I say, Roberts, I've been meaning to ask, who was that Caçadore officer you spoke to at Beresford's investiture, it looked like you knew him?"

Michael hesitated for a moment. "No, not really, just someone I ran into briefly at Abrantes."

"But the garrison were line infantry, not Caçadores?"

"Yes, he was at a ball."

"Good Lord," exclaimed van Hagen, "not the chap at the ball that we thought was going to call you out?"

Michael glared at him, but it was too late.

"Is that the business that saw you sent off to Lisbon?" Buchanan chimed in. "We never really knew what that was about. Didn't it involve that Senhorita, What was her name?"

"Come on, now, Roberts," Persse joined in. "You have to tell us about it, van Hagen and Keating have been very coy about it."

Michael looked at Henry van Hagen and George Keating, who both shrugged.

Alexander tried to change the subject and help his friend. "That's a long time ago, I'm more interested in what to do next time I get leave in Lisbon. Bence, tell us about that tavern you and Tomkinson found, is it worth a visit?"

"Oh, be quiet, Alexander," said Persse, "this sounds far more interesting."

Michael looked around the table. It was too well known that there had been some sort of trouble at the ball, and that a woman had been the root cause of it. He would have to tell, but that didn't mean he couldn't make light of it, laugh it away.

"Oh, very well." He laughed. "It was nothing really. It was the niece of the lady I was billeted on. Senhorita Maria Barros. I fear she set her cap at me, encouraged by her father. I think they saw me as a desirable catch, I can't think why."

"Oh, come on, Roberts," Buchanan interrupted, "none of us has a fine house in Lisbon."

"Well, yes, I suppose there is that." There was laughter. "Anyway, they made a damn nuisance of themselves, and I suffered for it from Stanhope."

"Oh, yes," laughed Persse, "we all heard about you nearly shooting her when she followed your patrol."

"Yes, well, it wasn't quite that close, but we gave her one hell of a fright, and I swore like a trooper at her. You should have seen her face!" There was more laughter.

"So, come on now," insisted Persse, "what about the ball?"

"Nothing much really. I got rather boxed into escorting her, but I thought to myself, a dance or two, and then leave her to the attention of anyone who cared to ask her. Frankly, I knew she was a treasure hunter and I just wanted rid. So that's what I did. Then that Caçadore officer approached me, and I persuaded him to take over as my escort, and then got myself out of there as quickly as I could."

"But why was there such a fuss? There must be more to it than that?" insisted Buchanan. "Van Hagen, you were there, weren't you? What happened?"

Van Hagen managed to get as far as "Err" when Michael finally gave in.

"If you must know, the Senhorita had put it about that this." Michael pointed to the scar on his cheek, "was a duelling scar and that I had killed several men. I thought he was going to call me out over neglecting the Senhorita. I simply persuaded him that he didn't want to fight me, and that I would be grateful if he took over my duties as her escort."

"What did you say to persuade him?" asked Persse.

Michael heaved an exasperated sigh, he was getting irritated, was a little drunk, and didn't think too clearly about what he said next. "If you must know, I took Stanhope's view of me, and the Senhorita's rumour, and I suggested he really wouldn't want to die at the hands of someone who wasn't a gentleman, but was a killer. And d'ye know, he believed me!" Michael laughed out loud at the recollection, but realised that no one else was so much as smiling.

"What? What's the matter."

It was Henry van Hagen who finally answered. "Well, the thing is, Michael, I believed you as well, and now there has been that business at Obidos, and there are all sorts of rumours about those special missions that you go on." He shrugged. "I'm sorry, Michael, but that's how it is."

The smile died on Michael's face. He looked around the serious, but expectant faces of his fellow officers. Alexander and van Hagen looked away. He had been irritated by his comrades persistence. Then he had begun to get angry. Now he was shocked to his very core by the implications of van Hagen's words. In a flash of perception he realised that there was a lot of truth in what his friend had said. He struggled with the idea of what he might have become. He felt he needed to explain.

"Gentlemen," Michael began, "there are things at work here, which, regrettably, I am not able to share with you, however…"

The door flew open and Archer strode in, followed by Ashworth and Hay. The subalterns all leapt to their feet, as Archer spoke. "Gentlemen, I am glad to find you all together. Massena has commenced a retreat. We will be marching after him at first light. Go and prepare your troops immediately. I want the whole regiment mounted and ready to move at seven o'clock. Captain Murray will be returning to command his squadron despite his wounds; he insists he is fit enough. A messenger has been sent to Captain Cocks, and he will be joining us by and by. Gentlemen, you are dismissed."

There was confusion as everyone made for the door, following Archer and the two Captains out into the cold of the night. Michael headed for the quarters of the squadron, along with van Hagen, Alexander, Sawyer and Keating. Ashworth was already far in front, bellowing for Sergeant Major Flynn. As they approached their billets, van Hagen put a hand on Michael's arm.

"Michael, stop a moment, please."

Michael turned to face him. "Look, I really don't know what was going on back there, Michael, but I want you to know that I most sincerely apologise for any difficulties I might have caused for you. I should have kept my damn mouth shut."

"No, Henry, it is better that I know how people feel." Michael paused. "Between ourselves, and no one else," he looked at van Hagen who nodded his agreement, "there are, as I said, things at work that I cannot share. I am what I am, I am who I am. But know this, I will fight the French and that bastard Buonaparte every way I can. I owe it to my parents," he paused, "and others. Now, let's go and prepare for the morning."

Chapter 8

The first grey light of dawn was just beginning to show over the hills away to the east. It was a dull and cold morning. The three squadrons present were drawn up in their two ranks, told off into threes and divisions, and squeezed into the small town square, filling three sides, leaving empty the narrower side, where the church was. It was a tight fit, and one flank of Murray's squadron was partly down a side road. Michael was back in his accustomed post, sitting on Duke, on the left flank of Ashworth's squadron, Sergeant Taylor behind him, Lloyd to his right. Ashworth sat alone just in front of the centre, Keating behind him, marking the centre of the squadron. Back home in England he would have been carrying a guidon, the squadron's colour. Out here they didn't use them. It was quiet save for the occasional stamp of a hoof on cobbles. Somewhere a cock crowed.

Colonel Archer sat on his horse in the middle of the square with the Adjutant, Lieutenant Barra, Quartermaster Harrison, RSM Williams and the orderly trumpeter. There was a clatter of hooves and General Anson appeared with his aide de camp, Lieutenant Osten, also of the Sixteenth. Anson didn't stop. As he rode through the square, he called out, "Follow me, Archer!" and set off down the road towards Santarem and the French.

Archer ordered the squadrons to wheel by threes, and moments later the Regiment marched out of Ramalhal, Hay's squadron first, then Ashworth, and Murray bringing up the rear, followed by the regimental baggage. Ahead of them were the hussars, and Michael knew that Linsingen, now recovered from his illness, was out in front of all, his squadron forming the advanced guard.

By the time they were marching through Ermegeira it was fully light, or as light as it was going to get. It was a cloudy, chilly day. Once through the village the road narrowed, forcing the squadrons from six abreast to three, and it began to climb, giving views of a rugged, tree covered landscape. All around the hilltops were shrouded in low cloud. It began to rain. A steady, persistent, penetrating rain.

Michael had little to do. They had marched by the right, making him and Sergeant Taylor the rearmost men of the squadron. There was a lot of time for him to think. His circumstances were preying on his mind, going round and round, unresolved, building up into huge, overwhelming difficulties that he could not cope with. He had thought he knew what he was going to do, fight the French, drive them out of Portugal, and avenge his parents. Then he had found himself hunting a man to avenge the murder of the woman he had loved, no, not had loved, still loved, and who he could not let go of. He had been going to fight the French with his Regiment, serve with his comrades, live his life with the Regiment. It was simple. Then Musgrave had interfered. But without him he would never have met Elaine, never become involved in the intelligence war. It seemed that had brought him mixed blessings, great love, but great sadness as well. It had brought him to the attention of Viscount Wellington, earned him the offer of promotion, if he left his Regiment, which he didn't want to do. And now he had learned how to kill. Not the killing of a soldier in a battle, but something beyond that, a cold, ruthless killing without remorse or conscience.

And then there was the question of Catarina Cardoso. She was undoubtedly an attractive young woman, although he did not know what she thought of him, did not know if the attraction was more than superficial, but it didn't matter. Whatever it was, it simply drove home to him that he had not yet freed himself from the bonds of love that tied him to Elaine. Tomorrow was the second anniversary of her death. Two years, but he could still feel the squeeze of her hand, the touch of her last kiss, that last, radiant smile she had given him before she had slipped so quietly away. It would not be a good day for someone if he let himself give vent to his feelings.

Michael was getting wound tighter and tighter, without knowing it. He was chasing around and around fruitlessly, he was slowly getting angry, beyond angry, with himself, with his feelings of helplessness, of impotence, but he didn't realise it. He was on the edge, on the verge of snapping. Tomorrow was not going to be a good day for someone.

A long, but uneventful days march brought the brigade to the Quinta Da Torre, and its bridge over the Rio Ota. It was a small quinta, with room only for the brigade's senior officers. The rest of the Brigade had to make the best of what cover they could find in the surrounding woodland. They were at least able to unsaddle and groom the horses, and there was an adequate supply of fodder. Later in the evening the baggage caught up, and along with them the commissary arrived to distribute rations. With a few fires going, it could have been worse.

Parra and Francisco arrived with the Regimental baggage and found Michael and Lloyd huddled over a small fire, and Francisco set about producing food for Michael. Lloyd had already received rations from the commissary. It had been a long days march, so Michael decided to change horses and ride Johnny. Duke was good, but as they were approaching near to the French, Michael wanted the additional confidence of being on Johnny. He was wet, but then everyone was wet. He tried, like everyone else to get some sleep. He changed his tarleton for his forage cap, wrapped himself in his cloak, sat with his back against a tree, pulled his knees up, folded his arms in close, and tried to sleep. His mind was awhirl, images of Elaine and Catarina came to him. He would have sworn he hadn't slept, but suddenly Lloyd was shaking him by the shoulder, and offering him a mug of coffee laced with brandy.

"Bore da, sir, time to be stirring. Francisco has some breakfast for you, sir, but we are running low on rations, sir. That was the last the commissary had. Seems he didn't expect us to move so sudden, like."

"Diolch, Lloyd." Michael heaved himself, tired and bleary eyed, to his feet.

"Begging your pardon, Mister Roberts, sir, but are you alright this morning?" Lloyd was well aware that it was the anniversary of Elaine's death, he had been there.

"What?" The question momentarily surprised Michael. He looked at Lloyd by the light of a flickering fire, it was still dark, and saw only genuine concern in his expression. "Yes, Lloyd, Emyr, I think I am, diolch yn fawr." He wasn't really sure.

Soon after daylight they met up with Cocks and his squadron. Back up to full strength, the Brigade advance towards Santarem, Cocks squadron taking the lead. A couple of hours later two of Cocks' dragoons came in sight, herding towards the brigade eight French infantry and their sergeant. They had been surprised by Cocks' advance guard, and had simply laid down their arms. They had no idea where the French army was, they had been an outlying picket, and hadn't been relieved when they were supposed to be. They had not been told the army was retreating. They were very thin, uniforms in rags, and seemed quite happy to be prisoners, even as the rain started to fall again.

The Brigade passed through the small village of Almoster, it was a scene of destruction and desolation. It was completely empty, but filth, human ordure, and rubbish lay around everywhere. There was a stench of death about the place. Houses had been stripped of doors and windows, apparently for firewood, and now stood open and derelict.

It was clear that the small town had been occupied by the French who had wreaked destruction upon it. Up until now they had been retreating away from the French, but now, for the first time, they moved into territory that had been occupied by the French army, and an army that was, thanks to Wellington's strategy, hungry and ill supplied. Michael was shocked, and upset, perhaps more than his comrades because this was Portugal, his home, his adopted country. He was overcome with a terrible loathing for the enemy.

They found Cocks and his squadron waiting on the far side of the town. All Michael knew from his post at the rear of the squadron was that the Brigade deployed into line on open ground, a long gentle slope, covered in scrubby undergrowth in front of them, and running up to a distant ridge line. Michael watched as Anson, Archer and von Arenschildt conferred with Cocks out in front of the Brigade. A few minutes passed and the group broke up. Archer rode straight to Ashworth, and then the two rode together to Michael.

They exchanged salutes and Archer explained to Michael. "It seems we are only five or six miles from Santarem. It the French have abandoned it, our orders are to occupy it and wait for the infantry to come up. Cocks is sending out patrols directly towards Santarem, and away to the left. Mister Roberts, take Sergeant Taylor and twelve men, ride south and see what you can find." He looked at Michael, and saw something in his face. "Are you alright, Roberts?"

"Yes, sir. It's just that the state of that town, sir, it was a bit of a shock."

"Yes, well, I think we can expect more, and worse. I particularly want you to go, you can question any Portuguese you come across." Archer pulled out his watch. "It's just eleven o'clock, be back by no later than three o'clock, that should give you plenty of time. Ashworth, I shall leave you to send Mister Roberts on his way." Archer wheeled his horse and rode off towards Anson.

"Are you sure that you are alright?" Ashworth asked.

"Yes, sir." Michael bridled, cross at being questioned in front of the men.

"Very, well, take the two left flank threes, both ranks. Off you go."

Michael ordered his small patrol to ready their carbines, and they quickly freed them from their saddles, attached them to their carbine belts, and loaded, resting the loaded guns in the crooks of their arms. While they did that, Michael loaded his single pistol. One of his two holsters now carried a telescope, which he found to be far more useful. Riley was one of the dragoons, and trusting him to scout ahead carefully, Michael sent him ahead with Williams, following with the rest of the patrol about fifty yards behind.

Their route took them along a narrow track through a narrow valley with steep, wooded slopes on both sides, the bare trees dripping with water. They had barely gone half a mile, when Riley and Williams halted, Riley looking back and pointing to the left. As he came up to them, Michael could see fields through the trees bordering the track. On the far side there seemed to be quite a large quinta. There was no sign of movement. He halted the patrol and listened carefully. There were no sounds, but they were a hundred yards or so from it.

"We had better have a look, don't want to leave any French behind us." Michael pointed a little way ahead. "That track seems to go to it. Lead the way, slowly, we will be right behind you, if you see or hear anything, halt."

The straight, tree lined track led towards a two story house, with farm buildings scattered around it. There were no sounds, no shouts, no shots. As they reached the house

Michael could see that, like the houses in Almoster, all the doors and windows were missing from all the buildings. Riley and Williams reached the house, and Michael halted the patrol. He watched as Williams slipped off his horse, passed the reins to Riley, and, carbine ready, stepped through the open door of the house.

Seconds later he shot back out, spun to the wall, and vomited. Michael spoke quickly to Sergeant Taylor, "Put a few vedettes out, dismount, be ready," and rode forward. He reached the house and dismounted. He started to walk towards the door when Williams gasped out, "Don't go in there, sir, for God's sake don't." Williams, heaved again, retching.

Michael approached the door, cautiously, and peered in through the door. He felt his gorge rise, and with difficulty avoided joining Williams. He took a deep breath, and stepped into the house. The door opened on a large hallway, stairs ran up against one wall, and at the top was a short landing. Hanging from the landing was the body of a man. He was hung up by his wrists. A fire had been lit below him; the lower half of his body was a charred mess. The air was full of the smell of cooked flesh. A little smoke still came from the fire. To his right was a doorway. Michael glanced in, and gasped. There were bodies, a woman, children, and there was blood everywhere. He staggered back and out into the fresh air.

"The bastards," he shouted, "you fucking bastards!"

There were no tools to be found, not a shovel or a mattock. They cut the man down, laid him and, they supposed, his wife and three children together in the main room. There was nothing else they could do. A check of the farm buildings revealed nothing else, no one hiding, no more bodies, and everything stripped out, leaving empty buildings.

The patrol moved off down the road towards the east, Riley and Williams in front again. There was complete silence from everyone. Michael's nerves were as taut as bow strings. He wanted to scream at the world, he wanted to put Johnny into a gallop and ride until they dropped, he wanted everything to just stop. He wanted to cry for the dead family, he wanted to cry for himself. He wanted someone to tell him what to do. What to do about Quintela's offer, Wellington's offer, about Catarina, about his love for Elaine, his future. He felt physically sick, he felt angry, he was absolutely cold with anger. He knew he had to hold himself together until there was a reason to let himself go. He rode out in front, looking straight ahead, watching Riley and Williams.

Suddenly the two men stopped, and rode into the trees. Michael halted the patrol and waited. The minutes passed, slowly, Michael looked at his watch. They would have to turn back soon, and they hadn't discovered anything, nothing useful anyway. Ten minutes or so passed, then Riley came out of the trees half way back to them and trotted to Michael.

"There's a party of French infantry, sir, about a dozen and a half it looks like, with an officer. They've a small cart with a mule. They're stopped by a barn a little way down the road, sir."

Riley's report brought a little distraction to Michael's mind, brought him back to his duty. He turned to Taylor. "Sergeant Taylor, wait here with the patrol while I go and have a look. If there's any trouble, come on fast."

Pushing their way through the trees, Michael and Riley joined Williams. He was a few yards back from the edge of the tree line. In front, the small valley opened out on to a wide, flat plain. A quarter of a mile away was a small barn, and Michael could just make out figures moving around, and the shape of a cart. He pulled his telescope out of its holster, back in the shade of the trees there was little chance of the lens reflecting the sun, and giving them away. He pulled the telescope open, twisting the tubes to get the image into focus as he looked for the barn.

He found it, and studied it intently for a moment, and then he cursed. "Bloody Hell, they've a woman with them, looks like she's tied to the tail of the cart. The bastards, I'll wager they've just come from that farm." He closed his telescope and put it away. "Follow me," he ordered the two dragons, turning his horse back the way he had come.

When he got to the patrol he told them what the situation was, and then gave his orders. "We are going to attack them. If they are the bastards from the farm…" He left the rest unsaid. He looked at his men, some looked a little pale still, but everyone had a look of grim determination. "We will trot up to where Riley and Williams were, just beyond there the trees end and it's open country, we will form a line, quickly, open order, and then gallop in. Any resistance and we charge. Got that?" Heads nodded, Michael wheeled Johnny round, "Draw,…Swords!" A moments pause, "Patrol, trot!"

They quickly covered the road to the edge of the trees, and as they came out onto the open ground a line quickly formed. Michael glanced behind him, then shouted, "Gallop," and the patrol was moving fast across the ground towards the barn, the sounds of their hooves muffled on the rain sodden ground. They were half way there, only a couple of hundred yards to go, when they were spotted. There was a shout, then a cloud of smoke followed by the crack of a musket. More followed. Good, thought Michael, too far away to worry about, and now they want to make a fight of it. More muskets cracked, smoke billowing, he heard the whizz of a ball. With a hundred yards to go, Michael screamed "Charge!", and urged Johnny on. The horse surged forwards, hooves drumming a fast, staccato, four beat rhythm.

Michael saw some of the infantry throw down their muskets and turn to run, then he was amongst them, and all restraint failed, he gave in to the anger that had been bubbling away inside, he just wanted to kill. He parried a half-hearted bayonet thrust from his right, and turned in the saddle to cut back, feeling the blade bite into the man's forearm. An infantryman to his left tried to raise his musket to fire, but Michael shot past him, turning to his left and delivering a backhand cut that took the man in the shoulder. He pulled Johnny up as another thrust at him with his bayonet, he parried and thrust, sending the point of his sabre into the man's throat. Another had dropped his musket, but Michael was in a cold rage, and cut across the man's face, sending him screaming to the ground. Another man threw his musket away and raised his arms. Michael rode straight at him, snarling, his face a mask of rage, his sabre raised to kill. Then another horse and rider got in the way, forcing Johnny to swerve, and Lloyd seized his sword arm, shouting at him, "Stop, sir, for God's sake stop! It's over, sir, it's over, we've got them all."

Michael stared at Lloyd for a moment as if he didn't know him. Lloyd clung to Michael's arm, his grip firm. More quietly, he said, "It's over, sir, it's over, you can stop now." Taylor appeared on Michael's other side. "Begging your pardon, sir, but there's a young lady here as needs someone who speaks Portuguese better 'n I do, sir."

"What? Oh! Yes, of course." Michael looked at Lloyd, who slowly let go of Michael's arm. "Thank you, Lloyd," he shook his head as if waking up. "Yes, diolch yn fawr, Emyr." He took a deep breath and looked around. All his dragoons were still on their horses, no one appeared to have suffered so much as a scratch. Half a dozen French infantry were laid on the ground, more, many badly cut about, were standing in a small huddle, dragoons, with carbines at the ready, watching them.

Michael walked Johnny to the back of the cart, standing with a mule in the traces. There he found a young girl, wide eyed, looking terrified. "Senhorita, we are English soldiers, you have nothing to fear from us." For a moment she just stared at him, and then she began to cry, huge, deep sobs wracked her small frame.

It took a little while, but all the French who could walk were tied together, two others were thrown in the cart, onto a pile of tools, including shovels. The officer had suffered a cut to his shoulder. His horse had been tied to the side of the barn, he was left on foot, and the young girl put on his horse. She had recovered herself a little, and, sobs still heaving her shoulders, she told Michael what he had suspected. These French had been at her farm, she knew her family were dead, she asked him for a knife to kill two who she pointed out. They looked scared when she pointed to them. The worst offender had been a sergeant, now lying dead. The officer, she said, had lost control of his men, and the sergeant had tortured her father to get him to reveal their hidden supplies of food. There weren't any, and so her father had died.

Grim faced, Michael walked across to the officer who was standing a little away from his men, one of the dragoons behind him, carbine resting on his arm. "Monsieur, your name and rank, if you please."

"Lieutenant Gerard."

"And you are responsible for what we found at the farm up there?" Michael nodded up the road.

Gerard looked down at the ground. "They are my men, monsieur," he looked Michael in the eye, "but I could not control them, monsieur. We have had no rations for more than a week, only what we can find and forage. The sergeant, there," he indicated a body, "he would not listen to me, he persuaded some of the men that there was food hidden at the farm, and he tortured the family, took the girl. I could not stop them." His head dropped with the shame.

Michael felt no pity for him. "Lieutenant, how far is your army retreating?"

Gerard shrugged. "We didn't even know there was going to be a retreat, the army just went. We were trying to get back to it."

Michael decided there was nothing to be learnt from the man, and time was pressing. Taylor already had a man at the reins of the cart, his horse tied behind. He mounted Johnny, and moments later they were heading back the way they had come. As they approached the turning to the farm, Michael spoke to the young girl.

"Senhorita, would you like us to see to burying your family?"

She just nodded, tears running down her face.

They used the tools on the cart, made the French dig the graves, place the bodies in them, and fill them up after. The girl just watched, crying silent tears.

Afterwards Michael asked her. "Senhorita, what will you do now? Do you want to come with us? It might be safer."

"No, Senhor, thank you." She looked around the devastated farm buildings, the rain still falling. "This is my home, it was my father's farm, and now it is mine." She turned her gaze on Michael. "I will stay."

"Are you sure? We can't stay any longer, our Regiment will be waiting for us."

"I am, Senhor, and thank you."

Michael mounted up the patrol and lead them away from the farm. The girl stood in the rain, watching until they were out of sight. Michael was glad of the rain, as tears ran down his face.

Almoster was in such a filthy state that the Brigade had bivouacked nearby, taking what shelter it could under trees that dripped with water. Michael saw to his patrol and securing the prisoners, then went in search of Archer. He found him with Arenschildt and Anson, sheltering in a very small hut that somehow had escaped the depredations of the French. He reported on what had happened, how the French officer hadn't known about the retreat, about the poor state of French supplies, the breakdown of discipline, and what they had found at the farm. Anson thanked him, and dismissed him, suggesting he go and get something to eat.

He found Francisco with his baggage sheltering under a scrawny olive tree that really did little to keep the rain off. Parra was nearby with the horses. Lloyd had disappeared somewhere, but probably not far as Rodrigo was with the other horses. The Regiment had quickly become accustomed to seeing Lloyd on Rodrigo, as had the whole Brigade. It no longer attracted any comment. As he took care of Michael's baggage, Francisco seemed unusually quiet.

"What's wrong, Francisco, you are very quiet?"

"Senhor, it is that town," he pointed in the direction of Almoster, "never have I seen anything like that. And I have heard what the French did to that family, Senhor. I do not like it. It frightens me, Senhor."

"It is bad, Francisco, you are right. But you do not need to fear anything, not here, not with the Regiment."

Francisco, gave a small smile. "Yes, Senhor, that is true, it is like a very, very large family Senhor. I am glad that I came with you."

Michael felt disproportionately cheered by Francisco's simple statement.

Gradually all the other patrols came in, they had been slowed because, like Michael's, they had run into small bands of French troops wandering around the countryside, some out to plunder, others simply lost. Some of the groups of prisoners weren't so small. Sergeant Baxter of Cocks' troop had gone out with just four men. He had come across a picket of French infantry in a remote house. They had piled arms outside, and he thought he could get close enough to get to their arms before the infantry could. With his four men he had charged, and some of the infantry had fired at him, wounding one of his men. Then they were in amongst them, killed one, and the rest surrendered. In all he captured forty one men and an officer.

Sergeant Blood had the closest call. He got too close to Santarem, and was trapped by the French pickets. He and his party managed to cut their way out, but lost one man made prisoner. The common theme was that the French were tired, hungry, ill supplied, and thoroughly demoralised.

As the day came to an end, the rain finally relented, and a few more fires were kindled. There was hot coffee, but no sign of the commissary with any supplies. A few dragoons were sent back into Almoster to see what they could forage, they returned empty handed. Murray's squadron was providing the pickets, and Michael managed to find a broken down shed to make his bivouac in. Parra and Francisco went looking for wood, and Lloyd succeeded in getting a fire going, with the help of the contents of one of Michael's pistol cartridges. Francisco produced some stale bread and hard cheese from Michael's supplies. It didn't go very far between them.

Michael huddled up in his cloak for another miserable night. He was cold, his uniform was soaked through, he was hungry, he was tired, emotionally exhausted. Sleep came quickly.

Chapter 9

The following day was another day of rain with occasional dry periods. Michael had changed horses, and was now riding Duke. The Brigade formed before dawn and waited in front of Almoster. Patrols were sent out again. Van Hagen was sent on the road Michael had taken the day before. He told him about the farm, and the girl. Van Hagen promised to check on her. The day passed slowly, and slowly the story of the patrol the day before filtered through the Regiment.

Will Alexander heard, and came to talk to Michael. He did not beat about the bush. "Michael, what the Hell has got into you? Your patrol yesterday is the talk of the Regiment. It's Obidos all over again. What's going on?"

Michael couldn't reply. He just shook his head. Alexander stood looking at him for a moment, and then walked away without another word.

Van Hagen and his patrol returned, and after he had made his report and dismissed his men, he came looking for Michael. "Hello, Michael, I went to that farm. There was no one there."

"What?" Michael was aghast.

"There was no one there. Place was in a Hell of a mess. Pretty much uninhabitable." He paused. "Michael, what's wrong? You really are out of sorts. There are all manner of rumours flying around." He waited for an answer, but none was forthcoming. "Look, Michael, people are worried about you, really worried. Everyone knows there is something wrong, but what is it?"

Michael thought, they care for me? Do they? He looked at van Hagen. "Henry,…"

"Yes?"

"Do you think I belong here?"

"What, in Portugal, well, I suppose you do, in a way."

"No, not Portugal. Here. In the Regiment? Stanhope thinks I don't. Is he right? Should I do something else?"

"Michael, of course you belong. You don't want to take any notice of what Stanhope might think, the man's high in the instep, even if he is a good field officer. He's probably spending all his time on Bond street, mixing with the Ton, and looking for promotion. Come on now, what would Will and I do without you?"

At that moment Lloyd appeared, and saluted. "Begging you pardon, sir, Colonel Archer wants to see you."

Michael's spirits sank to a new low.

Eventually the story of the patrol had reached Colonel Archer. He was a worried man. Michael was well thought of, in the Regiment and out, that much he knew from Sir Stapleton. He was a good troop officer, well-liked by the men, and respected by the NCOs. Blood thought he was an excellent horseman, and he had worked wonders with Lloyd. He wondered for a moment if he might ask Lloyd if he knew what was going on with Michael, but dismissed the idea as outrageous. He had a suspicion that most, if not all, of Michael's current problems stemmed from whatever it was he got up to when he got sent off on some confidential mission or other. Things had been hinted at, back in England as well as out here. What Archer did know was that something was preying on Michael's mind, and in danger of destroying him as a useful young officer. In the end he decided he would just have to grasp the nettle, it could not be ignored, not without risking damage to the Regiment. He happened to see Lloyd, and sent him for Michael.

When Michael arrived at Archer's small, derelict, but dry quarters, he was quickly invited in and offered coffee. Archer dismissed his servant and the orderly, and then there was just the two of them. There was nothing to sit on, save a couple of tree stumps that Archer's servant had found. Michael though it was appropriately uncomfortable for the circumstances.

"Now, Mister Roberts," began Archer, "it does not take any particular observational skills to know that all is not well with you, not well at all. Frankly your conduct of late has, at times, been positively alarming. I gather that, yesterday, Lloyd had to physically restrain you from cutting down a Frenchman who had surrendered? And before you ask, no, Lloyd did not tell me. He has been singularly tight lipped." Archer stopped to take a mouthful of coffee, and to give Michael a chance to speak. He didn't.

"Is there anything that you would like to discuss?"

"No, sir, thank you."

For a moment Archer's patience failed him, and he snapped at Michael. "And is that because you can't, or you don't want to." He took a deep breath. "No, that's not fair. It's this bloody weather, I wish to God it would stop raining!" He took another gulp of coffee. "Look here, Roberts, you have a bright future in this Regiment, and it's a damn good regiment, if I do say so myself. You could do a lot worse that make this your home, ye know."

"I hadn't thought of the Regiment quite like that, sir."

"Don't see why you wouldn't. Look at the length of time some people have been with the Regiment, even the Colonel, Earl Harcourt! And look at the way your grandfather could write to him, and get an answer. Eh? Oh, yes, I know all about that. Look at Lloyd, a good man. But he kept going to the bad, not anymore, and you did that, Roberts. There's bad apples, of course there are, number of men we have in the Regiment, bound to be, but look at all the good men we have, eh? You are part of that, one of us, just don't go to the bad, will you?" He paused. "Please?"

Michael sat silently for a moment, deep in thought. Archer knew better than to push him. Michael was realising the truth in Archer's words. Quintela's offer would, might, make him wealthy, but was that all there was? Of course not. And Wellington's offer, promotion, but at what price? Scovell was a decent enough man, had always been good to him, but the Corps of Guides? From what he had heard it had become a glorified Post Office. No, the Regiment was where he wanted to be, and if Wellington wanted him for his talents, then he would have to order him from the Regiment.

Michael raised his head and spoke to Archer. "Thank you, sir, that has been a great help. I can tell you, sir, that there really is nowhere I would rather be than with the Regiment."

Archer sighed a quiet sigh of relief. "Good. I hope that's all helped?"

"Yes, sir, it has."

"Then you'd best get along and see to your men, off you go, now, and on your way, tell my orderly I need some more coffee!"

Michael walked back to the woods where the squadron was making the best of the atrocious weather. He saw Lloyd. "Lloyd!"

Lloyd marched over to Michael and saluted. Michael returned the salute, and said, "I just wanted to thank you again, Lloyd, I don't know what came over me yesterday."

"Diolch, sir, but I think we were all a bit on edge, yesterday, sir. Dreadful what those French did, sir. And Francisco is out of sorts, sir, seeing that town has really affected him, sir, and he's still only a lad."

"Yes, I've spoken to him, I hope I helped."

"Yes, sir, it's what we do, isn't it, sir, in the Regiment, we help each other, sir."

That night was another miserable one. The only good thing, thought Michael, was that he wasn't out on picket duty. He huddled up under his cloak, and closed his eyes. He felt better for having resolved one issue, he was going to stay with the Regiment, if at all possible. He had no objection to being involved in the dirty war of counter intelligence, it had led him to Elaine, it had allowed him to avenge her killing. He had to admit that Wellington was right, he did seem to have a talent for it, but with the Regiment was where he wanted to be. As for Quintela's offer, that was a mirage. He hadn't found the mysterious Augusto and the missing diamonds in the last eighteen months, there was no reason to expect that he would in the next twelve. He would put that out of his mind. Proper soldiering was what he wanted, perhaps spiced from time to time with a little extra, something a little different. That settled, he turned his mind to thoughts of Catarina, and soon he was recalling the short time he had spent with Elaine, how much he loved her, and he drifted off to sleep.

He was woken by Ashworth. "Roberts, Roberts, come on man, wake up!"

"What? What is it? Beg your pardon, sir."

"We've got orders to move, in half an hour. Find Sar'nt Major Flynn, get Sawyer and Keating up, rouse the troop, Mister Roberts. I am off to find Mister van Hagen." Ashworth disappeared into the darkness.

The noise had woken Lloyd who had been asleep nearby. "Morning, sir, I think. Duw, it's a dark night."

"It seems we have orders to move, Lloyd, wake up Parra and Francisco, I shall need some coffee, quickly. Get the horses ready, I'll ride Duke again, I expect the baggage will follow when it's light. I'm going to find Mister

Sawyer, young Keating and the Sar'nt Major, we've half an hour before we move."

Michael wasn't sure if they managed it in the half hour, it was too dark to see his watch, he didn't even know what time it was until he was able to see by a barely alight fire. It was a quarter to four o'clock. But they were ready to mount at the same time as all the other troops, more or less. A march in the dark was never an easy thing to mange. The squadrons of the Brigade marched closed up, with barely any intervals. The road was narrow and rough, and they marched three wide, the eight squadrons of the Brigade stretching for half a mile behind Anson, leading the way. Their route took them north, across a small bridge, splashing through flood water to reach it, through another deserted town, the buildings barely visible, except as darker shadows, but the smell of death and filth hanging in the air.

Another mile and they turned east in a small village, dropping down to cross a river. The bridge was long and narrow, and the wooded valley was full of roaring flood waters. On the other side the road wound up, cut into the side of a steep hill. As light began to appear on the sky ahead of them, they passed another hamlet, and the countryside levelled off and opened up. A mile and a half on from the bridge, Anson halted the Brigade and deployed it, facing south east towards Santarem.

Once it was clear there was no immediate danger of being attacked, patrols and pickets were sent out in all directions, and the Brigade was dismounted. The rain continued to fall, it was unrelenting and soaking. On the high ground where the Brigade waited there was no escaping it. The wind was light, but blowing straight into their faces. Archer rode over to Ashworth, and waved for the squadron's officers to join them.

"Gentlemen," he began when they were all gathered. "There is to be an attack on Santarem some time this afternoon. General Pack and his brigade of Portuguese infantry are joining us, and we are to make nuisance of ourselves on this side of the town while the main attack goes in along the main road from Lisbon. We are five or six miles from Santarem, and patrols have found outlying French pickets no more than a mile away. The signal for us to move will be a gun. Well, more than one, I suspect." He smiled. "That is all I can tell you. Let the men know we will be here for a few more hours yet."

In the early afternoon a dragoon came in from the picket that had been left at the first bridge they had crossed in order to guide Pack to where the Brigade was. The flood waters had risen and now covered it. General Pack and his brigade were on the other side, unable to cross. He had indicated to the picket that he would march upstream and try to find another, practical, crossing point. The Brigade continued to wait, and nothing happened. A few small parties of the enemy were captured by patrols and pickets, and they were in bad condition, and seemed happy to be captured.

Night fell without any orders being received, and no sign of Pack and his Portuguese. Anson had no wish to spend the night so close to the enemy, a river behind him, and no infantry support. Cautiously, the Brigade retraced its steps. At the bridge every man dismounted, and led his horse across, the fast flowing water only just below the bridge. It was a short march, but unpleasant.

They hadn't seen the Regimental baggage all day, but found it waiting for them across the river. They had found a grove of olives, and done their best to prepare for the Regiment. The dismounted dragoons, officers' servants and soldiers wives had all set to in the atrocious weather to make sure there was something hot for the men. It was only coffee, but it was welcome. Of the commissary and rations there was no sign. Picket lines were quickly strung between the trees, and the men set about scavenging more wood and getting a few more fires going. They learnt that they were at the Bridge of Calhariz.

In the morning the Brigade sent a squadron of the hussars back across the bridge to keep watch towards Santarem from the heights across the river. Michael changed horses again, to ride Johnny. General Pack found another crossing point, and occupied the village of Cozembrigera, a mile away, posting an infantry picket on each side of the bridge at Calhariz. The rain continued to fall. Two squadrons of the Sixteenth and the hussars marched away to be billeted in the nearby town of Malaqueijo. Ashworth and Cocks' squadrons were left at the bridge with two squadrons of the German hussars.

Some of the hussars explored a nearby quinta and found a huge cask of wine, there was plenty for everyone in all four squadrons, and it helped to raise spirits. Ashworth's servant, Brown, aided by Francisco, even managed to mull some of it over a small fire. The six officers of Ashworth's sat companionably around the fire, under a dripping tree. In the morning they would be taking over the picket across the bridge. They hadn't seen the commissary for three days, and everyone was hungry. Some of the men were the worse for wear as they drank on empty stomachs.

Shortly before dawn the squadron prepared to replace the squadron of German hussars on picket duty across the river. Michael changed horses again to ride Duke. As the first glimmerings of grey light appeared in the sky beyond the river, they formed the squadron and prepared to march the short distance down to the bridge. The narrow road and bridge forced them to march only three abreast. As they climbed the steep road up from the valley, the sound of firing was heard ahead. Without hesitating Ashworth ordered the squadron to trot, and they pushed on up the winding road.

Immediately at the top of the valley side there was just enough open ground for Ashworth to deploy the squadron at the bottom of a long slope covered with olive trees. It was not an ideal post. Michael was in his habitual position on the squadron left, Sergeant Taylor covering him, Lloyd to his right. More firing was heard, and then the head of the German squadron appeared over the brow of the hill, trotting fast down the road. Ashworth ordered the half squadrons to wheel by threes outwards, marched them a few yards apart, and wheeled them back into line, opening up a gap in their centre where the road was. The Germans slowed to a walk for the steep descent and passed through the gap. The last man was Captain Gruben.

"Danke, Ashworth, I am very happy to see you." He smiled and wheeled his horse around so he could look back up the hill. "Ach, gut, here come my skirmishers."

Half a dozen hussars appeared at the gallop and came quickly on down the road. A minute later a dozen green coated French dragoons appeared, but they reined in at the sight of the dragoon squadron. Gruben waved his skirmishers on, through the dragoons.

"There is a dragoon regiment, and supporting infantry behind them. You do not want to wait here, I think." Gruben informed Ashworth. "I shall see you across the river. Viel glück!" And with that he followed his skirmishers.

Ashworth called out to van Hagen with the right hand half squadron. "Lieutenant van Hagen, wheel your half squadron by threes and get them back across the bridge." He turned towards Michael, "Lieutenant Roberts, take a dozen men, form a skirmish line. Once we are away, follow fast."

Michael took the twelve dragoons on his flank, along with Sergeant Taylor, and marched them clear of the squadron. Behind, Ashworth wheeled the remaining men by threes and set off down the road after van Hagen. Michael quickly strung his men out across the road, and ordered them to ready their carbines. He watched the French skirmishers carefully. They were sitting looking at him, showing no inclination to advance. Minutes passed, Michael thought Ashworth and the rest of the squadron must be at the bridge by now.

A movement on the road caught Michael's eye, and he saw a single dragoon ride a little clear of the skirmishers. The man reined in his horse, and put a telescope to his eye. Now why would he do that, thought Michael? He could see perfectly well what the situation was with the naked eye. A nasty suspicion arose in his mind. As he watched the man put the telescope away, and drew his sabre. He turned and appeared to shout behind him. Then he faced the front, and suddenly spurred his horse into a flat out gallop down the road towards them. Behind him a column of French dragoons breasted the skyline, coming on down the road at a good fast trot and then breaking into a gallop. Michael didn't wait. "Skirmishers, right about, gallop!"

They cantered to the brow of the steep drop, and slowed around the corners and steepest part of the road. Michael was the last man, and his heart was in his mouth as one dragoon's horse stumbled and nearly fell. The dragoon hung on and they were safely around the worst corner. As they neared the valley floor, the road flattened and straightened, and they all urged on their horses to a full gallop for the last two hundred yards to the bridge. The river was lined with Portuguese infantry who cheered them on as if it was a horse race.

On the far side of the bridge Ashworth was waiting. Michael reined up. "Well done, Roberts. Good thing you didn't hang about up there." He nodded back across the river. Michael twisted in his saddle to look back. The column of dragoons was just appearing a few hundred yards away, and deploying into the valley bottom. At the near end of the bridge the Portuguese infantry were hurriedly building a barricade of logs and bits of furniture dragged out of nearby houses. Out in front of the French dragoons sat a solitary officer, staring across the intervening bridge.

"I do believe," said Ashworth, "that is your dragoon Colonel. He appears to mean business." Ashworth and Michael watched until the man turned his horse and rode back to the deploying dragoons, then Ashworth said, "The squadron is at the top of the rise, I think we should go and join them." Side by side they rode up the narrow lane in the wake of the skirmishers.

Ashworth found Captain Gruben, and the two of them set about establishing a line posts along the river to watch for any attempts by the French to cross. Gruben took downstream from the bridge, Ashworth upstream. Anson arrived, along with Archer and Arenschildt. They had a good look along the river, and at the height of the water, concluding that with the bridge guarded, they were safe from attack.

Once he was satisfied with arrangements, Anson took another two squadrons of the brigade and rode off to establish himself in another village to extend the line of posts and protect the flanks of the army's position. One more cold and wet night followed, and then Wellington decided that no more operations would be undertaken that winter, and ordered the army into winter quarters. Ashworth's rode happily away from Calhariz, leaving a single hussar squadron there. They passed through San João da Ribeira, where Anson was with the Brigade headquarters and two squadrons, and rode on to the small village of Anteporta, a short eight or nine mile ride in all.

Anteporta wasn't the largest village, the small square in front of the church was only just large enough for the squadron to parade, but they found two houses on the square large enough for all the officers and their servants. A number of large, agricultural buildings supplied cover for all the horses. It was cosy, but adequate. Like most villages, it had suffered dreadfully from French occupation, but as they were likely to be there for some time everyone set too with a will, cleaning out buildings, and boarding up windows. Michael took the opportunity of dry quarters to write to colonel Murray, confirming that he was staying with the Regiment. He hoped it was the right decision.

Word reached them that when the hussars had got to the bottom of the huge wine barrel they had found near the bridge at Calhariz, they discovered a dead Portuguese peasant in it. There were a few queasy faces at the news, and Captain Ally of the hussars was reported to have sworn never to drink red wine again.

Mid-December was approaching when Michael was summoned to the small parlour serving as Ashworth's office. Colonel Archer was there as well, and he addressed Michael.

"Ah, Roberts, I have a little job for you."

"Sir?"

"Yes, the new issue of uniforms is expected to arrive in Lisbon imminently, which presents us with a bit of a problem. We are spread out all along from Calhariz to Rio Maior, and that will make issuing difficult, and the fitting of the uniforms even more so, and we have to get them out here first, and Lisbon is what, fifty miles away?"

"Yes, sir," answered Michael, beginning to see where this was going.

"Yes, so you are to take yourself off to Lisbon first thing tomorrow, receive the uniforms, check the consignment, organise transport to get them out here, and, if you can, hire some Portuguese tailors to come out here for a week or so to fit everything."

"Yes, sir."

"Good, off you go then, and I expect we will see you back here in three weeks or so, with good luck."

Once Michael had left, Archer said, "Well, Ashworth, there's no one better to send, and I hope that a few weeks in his home will settle him, give him a break, I think it's what he needs. We've had a hard campaign since Buçaco ridge, and he had a hard time before that, whatever it was he was doing, or so Sir Stapleton tells me."

"Yes, sir. And it won't do Sawyer any harm to have to take a little more responsibility."

"No, it won't. I tell you, Ashworth, sometimes there is an edge to young Roberts, a look in his eyes sometimes, that just gives me the shivers. It makes everyone uncomfortable, and that's not a good thing, we don't need it in the Regiment."

Chapter 10

Michael and his small party left at dawn the following morning. He rode Duke, with Lloyd next to him on Rodrigo. Then came Parra on Harry, leading Johnny, with Francisco on Fred the pony, leading the two mules. As they rode south the weather slowly improved, getting a little warmer, raining a little less frequently. They broke the journey at an inn at Carregedo, left early the following morning, and entered Lisbon in the middle of the following afternoon. As they rode through the city, it seemed to Michael to be a little less crowded, and he guessed that a lot of refugees had taken the opportunity of Massena's retreat to return home.

They rode around to the back entrance to Michael's home, dismounted at the stables, and began unloading the mules. Senhor Santiago appeared.

"Senhor Michael, it is good to see you, and all of you," he beamed at them. "My Senhora saw you from upstairs, she is even now putting the kettle on for tea!" He got smiles from everyone at that news.

"Thank you, Senhor, I think we are all ready for that" Michael laughed. "Parra, Lloyd, you see to the animals, Francisco, Santiago, let us get this baggage to the house, and then, Francisco, you can help Senhora Santiago get our rooms ready."

An hour later Michael was sitting down to dinner by a blazing fire with a good bottle of wine to hand. Francisco had gone off to Roberta's to see his sister and let Roberta know they were in Lisbon. Lloyd and Parra were eating in the kitchen with the Santiagos. Everyone was very happy to be in what was becoming home for all of them. He had barely finished eating, when noises from the entrance hall downstairs caught Michael's attention and he heard light footsteps on the stairs. He rose to his feet as Roberta burst into the room, a huge smile on her face.

"Michael!" She went swiftly to him and they embraced warmly. "It is so good to see you, and so well!" Lloyd appeared in the doorway, grinning, with an extra glass. "And Senhor Lloyd, it is good to see you."

"Thank you, Senhorita."

"Alright, Lloyd, thank you." Lloyd put the glass on the table and left the room.

"Michael, how long are you here for? More than just a few days, I hope?"

"Oh, yes, two weeks, I think, perhaps more, perhaps a little less."

Roberta clapped her hands as Michael poured her a glass of wine. "That's wonderful, I shall make sure you get lots of invitations. If you will be free to attend a few society gatherings, that is? What are you here for? Can you tell me?"

Michael laughed, "Yes, I can, this time there is no secret. I am here to collect the Regiment's new uniforms, and see if I can find a few tailors to travel to the Regiment and help to fit them. We've a few tailors in the Regiment, but not nearly enough to make the fittings quickly. We don't know when we might have to move again. But what about you? Are the Marcelinos still with you?"

Roberta looked unhappy. "Yes, well, the Senhora, the children and some of the servants still are. Now that Colonel Trant has retaken Coimbra, Senhor Marcelinos has gone home to see what the damage is to their house, and to get it ready for their return." She suddenly smiled, "But I am visiting an old friend who is unwell, and I shall be away all night."

Later, they lay together in Michael's bed, the room lit by a single candle. Roberta propped herself up on one arm, and ran a finger down Michael's chest.

"I think I am becoming jealous."

"Eh, what?" Michael frowned at her. "What are you talking about?"

"Oh, just a certain young Senhorita who has been asking me about you."

Michael thought for a moment. "Do you mean Senhorita Cardoso?"

"Yes, I do, she is quite struck with you, the poor girl."

Michael groaned. "I do hope that you haven't been encouraging her?"

"Well, I haven't told her that we are lovers. I think she would be devastated, to say nothing of mortified by embarrassment after her questions about you."

Michael groaned again.

Roberta went on. "I am sure she would be horrified; she would think I am far too old for you, young man." She chuckled. "No, I can't say that I am encouraging her, but I think I know who would if they thought it would do any good."

Michael lifted his head and stared at her. "Who, for God's sake?"

"The Venâncios, of course. They can't wait to marry her off to some eligible bachelor who can support her. They feel obliged to support her, while they live off her brother's fortune. If they didn't, society would be scandalised. It could affect the Senhor's academic career. But she is no blood relation, she has no claim on the inheritance. Her brother died unexpectedly, and made no provision for her. She is, in effect, penniless, although Senhora Venâncio did hint to me the other day that they might be able to manage a small dowry."

Michael groaned again. "God, it is, it's Maria Barros all over again, isn't it?"

Roberta put her finger to his lips. "Now, Michael, you don't know that. I am sure that I could discover their intentions with regard to a dowry, if that would help you."

"No, Roberta, it would not, and you know why."

Roberta fell away, onto her back, and stared up at the ceiling. "Yes, I do, of course I do." She was silent for a moment. "Where's her picture?"

"I put it away."

"Forever, or just while I am here?"

Michael was silent.

Roberta raised herself up and faced him again. She leant in to him and gently kissed him. "I'm sorry, that was unfair." She stared into his eyes. "But she set you free, I know she did, you know she did." She laid a hand on his chest and her head on the pillow, close to his. "Michael, you will have to let Elaine go one day, She has done all she can, God rest her soul."

"I know, my head tells me so, but my heart…"

"I understand, Michael, but one day you might find you need someone beside you, and not me. I am your friend Michael, and your lover, but I will not be your wife, we both know that. Who knows," she gave a little laugh, "perhaps I shall meet someone and be swept off my feet. What will you do then?"

Michael turned to look at her. "I should be very, very happy for you, if it is true love."

Roberta returned his look. "You really are the best friend I could ever hope for." She kissed him, his arms went around her.

The following morning Michael and Roberta breakfasted together. They talked lightly, making arrangements to meet again, nothing more was said about Catarina Cardoso. Roberta left to walk home, escorted by Senhor

Santiago. He would leave her near her home, but watch her safely in. Michael watched her go from a dining room window above the street. Once she was out of sight, he went up to his room. He could still smell her perfume. He opened a drawer in a chest, and took out a thin, leather covered diptych, and opened it. On one side was a miniature portrait of Elaine, on the other, a lock of her copper red hair. From behind the lock of hair he pulled her letter. He stood the diptych on the table next to his bed, and sat down to read the letter. He knew every word by heart, but he still felt the need to see it as well.

'My dearest Michael,

If you are reading this it means that I am dead, how, I cannot guess. I hope that this gift will keep my memory fresh in your mind for many, many years to come. I hope that I have had the time, and the courage to tell you what you have so very, very quickly come to mean to me. I never thought that I would love again, you proved me wrong, something I don't usually take kindly to, but in this instance I am only too, too happy to be wrong. My darling Michael, I love you.

I hope that you have loved me, I hope I know that you do before I die. If not, I hope you will remember me as a dear, dear friend. If you do love me, do not, my love, do not make my mistake of thinking love comes only once. I hereby, most sincerely, release you of any ties, real or imagined.

Remember me, your ever loving Elaine.'

Carefully, gently, he folded it up, and replaced it the diptych, which he left standing by his bed. He sat for a moment, looking at Elaine's picture. He knew Roberta was right, but despite the letter, he felt that he was still bound to Elaine, and did not know what might set him free, or, indeed, if he wanted to be free.

Accompanied by Lloyd, he rode out to the main depot for the British army at Belem, to see if there was any news of the Regiment's new uniforms. He learnt that shipments were starting to arrive, but not yet for the Sixteenth. He would have to be patient, and they rode slowly and gently back to the house. At the stables Michael left Lloyd with Parra to see to the horses, and walked up to the back of the house. Near the door he paused and looked over the garden. It was he had to admit, in a state of neglect. It had been his mother's pride and joy, and he should do something about it, he decided.

Inside he went to the kitchen, and happily accepted a cup of coffee from Senhora Santiago. Senhor Santiago came in from the cellar with firewood.

"Santiago," he began, "I have just been looking at the garden."

Santiago pulled a face. "Ah, Senhor Michael, your mother would hate to see it now." He shrugged. "But I have much to do about the house. Your mother had a gardener, and did a lot herself." He smiled at the memory. "In the spring she was always out there, your father always knew where to find her, usually on her knees weeding. He said it looked as if she was praying to the garden."

Michael gave a sad smile at Santiago's recollection.. "Then we must see what can be done, if not now, then in the spring. And I think I know where I might be able to find a gardener." He finished his coffee. "I am going to change and then go out for a while. I expect I shall be a few hours."

Dressed in his shabbiest civilian clothes, with his sword stick in hand, Michael set out for one of the poorer quarters of Lisbon, one he remembered well from his youth. It was where his boyhood friend Antonio Carvalho lived, or at least where his mother lived. He was in luck. As he approached the building where Senhora Carvalho lived, watched by curious locals, he saw his friend sitting on the doorstep, whittling a piece of wood with a wicked looking knife.

"Antonio!"

Antonio looked up to see who had called to him, and his face broke into a huge grin when he saw Michael. "Miguel! Ha, you remember where my mother lives!" He rose to his feet, and gave Michael a playful punch on his arm. "Come, come in and say hello to her. I told her that you were back in Lisbon." He practically dragged Michael in, shouting as did, "Mamã, mamã, see who is here!"

In a dark sitting room cum kitchen, Michael saw Senhora Carvalho, a frail looking old woman, sitting close to a small fire, a shawl wrapped around her shoulders against the cold and damp of the winter.

"See, mamã, it is my old friend, Miguel!"

"Hello, Senhora, it is good to see you."

The old lady stirred herself. "Ah, young Miguel. Antonio told me that you were back in Lisbon, and a British soldier, fighting those bastard French." The curse surprised Michael. "Come, sit down, but I have little that we can offer you."

"That is alright, Senhora, I am not in need of anything. But I would like to steal Antonio away from you for a little while."

"Ha, you boys, up to mischief again. Well, don't be too long, Antonio, I expect your father home soon."

Michael looked at Antonio in surprise. When he had met his old friend again, back in the summer, he had told Michael that his father had gone to fight the French with the Ordenança, and had not returned.

Antonio shook his head. "Don't worry, mamã, I won't be long," and took Michael out to the street.

Michael began to speak, but Antonio cut him short. "It's alright, Miguel, she has been like that for a while now. Come, let us find a coffee house, you can buy."

They found a small, quiet coffee house and settled themselves down.

"So, Miguel, what brought you to look for me?"

"Actually, I am not looking for you," he teased his friend.

Antonio put his hand on his heart in mock horror. "Now, Miguel, I am hurt, I do not know if I will recover."

Michael laughed. "Hurt? You? Ha! But, no, I remember that you told me Bernardo was now a gardener?"

"Yes, that is so, why do you ask?"

"That's easy, I need a gardener. My mother's garden has suffered, and I would like to see it back as it was. I thought Bernardo might be interested?"

"I don't doubt for a moment that he will be. He has had very little work for some time." He paused to gather his thoughts. "The last three years since the French came have been very difficult for we working people. All the wealthy people, and all their money, fled to the Brazils with the court. That was difficult, the French wanted to tax us to pay for their war, but there was no money, although that did not stop them taking what they could. People who refused to pay were shot." He sipped his coffee and Michael remained silent.

"The people who were left to govern us did nothing to stop the French, rather they helped them. There was no work for anyone, people starved, we had to beg from those who had a little. The city was almost empty because people fled across the river or into the countryside to escape!" Antonio stared at his coffee, lost in the memories of that awful time. "I went into the countryside; I know it well." He gave Michael a wry smile. "I have travelled it a lot, especially the little known paths. But my mother stayed. She survived on charity. And while the people starved, Junot was living in the Palácio da Quintela, living in luxury, giving balls, entertaining the aristocracy. And all the time his secret police run by Pierre Lagarde were everywhere, spying on people, arresting them, and many never reappeared. Did you know he replaced General de Silva?" Michael shook his head. "Well, even the General suffered. He could do nothing, there were French spies and sympathisers everywhere, they say there still are." He took another sip of his coffee. "French soldiers beat my mother. Some bastard told them my father was with the Ordenança. They thought she might know something about where they were. Of course, she didn't, but they still beat her."

"I am sorry," said Michael, "I had no idea it was that bad."

"It was, and it reminds me, did you find out what happened to Jean-Paul Renard?"

"Yes. He's dead"

Antonio looked closely at Michael. There had been something in his voice. "And how do you know that?"

Michael met Antonio's stare. "Because I killed him, Antonio."

The two friends stared at each other for a moment. Then Antonio spoke, "Good. And thank you for coming to Portugal to free us from the likes of him, Miguel. Thank you."

Michael broke the spell of the moment. "Now, Bernardo, do you know where I can find him? And while I think about it, did you say that Jorge had gone into the tailoring business?" Antonio nodded. "Then I need to find him as well."

They found Jorge first, in a small shop down a scruffy backstreet. He was working for an established tailor,

Senhor Tavares. As they walked in, Tavares looked up from where he sat crossed legged and sewing.

"Senhors, can I help you?"

"Senhor," Michael began, as Antonio lounged near the door, "I believe that you employ an old friend of mine, Jorge Pires."

The man shrugged, glancing at Antonio. "And who are you that asks?"

"Lieutenant Roberts of the British Sixteenth Light Dragoons."

The man laughed, "And I am the King of Spain."

Antonio pushed himself away from the wall, "Senhor, I can assure you that my friend is who he says he is. Unfortunately, he speaks Portuguese like a native, having been born here, so I forgive your insult for not believing him. If you will excuse me." He walked towards the bottom of some stairs in the corner of the small shop. "Jorge," he bellowed, "it's Antonio, get your raggedy arse down here!"

Tavares began to protest, "Senhors, I must ask you to leave, now."

But there was a clatter on the stairs and a small man with a mop of thick, black hair and a long moustache appeared. "Antonio? What are you doing here?" Then he eyes fell on Michael, and he paused for a moment. "Miguel? Is that you, Miguel?"

"Hello, Jorge, yes, it's me." Michael grinned, and Jorge rushed across the shop to hug his old friend. "Now," said Michael, untangling himself from Jorge, "perhaps you can tell Senhor Tavares who I am?"

"Eh? Yes, of course. Senhor Tavares, this is my very old friend, Senhor Miguel Roberts." He spun back to Michael. "But, Miguel, are you really in the British army?"

"Oh, yes," he addressed Tavares, "I apologise for not being in uniform, Senhor, but I did not really expect to be discussing business today."

Michael explained to Tavares the Regimental business that he was on. "So, Senhor, I am looking for some tailors who are willing to travel to where my Regiment is, near Rio Maior, and to fit about four hundred new uniforms to our men."

Tavares looked stunned. "Senhor, you do not jest with me?"

"No, Senhor, not at all. The uniforms are due to arrive in Lisbon from England any day now. They are roughly sized, but need to be fitted to each man. It needs to be done quickly, and my Regiment will pay you well."

Tavares thought about it. "Senhor, I cannot go, but I think that I might be able to find some young men like Jorge here, from other tailors. Your Regiment can pay us and we will pay our employees."

"And pay them a little more than they get working in Lisbon, I hope?"

"Ah, Senhor, I will talk to my friends, and see what we can do."

"Very well, Senhor, I will return the day after tomorrow, at nine o'clock for your terms. Is that enough time?"

"Yes, Senhor, I think so."

"Excellent, Senhor Tavares." Michael turned to Jorge. "Jorge, will you dine with me tonight? And Antonio, that big tavern on Black Horse Square, I think. In the meantime, let us go and find Bernardo, and he can join us as well."

It was a good evening. Bernardo agreed to come and look at Michael's garden in a few days' time with a view to coming to work for him. He could also help Senhor

Santiago. Then the old friends talked about their boyhood escapades, about their friends who were not with them. Carlos was off with his mule train somewhere, supplying the British army. Michael was not surprised their paths had not crossed, there were score of muleteers, different trains attached to different army divisions and units more or less permanently. Marco was apparently in command of a small detachment of militia at one of the forts on the Lines, almost on the Atlantic coast. Of Ricardo, their old leader, there was no news, his regiment was thought to be with Beresford, but no one was quite sure which regiment he was with. They drank a toast to him and wished him well.

It was a slightly drunk Michael who got home later that evening. He had enjoyed the evening, it had felt so right, sitting with his old friends, eating, drinking, telling stories, laughing together. There had been a few stories about the hard times in Lisbon under the French, Bernardo had been saved by his bad leg, but had seen a lot of cruelty inflicted by the French. Marco and Ricardo, it transpired, had been fortunate not to end up in the Portuguese battalions the French had formed, and then marched away into Europe. Many had deserted and were now with the Portuguese Ordenança. But there had been much more light hearted talk and joking, much more. It had brought back to him that Lisbon had, for a very long time, been the only home he knew.

The following day, Michael and Lloyd rode out to Belem again to see if the uniforms had arrived yet. They hadn't. He was able to enquire about transport, and was advised that was a matter for his Regiment. He swore, under his breath, at the commissary officer in charge of transport, thanked him politely, and went to see Deputy Commissary General Dunmore.

Michael had come across Dunmore in the hunt for Renard, when he had been impressed by Michael's orders from the

Quartermaster General, Colonel Murray, and Michael hoped he might be able to use his apparent connections to his advantage. As it was, he need not have worried.

"Lieutenant Roberts," exclaimed Dunmore, "you need have no qualms on that account. We have just received instructions from Mister Kennedy, the Commissary General, to assist with the delivery on uniforms, although it is, strictly speaking, a regimental responsibility. But, please, tell me, did you find that fellow you were looking for?"

"I did indeed, Mister Dunmore, and I am grateful for the help that you and your clerks were able afford me," he smiled. "And I was happy to report your assistance to Colonel Murray," Michael lied.

That settled, and the tailors organised, more or less, Michael was able to relax a little. Consequently he was very happy on his return home to find a note from Roberta inviting his to join her at a little soiree a friend of hers was giving, and asking him to call for her at six o'clock. He changed back to his civilian clothes, dined at four o'clock, and left for Roberta's in good time.

If there was one thing you could say about Roberta, it was that she was punctual. He knocked at her door as the church clocks chimed six, Constanca opened it, and there was Roberta in a warm coat, just pulling on her gloves. She took his arm with a smile, and they set off together, Roberta directing their footsteps.

Michael asked, "Is Senhora Marcelino not coming as well?"

"No, she prefers to stay with her children, and to only go out with Senhor Marcelino."

"So, tell me, where are we going?"

"To Senhora Lourenco, she is a very dear friend. It will be a small gathering, relaxed, and lots of time to talk."

"Will there be anyone I know there?"

"Oh, I am not sure," Roberta replied, with a slight smile that Michael did not see.

Senhora Lourenco's house was more of a grand Palacio, with several carriages drawn by teams of mules outside. Michael challenged Roberta, " I thought you said this was a small soiree?"

"Oh, but it is, at least by my friend's standards. Come on, now, Michael, don't be shy." She laughed.

Michael merely growled in reply, and Roberta laughed even more.

Inside the grand entrance hall a liveried footman took hats, gloves, coats and Michael's cane, and directed them up the stairs, towards the sounds of a rather lively party. Entering a large and exquisitely decorated salon, they found themselves with about thirty other guests, all standing or sitting around and chattering away to each other. A few were playing cards in a corner, and a footman was circulating with drinks. A short, plump, and very jolly looking woman in what even Michael realised was a very fine dress, bore down on them.

"Roberta, my dear, I am so glad to see you, and this must be the handsome Lieutenant Roberts?"

Michael gave her a small bow. "Senhora Lourenco, it is a pleasure to meet you, and thank you for inviting me to your wonderful home."

Senhora Lourenco tapped him playfully on the arm with her fan. "Lieutenant, you flatter me. She turned to Roberta. "Now, my dear, I know I can leave you to your own devices, you know everyone here, I think?" Roberta nodded, looking around, and waving at someone. "Then I will take the Lieutenant away from you, and introduce him to one or two people." Unnoticed by Michael, distracted by taking a glass of wine from the footman, Senhora

Lourenco winked at Roberta, who smiled in return and gave an almost imperceptible nod.

"Now, Lieutenant, your arm?" Michael decided that he rather liked Senhora Lourenco, and happily took her arm, and she led him further into the room. As they moved slowly forward, the Senhora introduced him briefly to a few people, but kept up a general movement across the room. She raised her fan to her face, leant in to Michael, conspiratorially, and whispered. "I have a little confession to make, Lieutenant, there is a young lady here who particularly wants to meet you."

Before Michael could react to that statement, she turned him to one side, and there, sitting alone on a couch, was Senhorita Cardoso.

"I believe," went on the Senhora, "that you and Senhorita Cardoso have already been introduced, so I shall leave you to become reacquainted." With that she released Michael's arm, hailed a friend, and was gone.

Michael and Catarina looked at each other for a moment. Catarina's eyes were sparkling with amusement, although Michael was feeling that he had been led like a lamb to the slaughter.

"Oh, Lieutenant, the expression on your face, please, forgive me, but...," and she laughed. "Please, sit down." She patted the empty couch next to her.

Michael had no choice but to comply. "Senhorita Cardoso, it is a pleasure to meet you again." He spoke and sat rather stiffly.

At the tone of his voice the laughter left Catarina's face. "I am sorry Lieutenant, if you do not wish my company, I am sure there are others here who will." She turned away from him, and fanned her face.

Michael sat, stony faced for a moment. He glanced across the room and caught sight of Roberta looking at them over the shoulder of a man and woman she was talking to. She arched her eyebrows, and gave him a questioning look. Damn it, he thought, she knew Catarina would be here, and Senhora Lourenco, he had been expertly ambushed. Well, he thought, the best way to deal with an ambush was to close rapidly with the enemy, and he was an officer of light cavalry, and a gentleman to boot.

He turned to Catarina. "Forgive me, please, Senhorita, I was simply taken aback, I did not expect to meet you, Roberta said nothing to me about you being here."

Catarina turned back to him, looking surprised. "She did not? But she told me you would be here, and that she had expressly asked Senhora Lourenco to invite me so that we might meet again. I assumed that you knew."

"No, Senhorita, she did not tell me. However, might I say, that it was the surprise of the unexpected pleasure that threw me off balance." He gave her a smile. "Of course I am delighted to see you again. Tell me, how are you finding life in Lisbon?"

"It is not home; there I can escape on my horse. My sister in law and her husband are more used to the town, to the city, to this sort of affair. For myself, it is dull. But tell me, how are your horses, Johnny and Duke?"

Michael was impressed. "You remembered their names!"

"Of course."

Michael told her how they were, and a little of the difficulties of the retreat. She laughed at his description of the horses being stabled in the cloisters at Mafra. She had been to Mafra and knew the convent. The conversation flowed easily between them. Supper was announced, and he took her in on his arm. Across the table he caught sight of Roberta who gave him a little smile, he tried to scowl at her, but failed.

As the evening drew to a close, Michael realised that he had barely spoken to anyone else. Roberta finally came over to where they were again sitting together.

"Michael, I wonder, do you think you could escort Senhorita Cardoso home? I have been offered a ride by friends in their carriage, so you need have no concerns about me."

"Certainly," Michael replied, "it will be my pleasure."

They walked side by side through the dark, wintery streets of Lisbon, not arm in arm, but there seemed to be an understanding that that would not be appropriate. As they neared their destination Catarina explained the Venâncios had been given the use of a house by a fidalgo that Senhor Venâncio had some acquaintance with through the university. They were, she added, a little out of sorts that she had received an invitation, but they hadn't. Arriving, she knocked on the door and it was opened a few moments later by Senhor Venâncio. He seemed surprised to see Michael, but invited him in.

In the hallway, Catarina bid Michael a polite goodnight, for the moment, and disappeared upstairs. Venâncio led Michael into a small study, and poured them both a glass of brandy.

"Senhor Roberts, thank you for escorting Catarina. I trust the evening was a pleasant one?"

"Indeed it was, Senhor. Senhorita Cardoso is excellent company.

Venâncio raised an eyebrow. "Really, Senhor? I suppose you have much in common, a love of horses. I am a man for books, for philosophy, the more intellectual pursuits, not the countryside." He smiled. "I hope that Catarina will find someone with whom she can share that, it is something that both her sister and I hope for."

Michael noted the use of sister, not sister in law, but let it go. He was more worried about the hint that seemed to be hanging in the air. He chose to ignore it, and finished his brandy before rising from his chair. "I hope she is one day fortunate, Senhor, but now, I must bid you goodnight."

Michael strolled slowly home. Well, that, he thought, had been an interesting evening, and he had to admit, to himself, that he had enjoyed Catarina's company. She was far more mature and interesting than Maria Barros, and no Sofia either. No, she was a very nice girl and he could happily be her friend, but no more. His love for Elaine would not allow it. Under other circumstances, who knew, but, no, not until he really believed himself free could he seek true love again. And in a week or so, all being well, he would be returning to his regiment, he would probably never see her again.

Tavares did well. He found six young tailors, including Jorge, all with enough experience to manage the fitting of dragoon uniforms. Terms were discussed and agreed, although it took most of the day, with much toing and froing between tailors and their employees. Archer had told him exactly how much was available, and Michael was pleased that he was able to be a little generous, but stay well within what he had been allowed. It was a long and at times exasperating day, and he was glad to dine quietly and retire early.

Chapter 11

The day after making his arrangements with Tavares, Michael once again rode out to Belem with Lloyd. For once, the rain had stopped, and with all the dust laid low, the air was warm and clear. At Belem Michael was pleased to hear that the uniforms had at last arrived, and he was taken to see them. Thirty six bales, each weighing ninety pounds were stacked up in a store house. He carefully checked that everything was there and that all the packing and seals were intact.

The same commissary officer dealt with him that had refused to help with transport. He grumpily advised Michael that if he went to see Deputy Commissary Dunmore, he would tell him about the transport arrangements.

Dunmore seemed to be pleased to see Michael. "Come in Mister Roberts, come in. I hear that your new uniforms have arrived, now, let me see, transport for you." He started shuffling though papers, without success. "Ellis!" he called out. "Where are the transport arrangements for the Sixteenth's uniforms?"

Ellis rushed forward with a sheet of paper. "Here you are, Mister Dunmore, a brigade of two dozen mules, sir, eighteen for the bales, the rest for fodder for the brigade." Ellis gave the paper to Dunmore, gave Michael a smile, "Pleasure to see you again, Lieutenant," and rushed back to his desk.

Dunmore looked over the paper. "Yes, this is in order. You should be able to leave in, oh, five days, I think." He beamed at Michael, and spoke conspiratorially in a low voice. "Quicker than we usually manage, Mister Roberts, but for a friend..." He left any more unsaid. "Now," his voice returned to its normal volume, "if you would care to return tomorrow, we can over the details in more detail, give you the name of the mule train captain, and so on."

"Thank you, Mister Dunmore," Michael replied, "and you can be assured that I shall remember your help, and mention it where it needs." At this meaningless blandishment Dunmore looked even happier, and Michael made his exit.

Lloyd had been waiting patiently with Rodrigo and Johnny in the shade of a huge chestnut tree. "Let's go home, Lloyd. There's nothing more to do here until tomorrow. Dunmore thinks we should be away in five days."

Lloyd smiled. "Duw, another five days of Senhora Santiago's cooking, and a proper bed, that will not be a hardship, sir."

They rode in to the back entrance of the house, to be met by Parra at the stables. Michael left him and Lloyd to take care of the horses, and walked up to the house. Inside, Senhor Santiago presented him with a letter that had been delivered. Michael found that he had been invited to a ball at Senhora Lourenco's house in three days' time. He wondered who else might be there. It was, however, only two days before he was due to set off to return to the Regiment. From that fact he could take a certain amount of security, he could easily fend off any subsequent social invitation.

He changed out of uniform, and after an early dinner, told Lloyd he was going out for the evening, and that he, Parra and Francisco were at liberty to do the same, but he wanted to be ready to ride back out to Belem at nine o'clock.

A few minutes later and Michael was strolling past the Palacio Quintela. He carried on up the hill to the Praca das Duas Igrejas. From there he wove his way through the streets to the Praca do Carmo. He stood for a moment and looked at the fountain. He smiled at a memory, and then turned away, across the square towards a small tavern. It was quiet, and he sat at a table and drank a glass of wine.

Refreshed he, paid, and stepped out into the dark of the square. Heading downhill, a short walk brought him to the small square in front of the opera. A performance was underway, and there were few people around, save for a few women near the front of the opera building, looking optimistically for business, looking hopefully at him. But he knew about the whores of Lisbon, and, with a shake of his head, he walked on.

Another tavern, this time a bottle. It occurred to him that the problem was that he was bored, melancholic, and frustrated, a situation that made him feel angry. He was bored playing commissary to the Regiment. He missed the campaigning; he missed the dirty war. He was melancholic because he missed the love he had known with Elaine. He was frustrated at his inability to find any sort of, of, of…, whatever. He didn't know what he wanted, just that he wanted something more than he had, which made him angry. That made him angry with himself. He was angry at what the French had done to Portugal, to the people. The drink wasn't helping him, his self-control was slipping. He felt that he wanted to smash something. He paid his bill and left.

He wandered aimlessly. The streets were quiet in the cold December night. He heard a footfall behind him, and spun around. There were two men a few yards from him. Inside he smiled, but his face was expressionless. He held his cane in his left hand, his right on the top, his finger on the little stud.

One of the men spoke. "Good evening, Senhor, your purse, if you would be so kind."

"No."

The two men glanced at each other, and long knives appeared.

"Please, Senhor, do not be foolish."

"No."

They came towards him rapidly, together. Michael drew his blade, stepped quickly forward and right, and drove the wickedly thin blade into the side of the left hand man. He dropped his knife, and clapped his right hand over the puncture, gasping with pain and shock. Michael kept moving, placing the wounded man between himself and the second man. He kicked the wounded man in the arse, and he staggered forward, into his friend, who instinctively caught him. Michael's blade came over the wounded man's shoulder and into the throat of the second. He left them lying in the street, sheathed his blade, and walked quietly away, smiling and feeling much better.

The next two days were busy enough, particularly making the necessary arrangements to get six tailors with their baggage up to the Regiment. In the end he went to see Juan Moreno at his livery stable. Parra and Francisco had already called on him to give him news of his son, Pedro, and his friend Rafael Martins who served as grooms to the officers of Ashworth's troop. He arranged to hire six mules for the tailors at a daily rate, paying two weeks in advance. Moreno was happy to trust Michael for any more. With the pack mules it would take three days to get to the Regiment, and three to get back. Michael anticipated that it would take two, perhaps three weeks to fit the uniforms.

With three days to go before they set off, everything appeared to be ready. The mule brigade would be at Belem in two days, and ready to leave early the following morning, or so Mister Dunmore assured him. Knowing he would at last have a quiet day, Michael had arranged for Bernardo to come around to see the sad state of the garden. Bernardo was a big man, he had been a big boy, and looked as strong as an ox, but limped badly as a result of a badly set broken leg.

He greeted the Santiago's shyly, he had always been the quietest in their group, but Senhora Santiago fussed over him a little and he soon relaxed. Michael took him out to see the garden, and to meet Parra. It was only then that he realised they both limped, albeit on opposite legs. Parra came limping up from the stables as Michael and Bernardo came out at the back of the house. Parra and Bernardo both stopped and looked at each other.

"So, Miguel," Bernardo said with a very serious tone, "do you only employ men with a limp?"

Michael got as far as "Err…"

Then Bernardo laughed, Parra smiled, and Michael introduced them to each other, explaining that Parra would be away when he was, and would not be involved with the garden, or the house, just the horses, which was enough for any man. Leaving Parra to go on into the house on some errand or other, probably coffee, thought Michael, he led the way to the edge of the garden.

He waved an arm across the sight. "There it is, Bernardo, what do you think?"

Bernardo nodded slightly as he took in the sight. "It was a nice garden, once." He looked some more. "I think it could be a nice garden again, but it will take a lot of work." He pointed to some shrubs, "They should have been cut back two months ago," he shrugged, "but it's not too late to start now."

"Shall we take a walk around it?" Michael suggested. "You can look down to the stable and the land at the back from the far end. It will give you a better idea of what there is to do."

There was a partly overgrown gravel path leading through the garden towards the back. In one corner stood the bust on a pillar that Michael had seen from a distance, but never been to look at. Bernardo was peering around, looking at plants and shrubs. Michael looked at the bust and was reminded of the room full of them at Mafra. Who had they been, he asked himself? Julius, err, Hadrian, and Augustus, of course.

He moved closer, and with his hand he brushed moss and dirt off an inscription. Caesar Augustus. The realisation struck him like a blow. Augustus, Augusto! Could it really be so simple, yet so unobvious? He stared at the pillar; it stood some four feet high on a small area of flagstones. The base of the pillar was fair and square on a single large flagstone. He put a hand on the top of the pillar, and pushed gently. He felt a slight give.

Michael turned to Bernardo. Fortunately he was still engrossed in the bushes. He pulled himself together, "What do you think, Bernardo."

Bernardo pushed his hat back scratched his head, and took a breath. "It would be no great difficulty to restore this, a lot of work, but nothing difficult. It was well thought out."

"Then let us go and see Senhor Santiago, and work things out for you to work for me on this, if you are willing that is?" Inside Michael's head he was screaming, just go away, I need to get at that bust!

It took half an hour, over coffee in his father's old office, with Santiago in attendance, but finally it was agreed that Bernardo would start the day after tomorrow, before Michael had to leave, and that he would have a room in servants quarters in the roof of the house. All his meals would be provided, and a fair rate of pay was agreed. Finally, with huge smile, Bernardo was gone.

In the hallway, Michael said to Santiago, "Let's go down to the kitchen."

Parra was still there, and Lloyd and Francisco were also there, with Senhora Santiago. Michael addressed them. "Bernardo will be coming to work for me from the day after tomorrow. He will work on the garden, but also help Senhor Santiago with the heavy work in the house." He paused, and looked at them. "Senhor, Senhora, you are my family's oldest servants," there was something in Michael's tone that made them attentive, and a little nervous. "Senhora, you were like a second mother to me. I trust you both completely. Lloyd, we have fought together, and I trust you completely as well. Francisco, you have also proven yourself trustworthy in your time with me." He paused, wondering how to tell them, because he could be wrong.

"I think you are all aware by now that my farther left around half of his wealth in the care of someone he called Augusto?" There was nodding all around. Michael took a deep breath. "I think I know who Augusto is, and where he can be found."

Senhora Santiago gasped, and Lloyd quietly swore, "Duw." The others looked slightly stunned.

Michael went on, "Now, if I am correct, I must ask you all to say nothing, nothing at all, to anyone." He looked around as they all nodded in agreement, "No, Francisco, not even Senhorita Roberta." He smiled, "I want to do that myself." Francisco grinned and nodded.

"Very well. Senhor Santiago, we shall need a crowbar and a pickaxe, possibly a spade as well, can you find those please?"

A bemused Santiago replied, "Of course, Senhor."

"Good, off you go, take Parra with you, and join me in the garden.

Michael went up to his room, and rummaged around in his chest. At last he found it, a small leather pouch where he kept the key his father had sent. He hung the small key around his neck by its silver chain. Outside everyone had had gathered, Santiago with a crow bar, Parra with a pickaxe, and Lloyd with a spade, Francisco and Senhora Santiago with them.

With a brief "Follow me," Michael led the way to the bust of Caesar Augustus on its pillar. "If I'm right, this is Augusto."

Santiago exclaimed, "But senhor, it is just a statue, your mother had it put here."

"And exactly who did put it here?"

"Senhor, your mother and father together, no one else, they wouldn't let me help…" His voice tailed off.

"Exactly, why would they do that?" Michael turned to the pillar, put his hands on it at the top, and gave it a massive heave. It rocked, the bust fell and shattered a flagstone, the pillar rocked once more, and fell with crash.

"Lloyd, Parra, help me drag it clear."

While the three men pulled at with their hands, Santiago put his crow bar under it and heaved. Slowly the pillar rolled and slid until it was clear of the central flagstone. Michael took the crowbar from Santiago, worked the end into the narrow gap between it the next flagstone, then he heaved. The flagstone moved slightly, and Parra got the tip of the pickaxe into the gap, and heaved as well. Then Lloyd got the edge of the spade under, and they worked the crowbar and pickaxe further in. There was suddenly a gap as the flagstone was an inch or so higher than those around. Michael and Lloyd dropped their tools, grabbed the edge, and heaved. The flagstone came up and crashed over, revealing a small, square hole, lined with vertical slabs. In the bottom of the hole was a small strongbox.

Michael knelt at the side of the hole, and carefully lifted the box out. Nobody spoke as he stood up with it and walked towards the house. He took the box into his father's office and placed it gently on the desk. He took the key from around his neck, inserted it in the lock and turned it. It was stiff, it resisted, it gave, and the lock clicked free. Michael glanced at everyone; they had all silently followed him.

He lifted the lid.

An oilcloth wrapped package lay there, and Michael carefully lifted it out, to reveal five small, cloth bags, identical to one his father had sent to Falmouth. He put down the oilskin wrapped package, and picked up one of the small bags. It felt as if it was full of gravel. He fumbled with the cords of the bag. He pulled it open, and carefully poured its contents onto the desk. A shower of uncut diamonds fell out. "Begging you pardon, sir," Lloyd's voice broke the silence. "But what are they?"

Michael looked up at him. "Diamonds, Lloyd, uncut diamonds."

"Uffern waedlyd!" Lloyd swore.

Senhora Santiago's hands flew to her mouth and she gasped.

He swept the diamonds together, and put them back in the bag. The other four revealed exactly the same contents.

Michael untied the cord around the oilskin package, unwrapped it, and revealed a folded document. It was a legal document; it looked like the deeds to a property. At the top he made out a name, Quinta dos Cavalos Pretos, Quinta of the Black Horses. Close to that was the name of a town, Mealhada. Damn, thought Michael, it's not long since we rode through there on the retreat from Buçaco.

Slowly, carefully, Michael put everything back in the strongbox and locked it. he put the key back around his neck. Then he picked it up and turned to place it in his father's safe, standing empty and open, the key in the lock. Once the door was closed and locked, he took the key, holding it tightly in his hand.

"Very well." He looked around at everyone. "Now, not a word to anyone, anyone at all." He pulled out his watch, and checked the time. "Now, I have a ball to attend, Francisco, Lloyd, I want my dress uniform, I'll wear my bicorn, not the tarleton, can you get everything ready, I shall be up to change shortly. I shall need to shave as well. And my lightest hessians, no spurs, I may be dancing."

"Right you are sir."

"Yes, Senhor."

"Senhor Santiago, I would like you and Parra to put the flagstone back, and put the pillar and bust back up, if you can. My parents managed it, so you should be able to." They both acknowledged the instruction. "Senhora, some fresh coffee, please. No, I'll have tea, and some bread and cold meat before I go." She gave him a little smile. "Good, now, off you all go. I need to sit quietly for a while."

Once everyone had gone, Lloyd last, closing the door gently behind him. Michael took the key and placed it where his father had always kept it. It was a place that, as a boy, he had known existed, but he had never found it. Before he left for England, his father had shown him the secret. He wondered if his father had had some intimation? The key safely concealed; he sat down at the desk.

So, he thought, Augusto had been around all the time. He smiled at the inventiveness of his father, the calculated risk, just like a successful merchant. He imagined his mother laughing at the joke. And now he truly was a wealthy man. The diamonds should be worth about twenty five thousand pounds. A huge sum, to him at least. And the deeds to a quinta? That had been a complete surprise. Furtado had said nothing about a quinta, so, presumably, he didn't know. What was he to do? He could now afford to buy the next step in promotion, become a captain. An idea that brought its own difficulties. For the moment he would do nothing, he had a ball to go to, then he would sleep on it.

It was dark when Michael reached Senhora Lourenco's. The windows were ablaze with candlelight, a stream of carriages with magnificent teams of matched mules were pulling up at the front of the house, disgorging their passengers, and disappearing onto the night. He cut behind one carriage, scratched a mule in the next carriage team on the nose, and jogged up the steps to the front door. Liveried footmen were on duty, checking invitations, directing guests. He was directed to a room just off the entrance hall where he was able to leave his sabre, belt and sabretache, and his bicorn.

The hallway was lit by two huge chandeliers, and he made his way up the stairs and once again entered the salon where the soiree had been. As he walked in, a footman offered him a glass of wine. It was crisp, dry, and cold. A couple of dozen or more people were in the room, some standing, couples sitting, chattering away. Across the room a pair of doors stood open, and revealed the ball room. It was twice the size of his, with three chandeliers and numerous candle sconces around the walls. Music poured forth, and through a small crowd in the doorway he could see people dancing.

A couple standing by the fireplace caught his eye. Leaning nonchalantly with his elbow on the mantlepiece was Sir Stapleton Cotton. He had heard that Sir Stapleton was planning to go to England for the winter. Presumably he was in Lisbon waiting for a ship. Sir Stapleton saw him, and spoke to a lady who was standing with her back towards him. When she turned he realised it was Senhora Lourenco, and Michael went over to pay his compliments.

"Senhora Lourenco." He took her proffered hand and bowed low over it, and then as he straightened, "Good evening, Sir Stapleton."

Stapleton nodded an acknowledgement, but Senhora Lourenco retained a grip on his hand. "Lieutenant Roberts, I am so pleased that were able to come. Now, I will not let you go until you promise me a dance!"

"It will be my pleasure, Senhora."

"Good, because there are two ladies at the door who I think would otherwise monopolise you," she laughed.

Michael spun around to see Roberta and Catarina entering the salon together. They were a picture of elegance and beauty. Roberta was in a deep, dark red gown, with long, lace sleeves, and silver decoration on the bodice. A silver necklace adorned her neck. Her hair was carefully piled and sported a silver tiara. Catarina was in a dark blue dress, undecorated save for a gold belt, and with puffed shoulders, her bare arms covered by long, white gloves. Her hair was looser, but decorated with a gold tiara with blue stones that matched her necklace. They both had silk shawls and fans matching their dresses.

Michael was aware of Sir Stapleton pushing himself upright off the mantlepiece, and heard him mutter, "I say."

The two women spotted the group, and made their way over. Catarina hung back a little, but Roberta forged on, and greeted everyone. "Senhora Lourenco, such a pleasure to be here, and Sir Stapleton, how nice to see you again, and Lieutenant Roberts as well, this is splendid." She turned and brought Catarina into the group. "Sir Stapleton, allow me to introduce Senhorita Cardoso, a friend of mine from near Coimbra." She spoke to Catarina, "everyone else you know, I think."

Sir Stapleton beamed at the two ladies. "Senhorita Cardoso, a pleasure to make your acquaintance, and Senhorita Roberta, a pleasure to meet you again. Perhaps you would do me the honour of the next dance?"

Senhora Lourenco tapped him with her fan. "Sir Stapleton, and I shall have the one after that." She turned to Michael. "Why don't you take Senhorita Cardoso in, I have more guests to speak to, but I shall claim my dance later."

Michael had no real choice, but didn't mind. Catarina looked stunning, dancing with her would be a delight, and then he could dance with Roberta and Senhora Lourenco, and whatever else transpired he was going back to the Regiment the day after tomorrow.

Catarina was indeed a delight to dance with, and made Michael feel rather pedestrian as they danced the figures and turned, and crossed, and wove their way up and down the set. The dance over, they went in search of refreshment, and in a side room where drinks were available, Michael was a little surprised to see the Ambassador, Mister Stuart. He couldn't avoid speaking to him.

"Your Excellency, it's good to see you."

"Mister Roberts, sir, how are you."

"Very well, thank you, sir. Err, May I present Senhorita Cardoso, Senhorita, His Excellency Senhor Stuart, the British ambassador."

"A pleasure, Senhorita," Stuart gave her a slight bow, and Catarina returned a curtsy. "And, now, Mister Roberts, if you will forgive me, I need to speak to our hostess." He gave them both a smile and walked off.

"Lieutenant Roberts, I did not know that you knew such important people?"

"Oh! Well, Sir Stapleton is an officer in my Regiment, and I have known him for some time, the Ambassador I have been able to be of service to." He smiled at her. "I also know Viscount Wellington." Catarina looked very impressed.

At that moment Sir Stapleton appeared, and claimed a dance with Catarina. She went off with him, and Michael stood against the wall of the ballroom to watch. She certainly danced well, he thought. Then he caught sight of Roberta dancing with a man he never seen before, and she seemed to be looking very intently at him. Now I wonder who that is, he thought.

"There you are, Lieutenant, not hiding from me, I hope?" Senhora Lourenco tapped him with her folded fan.

Michael smiled. "No, Senhora, perhaps the next dance?" She looked pleased. "But, tell me, please, who is that dancing with Senhorita Roberta?"

She stared for a moment, "Ah, yes, Senhor Alexandre da Rocha. A delightful man, he has a significant landholding near Alcoentre. Another refugee from the French, I fear."

Senhora Lourenco proved herself a more than adequate dance partner, and Michael was enjoying himself. He danced with a number of other ladies, and noticed that Roberta seemed to have been monopolised by da Rocha, or perhaps, he thought, it was the other way around. The last dance before supper found Michael once again partnering Catarina. As custom dictated, when it ended he offered her his arm and led her in to supper. He saw da Rocha lead in Roberta. He had hoped to have a chance to talk to her, perhaps in his bed. He wanted to tell her about his discovery. She didn't even look his way. Instead he chatted inconsequentially to Catarina. He was only giving her half his attention, he was still slightly stunned by the discovery of the diamonds, and the deeds to the quinta. He wondered if Catarina knew of it. He decided not to ask. It would lead to questions that he couldn't yet answer, such as what he was going to do about it?

The ball continued well into the early morning. Michael had danced again with Catarina, and they were just taking some refreshment when Roberta appeared, with da Rocha.

"Michael, there you are!" She gave him her brightest smile. "Senhor da Rocha has kindly offered to take me home in his carriage. I wonder, could I impose on you to see Senhorita Cardoso safely home?"

Michael glanced at da Rocha, who was looking slightly embarrassed. So that's how it is, is it, he thought? Vexed with me so you are forcing me into Catarina's company and using this poor fool to do so. Well, he thought, Catarina is good company, and an extremely attractive woman. Under other circumstances... He gave Roberta an equally bright smile, two can play games. "Of course, it would be my pleasure, if the Senhorita is amenable to that?" He turned his eyes and his smile on Catarina, who looked more than a little confused, but simultaneously pleased.

Roberta smiled to herself. If Michael couldn't see that Catarina was perfect for him, well, she could. She could bring them together, but her problem was what to do about Elaine. Still, she had the most attractive and entertaining Senhor da Rocha to consider. It might have only been a few hours, but she felt something stirring in her, something not felt for a long time.

Catarina answered Michael's question. "I should be glad to have the Lieutenant escort me home," and this time it was Catrina's turn to smile brightly at Michael.

Michael retrieved his sabre and bicorn, and then helped Catarina with her cloak. They watched as da Rocha handed Roberta into his carriage, following her in, and tapping on the roof with his cane to tell his coachman to drive on.

Michael gallantly held out his arm to Catarina. "Senhorita?"

She took his arm, said "Thank you, Lieutenant," and they walked away. She leant a little on his arm, a bit tired, but also excited by the proximity of Michael and being alone in the night with him. Deliberately, she walked slowly, relishing the experience.

Michael had his sabre tucked under his left arm. He felt Catarina's hand seek his right hand, and took it, and gave it a little squeeze. It seemed to be the thing to do. He would not begrudge giving her a little adventure before he rode off to join his Regiment. Her perfume reached him, filled his senses. The drink was working its disinhibiting effect.

Their pace slowed. The grip of their hands grew firmer. Michael heard an upper window a little ahead of them open, heard the bump of something on the window frame. He dropped Catarina's hand, grasped her firmly around the waist, and spun her into a dark, recessed door way. She gasped, and her hands were on his chest, she could feel the roughness of the silver braid on his jacket. She looked up at him.

A few yards away the bucket load of waste splashed into the street.

Michael turned to her, and met her gaze. "That was close," he said, softly.

Catarina put a hand up to his cheek, and gently touched his scar. "How…"

"An accident, nothing exciting."

Catarina didn't reply, she didn't move, her fingers stayed on his cheek, she just gazed into his eyes. Her lips parted slightly; she lifted her head a fraction. Michael, hesitantly, lowered his lips towards hers. Her eyes closed.

Across the street a door opened, spilling light across them. Voices called goodnights to each other; several people came out into the street. Instinctively, Michael and Catarina stepped away from each other.

Silently, they continued on their way, Catarina once again held his arm, but something had changed, something had shifted for her. Michael was frightened, he had nearly kissed her! He had felt an attraction, a desire, different from Sophia, nothing like Maria, something like Elaine.

With something approaching relief, Michael realised they had arrived at their destination. He released Catarina's arm to knock on the door. It was opened by Senhor Venâncio, who looked surprised to see Michael standing there with Catarina. "Lieutenant Roberts, what has happened? Where is Senhorita Roberta? She said she would make sure Catarina got home safely!"

"And, indeed, she has Senhor. She was, err, unable to bring the Senhorita herself, and asked me to escort her home. It was my pleasure."

"Oh, very good, thank you. Come along in, Catarina." He stood aside for her. "Forgive me, Lieutenant, it is a little late, perhaps you would care to call one afternoon?"

"Thank you Senhor, that is kind of you, but I am afraid that I return to my Regiment the day after tomorrow, and there is much to be done. Another time, perhaps?" Behind Venâncio he saw a look of disappointment on Catarina's face.

"Of course, Lieutenant, of course. And now, thank you again, and goodnight to you."

"Goodnight, Senhor,"

Michael walked home slowly, and thoughtful. He wasn't quite sure what had happened. It was a matter of some relief to him that he was about to return to the Regiment.

The following morning, Michael was down at the stables with Parra and Lloyd when Francisco appeared. "Senhor, Senhorita Roberta is here, she wishes to see you, Senhor!"

She was waiting for him in the drawing room, coffee was already on the table. "Michael!" She greeted him, put her cup down and stood to embrace him. Michael kept the table between them. "Michael? What is the matter with you?"

"Roberta, I am sure you know very well."

She smiled coyly, "Are you cross because I left with Senhor da Rocha? You know, I couldn't very well leave with you, how would Catarina have got home?"

"No, Roberta, that is not why I am cross. What makes me cross is that you insist on throwing that poor girl at me, encouraging her, I don't doubt, raising her hopes, when you know very well that I am not a free man!" His voice had risen until he was practically shouting.

"Michael, please,…"

"No, Roberta. You have no idea, do you? No idea what is going on with me. No idea that everyone is trying to run my life for me. I've got Quintela, trying to get me into business with him." Roberta's mouth opened in a silent oh! "Wellington is trying to get me into the bloody Guides, for God's sake, so I'll be more convenient if he wants me to do some dirty fighting for him. I've got the bloody Regiment watching me like something dangerous because I killed a few Frenchmen who were going to rape a woman in front of her husband and her children! And you, you're trying to marry me off when you know damn well that I still love Elaine. Yes, I know, she set me free, I have read the bloody letter, you know. But it's not enough, Roberta, it's not enough!" He paused.

Roberta rose to her feet, her face stony. "How dare you speak to me like that. Of course I think Catarina is right for you, because she is, and you're a fool if you can't see it. And I don't need to encourage her, she is doing that quite well on her own. As for Quintela and Wellington, I am afraid that I can take no credit for anything they are doing in the mistaken belief that they might actually be helping you! I understand about Elaine. Damn it, Michael, do you think I didn't love my husband, that I didn't miss him, that I didn't cry myself to sleep for months afterwards? And, yes, I was happy to leave with da Rocha. Happy for me because he made me feel something that I haven't felt since my husband died, no, not even with you, love you as friend though I do." She gasped for breath, "And happy for you, because I thought Catarina might just be the woman to save you from a hopeless love. Yes, you loved Elaine, and I am happy for you that you did, but you must believe what she wrote to you!"

They stood looking at each other. Michael was expressionless, but ice cold with anger, anger at himself because he recognised the truth of what Roberta said. Roberta, chest heaving with emotion saw the coldness, saw a hardness that she had not seen before, and it scared her.

"What has happened to you, Michael?" She turned and left.

Later that day, later that night, Michael sat on his bed, and looked at the portrait of Elaine. It had not been a good day. There had a been an atmosphere in the house. Everyone was aware of what had passed. Even knew some of what had been shouted. They walked around Michael as if on egg shells. He picked up the picture and stared at it, at the lock of copper red hair, and he felt despair.

"Elaine, Elaine, please, help me."

Chapter 12

Roberta sat at a corner table, giving her a view of the window, and both doors, one from the street, one behind the counter. It was arguably the smartest coffee house in Lisbon, its customers representing the best of Lisbon society, but she had learnt to be careful. It was richly decorated, white cloths on the tables, red velvet covered chairs, and heavy curtains at the window. The table was for two, and she sipped her coffee as she waited for Catarina. She had met Catarina and her sister in law out shopping yesterday, and had suggested coffee today. Senhora Venâncio had pleaded a prior engagement, but suggested that Catarina go. Catarina had seemed very pleased at that, and Roberta was sure it was because she wanted to quiz her more about her friend, Lieutenant Roberts. Roberta was a little apprehensive, it would be their first chance to talk since the ball, and since Roberta had rowed with Michael. She knew he had left yesterday to return to his Regiment. For once she wasn't sorry. She loved him dearly, but his obsessive clinging to the love of a dead woman, no matter how deep that had been, was beginning to get tiresome, he needed to move on, and it wasn't as if the woman hadn't told him he could. And Michael had changed, he had become, she felt, unpredictably dangerous.

Roberta was supposedly getting to know Catarina and the Venâncios on behalf of her cousin, General de Silva. As head of the police in Lisbon, he was working through everyone who had fled to Lisbon from the French, looking for spies and traitors. In reality she had quickly concluded that Catarina was not involved in anything treasonous, and that she would make an ideal wife for Michael, if only he would free of himself of those bonds to the dead. She had to admit that she wasn't so sure of the Venâncios, but wondered if she was being unduly influenced by de Silva's dislike of intellectuals. What she wasn't now so sure about, was if this new, dangerous, unpredictable Michael would make a good husband for anyone.

Catarina entered the coffee house, and was soon seated opposite Roberta, fresh coffee on its way. They chatted inconsequentially about the ball for a few minutes until the waiter delivered the fresh coffees. Catarina watched him go, and once he was out of earshot, she said, "I think I can tell you, Senhorita, I am a little saddened that Lieutenant Roberts has returned to his Regiment."

"Please," said Roberta, "if we are to be friends and share confidences, you must call me Roberta, and I shall call you Catarina. In private, at least." She smiled. "Clearly the Lieutenant delivered you home without incident, the streets can be dangerous at night?"

Catarina blushed. "Not entirely without incident," she smiled. "He nearly kissed me!"

"Only nearly," asked Roberta, slightly surprised that he had even nearly kissed her.

"Yes," Catarina grimaced, "the moment was spoilt by some people coming out of a house."

Perhaps, thought Roberta, there was hope yet. "Never mind, my dear, I am sure he will get leave and be back in Lisbon before too long. It is his home, even if he is English."

"You've known him for a long time, haven't you?" asked Catarina. "I am not trespassing am I."

Oh, if only you knew, thought Roberta. "No, of course not, we are friends, very good friends, but that is all." She gave Catarina a reassuring smile. She would find it all out for herself in time if things worked out, if not, well, there was no need for her to know.

Catarina looked relieved, and said "May I ask about Senhor da Rocha."

Roberta was a little surprised to find it was her turn to blush. She sipped at her coffee to hide her confusion. "He is a very pleasant gentleman," Roberta answered. "I…, I find I like him a lot." She surprised herself with the admission, and sought to change the subject. "But, Catarina, I would not be a friend if I did not give you a gentle word of warning about Lieutenant Roberts." She had the decency to feel guilty, but also to know she would feel more guilty if she said nothing. Catrina looked at her, expectant, worried. "He is, of course, a soldier, and there is always the risk he may be killed, or severely disabled in some way."

Catrina waved dismissively, "I know that, but again he may not."

"Indeed," went on Roberta, "but soldiering can affect some men in an unfortunate way." She struggled for words.

"What do you mean?"

Roberta found a way. "As you know, I have known the Lieutenant, Michael," she gave Catarina a little smile at the use of Michael's first name, "for a very long time. I can tell you that since he returned to Portugal, he has changed. I think," and I know, she thought, "that he has had experiences that have changed him. I have seen a look in his eyes that I have not seen before."

"Oh, yes," exclaimed Catarina, " I know exactly what you mean. He has this look that makes the hairs stand up on the back of my neck, and I think I am glad I am not his enemy." Her eyes gleamed as she spoke, clearly excited. "He can look so dangerous, and it just makes him look more handsome, more attractive!" She realised how indiscreet she had just been, and her hand flew to her mouth.

Roberta stared at her, well, she had told her, there was nothing more she could do. They both sipped at their coffees and let the conversation move on to less controversial matters.

Christmas came and went in its usual social whirl, and Roberta's annual pilgrimage to Mass at the cathedral. Roberta frequently met Catarina at various social affairs, and their friendship slowly developed. Sometimes the Venâncios were also present, but increasingly Catarina appeared without them. That was alright with Roberta, she thought Senhor Venâncio to be a pompous, academic bore. She was also, to her increasing pleasure, increasingly escorted by Senhor da Rocha.

Two days after Christmas, Roberta attended a Soiree at the home of an acquaintance of hers, escorted by Senhor da Rocha. She had invited Senhora Marcelino to accompany her, and as she had expected, she had thanked her, and declined. She was not sorry. It was pleasant enough, she knew everyone there, and was well aware that her arrival with da Rocha had raised eyebrows. She didn't care. It was, she felt, an evening when she could relax without worrying about young lovers, spies or traitors.

Da Rocha was talking to a banker and a lawyer about the difficulties of land management. She yawned behind her fan, and wandered off to rest herself in a deep, winged armchair. She sat quietly and sipped her wine. She became aware that behind the chair two ladies were speaking to each other in what they thought were hushed tones, but in their excitement she could hear every word.

"… and apparently they are reduced to eating cats, dogs and even rats,"

"Oh, but that's awful!"

"And they are burning furniture, doors and window frames, and sometimes whole houses catch fire."

"Simply dreadful."

"Oh, my dear it is, and the absolute truth, you know. I heard it from a friend who is in correspondence with someone in Torres Novas," Now Roberta was very interested, Torres Novas was occupied by the French. The voice went on. "I can tell you, in the strictest confidence of course,…"

"Oh, yes, absolutely."

"… that they have a friend with," there was a pause, and the voice went on in whisper, "General Pamplona! There, what do you think of that?"

Now Roberta was very interested, Pamplona was a renegade Portuguese general serving with the French, and Torres Novas was some way behind the French lines.

The voice went on, "And they are entirely dependent on this correspondence for any word from the outside world, they are completely isolated, without essentials like sugar and coffee," Roberta heard the other woman give a little gasp of horror, "and so those things are smuggled to them, along with news of what passes here, in Lisbon. Do you know, they have been forced to create their own theatre for their entertainment, and the common soldiers act there!"

"That is dreadful, my dear, but look, is that your husband waving?"

"What, oh, yes, how tiresome, I had better join him. Now, not a word to anyone, please?"

"Oh, no, of course not."

"Shall we meet for coffee tomorrow?

"Certainly, in that little place on the south side of the Cathedral…"

The voices faded as the two ladies moved away.

Roberta leaned forward slightly, just enough to peer around the side of the chair, and see the two women who had been talking, and to see which one joined her husband.

She waited for a few more minutes, and then rose from her chair and walked the long way around the room, until she found her hostess. A quick smile, an inconsequential enquiry, and she had a name. Prates, Senhora Prates, wife of Senhor Prates, a notable lawyer, but one that Roberta knew was suspected of Republican sympathies.

The rest of the evening passed pleasantly, the Prates had left, and she was happy enough to keep company with da Rocha, very happy in fact. They were not far from Roberta's, and had walked rather than draw attention with da Rocha's fine carriage and mule team. They walked back, companionably, arm in arm, not saying much, just comfortable with each other's company. At her house, da Rocha bid her a goodnight with courteous peck on her cheek, and then was gone. Constanca, her maid helped her out of her warm cloak, and looked at her, questioningly.

Roberta grinned. "If the Marcelinos were not still here…" Da Rocha was comfortable to be with, intelligent amusing, a gentleman, and she felt safe with him.

The following day Roberta set about accidentally meeting Senhora Prates. They were not acquainted, so Roberta could not simply call upon her. Instead, the hour when the ladies of Lisbon habitually met for coffee found her lurking, there was, she thought, no other word for it, in a recess of the walls of the cathedral. From where she stood, she could clearly see the entrance to the coffee house only a few yards away. She had already strolled past it, and caught a glimpse of Senhora Prates deep in conversation with her friend. They had taken no notice of yet another figure passing by the windows. She was taking a chance, waiting so close to the coffee house, but was relying on the ladies being typically unobservant. It was cold and damp, but Roberta was warmly dressed in a heavy and nondescript cloak.

Eventually the door opened and the two ladies came out, spoke to each other briefly, and set off in opposite directions. Roberta passed unnoticed on the opposite side of the narrow street from Prates' friend, and was soon only a few yards behind the Senhora. She had a rough idea of where the Prates' house was, and, only a few feet behind Prates, suddenly turned into a narrow alleyway. Steps led steeply upwards, and were a short route to the street she wanted. She had been confident that the rather large Senhora Prates would not tackle the steps, but would take the longer, easier route home.

Panting hard, Roberta reached the top of the steps and turned right. She strolled gently downhill, catching her breath as she went. She couldn't see Prates. At the end of the street it turned to the right, into a small, open area at the front of a church. She began to worry that she had miscalculated, when Senhora Prates came around the corner in front of her. She let her get closer, and then, feigning surprise, greeted her.

"Senhora Prates! What a lovely surprise."

Prates started at being addressed, but then saw who it was. "Why, Senhorita de Silva, oh, you gave me such a start."

"My dear, forgive me, I am so sorry, but I am so relieved to see someone I know."

"Why, what ever is the matter?"

"Well, you see, someone was telling me about a delightful little coffee house by the Cathedral, and having nothing else to do I thought I would seek it out. Have a little adventure!" She gave a girlish giggle. "But I haven't found it anywhere, and now I am quite fatigued."

"Oh dear, but you are on the wrong side of the Cathedral. What a shame you didn't find it a little earlier, I have just this minute come from it."

"What? Oh, that is a shame."

"Listen, my dear, my house is just up here, and closer, why don't you come in and rest a while?"

"Is it? Oh, that would be so kind of you, Senhora." Roberta gave Senhora Prates her best look of gratitude. This was working better than she might have hoped.

Ten minutes later she and Senhora Prates were sitting together while a maid poured coffee for them. "Such a lovely house!" gushed Roberta.

"Thank you, my dear. Of course, being a little out of the way, we were not too inconvenienced when the French were here."

"You had no officers imposed on you?"

"No."

Roberta looked around, as if about to impart a secret. "I probably shouldn't say this, but I found some of them to be perfectly charming, quite gallant, unlike these cold Englishmen."

Emboldened, the Senhora joined Roberta's conspiracy. "Yes, I know just what you mean. We only met one or two, but they behaved quite correctly."

There was a moments silence, each wondering where to take the conversation. Roberta decided she had better keep the initiative, before the Senhora got cold feet and changed the subject. "Of course, my cousin, General de Silva, was relieved of his post while they were here." She shrugged. "He is, you know, only my cousin by marriage, and proved to be little protection for a single woman like myself."

"Oh, my dear!" Senhora Prates managed to looked horrified and curious at the same time.

"Fortunately, and you realise that this is something that I wouldn't share with just anyone?"

"You may rely on my discretion, Senhorita."

"Please, if we are to share secrets, call me Roberta."

"And you must call me Mariana."

"Thank you, Mariana." Roberta leaned forward and lowered her voice. "Fortunately, I found a protector!" She sat back looking triumphant, and Senhora Prates' mouth gaped open. "I shall say no more, I am sure you understand?" Prates nodded. "So, you see, I have no fear of the French returning." She sipped her coffee. "I do find myself wondering. One hears such awful stories about conditions in the French army."

"And they are true, Roberta, absolutely true!" Prates exclaimed.

Roberta put her hand to her mouth in horror. "But are you sure, how can we know what is true and what is not?" She thought the "we" was a nice touch.

This time it was Senhora Prates who leaned forward conspiratorially. "There are a few of us who feel like you do," she said, "and there are ways of knowing what is really happening."

"But how?" Roberta held her breath, this was the moment of truth.

Senhora Prates answered, hesitantly. "there is a regular salon, a small gathering, where those of us who feel like you do can meet and speak freely."

Roberta's eyes opened wide. "And do you attend, Mariana?"

"Oh, yes." She managed to look extremely smug and superior. "And we hear news direct from the French army."

"Then you are very lucky." Roberta looked sad. "However," she gave Prates a wan little smile, "I am glad to have found a new friend, a new friend I can confide in.

It is such a relief to find someone else who shares my thoughts."

"And I feel quite the same," beamed Prates, "and I shall see if I can obtain an invitation for you to one of our little gatherings.

"Oh would you? I would be so grateful!"

"I can make no promises," said Senhora Prates, "but I can try."

Roberta smiled back, gratefully, and thought, it doesn't really matter, Senhora, I already have enough! And then the conversation turned to more conventional matters.

Over a week later Roberta was at another soiree, with Alexandre da Rocha escorting her. There had never been such a social whirl in Lisbon, it was if the proximity and threat of the French had determined everyone to enjoy themselves as much as possible while they could. Perhaps that contributed to her feelings towards da Rocha. They had begun to meet whenever they could. She was feeling emotions that she had thought long lost. Emotions that Michael, dearly though she loved him, had never given rise to. She realised the consequences for him, but it had always been a possibility. She just hoped that he would prove to have meant what he said and that they would remain friends long after they were no longer lovers. After all, she had raised no obstacles, nor shown any jealousy of his romances, and she had tolerated his obsession with Elaine for too long. She could not help but wonder if anything could ever have come of that liaison. She thought it would probably have ended in tears, Michael's.

Roberta had been lost in thought, half watching da Rocha who was chatting away with someone, when she became aware of someone standing next to her. She turned to look.

"Mariana, how are you?"

"Well, thank you, Roberta." She looked around, and dropped her voice, holding her fan in front of her mouth. "I have an invitation for you. Next Monday." She glanced sideways at Roberta, who almost laughed at her attempt to be inconspicuous. "Can you be at my house for two o'clock? We can go together from there."

"Yes, there will be no difficulty with that."

"Until Monday then!" Senhora Prates sidled away.

Da Rocha came over to her. "What on earth did the strange looking woman want?"

Roberta laughed, and turned to face him. "Take no notice of her, she is a little eccentric, she was just inviting me to coffee next Monday."

"And shall you go?"

"Oh, yes, I think one should always be open to new experiences and possibilities, don't you?" As she spoke she realised the full implications implicit in what she had said. She and da Rocha stood only a foot or so apart, face to face, the crowded room of the soiree ignored. In a split second of silence more understanding was reached than might be possible in an hour of conversation.

"I think," said Roberta, softly, and slowly, "that you can, should call me Roberta, Alexandre."

He gave her a slight bow without breaking eye contact. "With the greatest of pleasure, Roberta. Thank you."

In that moment they became lovers. He hadn't asked, she hadn't offered, but they were, they would be, and they both knew it.

At two o'clock precisely on the following Monday, she could hear the Cathedral bells tolling the hour, Roberta knocked at the door of Senhora Prates' house. The door opened immediately and Senhora Prates stepped out, already in her hat coat and gloves. "Come, my dear, it's not far."

Somewhat to Roberta's surprise, they walked around to the coffee house by the Cathedral and went in. It was almost empty, and Roberta wondered what was going on. Then, a nod from the patron, and Prates led the way to the corner and up a flight of stairs. Through a door at the top was a private assembly room, with a score of people sitting around, engrossed in lively conversation. To her surprise, she saw the Venâncios sitting alone at one table. Senhor Venâncio saw her, rose from his chair, and walked over.

He greeted the two women. "Senhora Prates, and Senhorita Roberta de Silva."

"Senhor Venâncio." Roberta replied.

"I must admit," Venâncio went on, "to being more than a little surprised when our friend here," he indicated Prates, "suggested that you might be an addition to our little gathering."

"I quite understand, Senhor, but sometimes the company one keeps requires one to be discreet and perhaps deny what one really believes."

"Indeed, Senhorita?"

"Senhor, my cousin is General de Silva, and a British officer is one of my oldest friends. Of course I must be careful, even to the extent of denying some friendships. Sometimes it is necessary to be friendly to people for protection when none else is available." Venâncio considered her in silence. "Of course, if my presence is not welcome, I shall leave immediately."

"No, no, there is no need for that, we are all just friends here, nothing else. Perhaps you would care to take my chair by my wife. I know she would be delighted to get to know you better." He gestured towards Senhora Venâncio, who waved to Roberta to come over. "Senhora Prates, a word, please." He took the Senhora's arm and left Roberta to join his wife.

Senhora Venâncio was a little more welcoming, although Roberta thought she detected some reserve. "Senhorita, welcome, coffee?" She poured Roberta a cup. "I must admit that I was a little surprised when Senhora Prates suggested that we might have, err, friends in common? A shared desire when it comes to government?"

"I am not sure what you mean?" replied Roberta. "I do know that I find the company of a French officer preferable to that of an English one!"

"Really, my dear, that is very outspoken, you must be careful expressing such a sentiment."

"Must I? I thought I was amongst friends here?"

Senhor Venâncio placed a comforting hand on Roberta's. "Of course you are, of course you are. I quite understand a woman's needs… for protection." She arched her eyebrows. "One cannot expect a man to understand that."

"That is true." Roberta contrived to sound a little frustrated.

Senhora Venâncio continued, "And your English officer friend is away with the army, but you now have Senhor da Rocha to look out for you?"

"Yes, I do, but perhaps there is someone else I would prefer."

"Ah, so when you referred to the company of a French officer, you had one in particular in mind?"

"Senhora, I am amongst friends am I? If I were to admit to a French lover, it would be a terrible scandal. I have my place in society to consider."

"I quite understand, and so do some of our friends." She paused to drink her coffee. "If you were to give me a name, it might be possible to find out how he is."

"Really? Could you do that? How is it possible?"

Venâncio laughed. "Senhorita, you would be surprised what is possible. For instance, did you know that the French have set up a theatre in a church in Santarem and the ordinary soldiers put on performance for the officers?"

Roberta allowed herself a gasp of surprise. "But how do you know?"

"That's simple, there is correspondence."

"Could, might it be possible to ask after someone for me?"

"I cannot promise anything, but without a name I cannot even try."

Roberta, stared hard at Senhora Venâncio. She hesitated, as well she might. She wanted to look for any reaction to the name she was about to give. "Renard, Jean Paul Renard." Venâncio's face gave nothing away, not a flicker of recognition of the name. "He," she caught herself in time, hoped the pause would be taken for hesitation, not the realisation she was about to say "he was". "He is an officer in a chasseur regiment, but I think he may have been on the staff." She shrugged. "I don't really understand these things."

Venâncio gave her hand another reassuring squeeze. "No promises, my dear, but we will try. We will ask our friend if he can ask in his next letter."

"Can he do that? How? Is it not terribly dangerous, he must be very brave?"

"He is a great man of great principle. And that is all I can tell you for now. She looked across towards her husband. "We must go." She looked around the room. "But you should stay awhile, make some friends."

Roberta gave them ten minutes while she sat alone, and finished her now cold coffee. Then she quietly got up and left.

That night she met Alexandre for dinner in one of Lisbon's better restaurants. As he walked her home, her arm in his, he said, "You are very quiet. Roberta, is everything alright?"

"What? Oh! Yes! I was just thinking." She did not say so, but the meeting with the Venâncios had scared her more than a little. It could all have gone so very, very wrong. It had left her a little drained.

"And what were you thinking?"

Roberta paused for a moment; she hugged his arm tight in hers. "I was thinking that I would very much like you to take me home with you, please." She pulled them to a halt, turned to face him, lifted up her face towards him, and let him kiss her.

A few days later Roberta was sitting quietly at her usual table in her favourite coffee house. She was happy, she was in love. She looked up as the door opened, and Catarina came in. Roberta gave her a wave inviting her to join her. She was bursting to talk to someone, and just at the moment could think of no one better.

She stood, and gave Catarina a peck on the cheek. "Catarina, how are you? Coffee? Two more coffees," this to the waiter, "sit down, sit down. Tell me, how are you?"

Catarina laughed. "I am well, thank you, Roberta. But you look as if you are about burst. What is it?"

"Not what, who!"

"What? Then who?"

"Senhor da Rocha!"

Catarina squealed in delight. "That's wonderful, I am so happy for you. Tell me all about it?"

"Ah, well, that's it, really." She was not about to tell her everything. "But how are things with you?"

"A little difficult, to tell you the truth." She went on to explain that money was difficult. fortunately they house they had was being lent to them by a friend of the Venâncios. Roberta asked who, and the reply surprised her. "Baron Francisco de Barcarena. I gather he is quite an important man. I think Senhor Venâncio knows him through some university connection." Coffee arrived and the conversation paused. Roberta tried to grasp the implications of the name so casually given.

"Anyway," Catarina continued, "the Senhor is going away tomorrow, taking some trip that will solve the money difficulties, apparently." She took a drink of coffee. "Well, it's not the first time, and it did last time, so I expect it will this time."

"Oh, where is he going?"

"Caldas, I think. I heard Senhora Venâncio mention it to him, I don't think they knew I could hear them."

Roberta did not want to seem too inquisitive, so she asked Catarina, "What about you, how are you now?"

She looked at Roberta a little sheepishly. "I find that I am missing a certain lieutenant."

Across Lisbon Senhor Venâncio was talking to de Barcarena. "Don Francisco, I have to say that I am not happy about letting that woman into our little group. Look at who she knows, an English cavalry officer and General de Silva, her cousin no less!"

"Yes, yes, Venâncio, I can see that it might not look good. However, look at the possibilities. Think of the intelligence she might be able to get for us with connections like that? And we can easily check with this officer she mentioned." He gave Venâncio a knowing look. "It just so happens that I know him. He has been here before, he set up the agents we had until de Silva got them. He was here in September. I haven't heard from him since,

I assume he is back with the French army, he is on Massena's staff. So a note to Pamplona should get us a result quickly." He handed a sealed package to Venâncio. "Unfortunately everything is ciphered and sealed, it will have to wait until next time. I fully expect her story to be validated. How could she invent something like that? And you wife was convinced?"

Venâncio gave a reluctance shrug of agreement. "Then I suggest we trust her female intuition, and you can see what you can get from her, without her realising, of course. You can tell her we are enquiring about Renard. See how grateful she is. There is no rush, after all, Renard may want nothing to do with her, he may have gone back to Paris," he laughed, "he may even be dead. To be honest with you, I have been aware of her for some time. As a typical social butterfly, flitting here and there from party to ball to soiree. She has her own money, her own house, and that is all there is to her, you will see. Put your wife to work on her. Now, when do you leave?"

"First thing in the morning."

"Excellent. I shall expect you back in ten days or so."

Roberta received a note from Senhora Venâncio with mixed feelings. It was progress, she was suggesting meeting for coffee and a little talk at the coffee house by the Cathedral. On the other hand, as her feelings for da Rocha deepened, and their relationship blossomed, she found herself less in need of her role in the intelligence war against France. She decided that after this little adventure, there would be no more.

Senhora Venâncio was waiting for her. "Senhorita, how are you?" They were soon settled in a quiet corner.

Roberta decided to display a little stupidity. "Senhora, do you have any word for me?"

She got a slightly mocking little laugh in reply. "No, no, it will take a little while, but my husband has spoken with our friend, and enquiries will be made after your Renard." She hesitated for a moment. "Did Renard tell you anything about what he did?"

"No, well, he might have, I wouldn't have understood, so I wouldn't have taken much notice if he did."

Venâncio smiled. "Fortunately, our friend knows him."

That didn't entirely surprise Roberta, but surprise was called for. "Oh, my, really? But how, who?" Who was the big question, and she hoped it might get an answer slipped in like that.

"I can't answer that."

Her vanity, thought Roberta, that's the way in. She contrived to look thoroughly downcast. "Oh, I thought you and Senhor Venâncio were people who knew things, that you were important?"

"Well , we are, but it is de Barcarena who is our leader."

She had no difficulty in looking surprised. "Do you mean Baron Francisco de Barcarena? But, he's a very important man, he's a real fidalgo, he knows all the important people." She paused to look thoughtful. "He must know best, then, that sort of man." She put on her best sincere face. "And he must know what is best for Portugal." She smiled and looked pleased.

"Indeed, and you must show a little patience, writing to friends with the French is not a simple matter."

"Oh, I shall, Senhora, I shall."

"Now, tell me, how is your Lieutenant friend, and your cousin the General?"

"Oh, the Lieutenant has gone away, and the General is the same as ever. But I think the Lieutenant might be interested in your Catarina."

"Really?" asked Senhora Venâncio, "tell me more please?"

Forgive me, Michael, Roberta thought, but it is in a good cause, the war, and you. She then launched into a tale of how Catrina was all Lieutenant Roberts seemed to be able to talk about. In the process she made it quite clear that she had no romantic interest in the lieutenant herself, that her interests lay elsewhere. Senhora Venâncio seemed very pleased by it all.

The following morning, Roberta slipped unobtrusively into Police headquarters by a little used and very discreet entrance. She was shown into de Silva's office and proceeded to tell him all that she had learnt. De Silva was horrified.

"De Barcarena?"

"Yes, I'm afraid so."

"But he's got friends in the highest places, he knows half the Regency council personally, my God, the man is untouchable. And we have no evidence, just hearsay."

"He is related to Alorna." Roberta referred to the Portuguese general advising Massena.

"That's not enough to accuse one of Portugal's most important and influential fildago's of treason!"

"So what do we do?"

"We? You do nothing, just go along with them as much as you have to. And be careful, these are dangerous people." He paused and thought. "I'll put a light, very light surveillance on him, but a man like that isn't stupid. He won't do anything himself. He will always have someone to take the blame for him, always be able to deny everything." He paused again. "There is one other thing you might do, when you have the chance."

"What's that?"

"Tell Lieutenant Roberts."

"Ah…" It was only late January, Roberta had no idea when she might see Michael again, and it was a meeting that she was not relishing.

Chapter 13

It took three days to reach the Regiment's headquarters at San João da Ribeira. The weather was cold and damp, with intermittent rain. It matched Michael's mood. Despite the size of the party he felt very alone. There was no one he could talk to, share his situation with, he suddenly realised how much he missed his grandfather and his quiet way of guiding without judging. Perhaps he would see if he could be reconciled with his uncle, if his grandfather thought it right, and would help. He decided he would write to him, tell him everything, tell him about the diamonds, and beg his guidance.

As they plodded their way through the interminable cold and drizzle, Michael had plenty of time to think. He would not, could not end his love of Elaine, it would be, he felt, a betrayal of everything he felt for her. He recognised that Roberta's home truths were not without their validity, and he could not deny, at least to himself, that he had enjoyed holding Catarina in his arms, had enjoyed her company, a lot. But he would not betray his commitment.

Almost as an afterthought to all that, he wondered about the Regiment, how he was perceived. He did not want to be labelled a killer, even if that was almost the definition of a soldier, but he had no regrets about his actions, no pity for the dead Frenchmen, and he would cheerfully do it again. He could not make France pay enough for what had been done to Portugal. He was pleased that he had decided to remain with the Regiment, and reject Wellington's offer. Many would think him mad, if they knew about it, but he had decided where he belonged, and there he would stay. At least that solved one problem of the diamonds. He wouldn't be going into business with Quintela, although beyond that he didn't know what he would do. His sudden wealth was still more than a little unreal.

He had expected to deliver the tailors into the care of the adjutant, Mister Barra, and return to his squadron at

Anteporta. Colonel Archer, however, had other plans for him.

"Mister Roberts, good to see you back so soon, I thought you would be another week. Mister Barra tells me the arrangements you made are excellent, and quite economic. Well done. And since Captain Ashworth isn't expecting you so soon either, there's another little job you can do."

"Yes, sir?"

"Yes, I want you to take yourself off to Mafra, and bring back all of our men and horses who are fit, should be all of them by now, I hope. It will be useful to have Lloyd with you, he can check the horses for us as well, save sending the Vetenry, he's enough to do here."

"I was hoping to get back to the squadron, sir."

"I don't doubt it, Roberts, but you are here, they are there, things are quiet, as quiet as they ever are at least. Stay here tonight, you can get off in the morning. A good days ride will get you there. Have a couple of days there, no point in ruining your horses, and then come back here."

"Yes, sir."

Mafra was busy, full of British troops, but Michael was pleased to find that they were allocated billets in the convent again, which was also where all the Sixteenth's absent men and horses were. He left Parra and Francisco to sort out their billets and with Lloyd went in search of men and horses. The senior man was Sergeant Peters, from Murray's troop. He seemed pleased to see Michael.

"Lieutenant Roberts, sir!" He called the room to attention and saluted.

Michael returned the salute. "Good evening, Peters." He looked around the dimly lit room. "How is everyone, all fit for duty?"

"Yes, sir, be glad to get back to the Regiment, sir. It's a nice enough billet, but it's all infantry here now, and they don't really understand horses, sir."

Michael laughed. "No, I don't suppose they do, they probably think we just sit on them and do no work." There was laughter from the men. "Right, tomorrow I want to inspect all the horses, and their saddles and furniture. Then I'll want to inspect every man and all the baggage. Horses in the morning, men in the afternoon, Sergeant. We are in no rush, so we will leave at dawn the day after. Every man and horse that's fit, that is. Where's the surgeon looking after you?"

"A little way through the convent, sir, I can show you now, if you like, sir?"

"No, tomorrow will do." Michael looked around again. "and you're sure everyone is fit, subject to the surgeon's agreement, of course?"

"Yes, sir, one or two are still a little stiff and sore, sir, but nothing much."

"And the horses?"

"I'm afraid we lost three, sir, so we've more men than horses, sir."

"Damn. Well, we shall see what we do about that tomorrow. Now, can you show me where the horses are, I want to have a quick look at the stabling."

By the second day, everything was ready for an early departure the next morning. Michael had contrived to get all fourteen men away despite there being only eleven horses. He would put Parra on Duke, and one of the men on Harry. Two men at a time would march on foot, and they would take two days over the return trip. It would be a little difficult for a few of the men with leg wounds and injuries, but the surgeon had passed them all as fit, and all the men wanted to get back to the Regiment.

With time on his hands, Michael went to the library, hoping to find Father Nascimento there. To his relief, he found the Father sitting at his usual desk in a window of the library. "Hello, Father."

"What? Why, Lieutenant Roberts, what a wonderful surprise! How are you, my son? Come. come, sit down."

Michael pulled up another chair and joined the priest. "I am afraid that I am leaving tomorrow, Father, it's a short visit to collect up some men and horses that we left here to recover."

"Then we must make the most of this chance, my son. So, tell me, how are you?"

Michael hesitated for a second, and saw the concern that immediately washed across the priest's face.

"My son, I told you once that I am here to listen to you, and advise you if I can. And while I cannot give a heretic like yourself absolution, I can still keep secret anything that you say." He fell silent and waited.

Michael stared out of the window; a shower of rain spattered against the glass. "I…, I don't know what to say, Father." He paused, staring at the floor between his feet, avoiding the Priest's eyes.

"Say what you like, say what you feel."

"Feel, Father? I feel confused, uncertain, lost even. I feel angry all the time, feel it bubbling away under the surface. And sometimes it explodes, and…, well, it's not something I like."

Nascimento sat silently for a moment, then asked, "So, what makes you angry, my son?"

"Being told what to do all the time!" Michael blurted out without thinking.

"But you are a soldier, doing what you are told is what soldiers do."

"No, no, that's not what I mean, that's not a problem. I enjoy soldiering. It's everything else!"

"Then tell me, Michael, tell me and it will help,"

Michael looked up at Nascimento. "Will it Father, will it really?"

"In my experience, yes." He smiled gently at Michael.

Michael hesitated. Could he tell this Priest everything? Or even almost everything? He realised he might never see him again, never pass this way again. Would it help? He looked at the Priest's open, patient face, saw nothing but kindness in his eyes. He made a decision.

"It seems a long time ago now, Father, but there was a woman I fell in love with." Slowly, hesitatingly, Michael told Nascimento about Elaine, about their love, about her letter, about his continuing love for her. He told him about Roberta's advice, Roberta's anger with him. Nascimento said nothing, let him talk, nodding encouragingly from time to time, staring off into the dark of the library as he listened. Michael told him about his new wealth, about Quintela's offer, which got a raised eyebrow from Nascimento, but nothing more. He told him about his uncle, and his grandfather's request. He told him how he was torn by his love for England and Portugal, about Catarina, about how it all tormented him, fuelled his anger. He confessed to his loss of control, his violence, his killing. He hung his head and sat silently.

By the time he had finished it the afternoon was almost fully run, and it was getting dark in the library, he could hardly make out Nascimento's face, it helped.

Nascimento rose, found a tinder box, and carefully lit a solitary candle. It gave him time to think. Michael sat, unmoving, head bowed. Nascimento returned to his seat, and spoke softly.

"Thank you, Michael. I can see how that required all your courage, and I see how great a burden you have brought upon yourself." Michael's head came up in surprise at that comment. "Oh, yes, my son. You see it is your decisions that have brought you to this sorry pass. It is the decisions that you have yet to make that will unburden you."

"I don't understand."

"Michael, my son, you have decided to let yourself be torn by apparent conflicting loyalties. That frustrates you, which in turn makes you angry. And when you are angry you take any opportunity to vent that anger, to lash out. For instance, your feeling of being torn between England and Portugal. Why do you feel torn at all? You can perfectly well love two countries equally and at the same time. Of course, a conflict between England and Portugal might make that difficult, but at the moment such a pass seems rather unlikely. Your duality gives you much to enjoy. Enjoy it." Michael nodded, thoughtfully. "As for your uncle, your grandfather sounds to me a like a wise and perceptive man. I think you should carefully consider what he suggests, if only out of regard for him.

"However, I think that the thing that is at the root of your difficulties, what is slowly eating away at you, is your love for Elaine. She sounds like a remarkable lady. I should like to have met her."

Michael smiled. "That's what my grandfather said."

"And what else did he say?"

"That I was lucky to have known such love, no matter how brief."

"Your grandfather, young man, is a very wise man, for a heretic priest." He gave a little chuckle, before going on, speaking softly, with gentleness. "There is no doubt that she loved you greatly, deeply, and that is what you need to think about, Michael. Not your love for her, forget that for a moment, and think of hers for you. She wrote to you in love, in genuine, loving concern for you." His voice suddenly hardened. "Never mind your self-pitying love for her, what you are doing is denying her love for you, denying her last wish for you, given to you in love." He paused, and Michael sat still, his head bowed, stunned by Nascimento's words.

Nascimento went on, his voice softening again. "I ask you, Michael, to consider what I say. Which is the bigger betrayal of Elaine? Loving again, or refusing to honour her last wish for you?"

Michael remained silent.

"I realise that you find it hard to accept what I say. So, consider this, I hope it will help. I acknowledge what you said about her letter not being enough, but that you don't see how you can have anything more." Nascimento paused, struggling to find the right words. "My son, Michael, God moves in mysterious ways, even for heretics. I can only say to you that you must open your eyes and your heart and watch for some sign that will confirm for you what, in your heart, you already know. Elaine has gone, and you are free man. That is the truth, and you must come to acknowledge it. Now, I cannot hear your confession, you wretched man," he smiled at Michael, and placed a hand on his knee, Michael looked at him, "but I shall pray for you."

"Thank you, Father." Michael's mind was in a whirl. He had never looked at his situation from Elaine's point of view. What Nascimento had said had shaken him. What he wasn't sure about was accepting it, whether or not he could accept it as the truth of the situation.

Nascimento changed the subject. "Now, tell me, what is it that brought you here?"

They chatted inconsequentially for a while. Michael gradually relaxed, although he barely listened to the

Priest's chatter, which Nascimento knew full well. Then a distant bell began to toll.

"Ah, Vespers! I must hurry, Michael." They both stood and Nascimento took the candle and started to walk through the library with Michael. "No doubt you will be leaving early tomorrow?"

"Yes, Father."

"No doubt at Matins. Then let us part now, and may the blessings of God go with you, my son."

"Thank you, Father."

Michael and his party arrived back at San João da Ribeira on Christmas Eve. It was cold, damp and windy, and everyone was glad to finally get men and horses under cover, dry out, and get some warm food. Archer was more than happy, and told Michael to spend Christmas Day at headquarters before riding on to rejoin the squadron. He was pleased to see that, despite a damp, two day march, Michael seemed a little lighter in his general disposition.

Michael was, indeed, a little lighter, less discontented with his lot. He had spent a lot of the slow trip back to the Regiment huddled up in his cloak and mulling over Nascimento's words. He could see some truth in what the Priest had said. His decision to stay with the Regiment and to forgo the offered transfer and its accompanying promotion had certainly lightened his mood. His return to the Regiment only reinforced that as he was warmly welcomed by his friends in the Brigade and Regiment posted there. What he wasn't at all sure about was Nascimento's suggestion that he look out for a sign from God. He did see that he was correct about seeing things only from his own position, and not considering what Elaine had wanted for him. That he would think about, but he acknowledged to himself that he would be keeping an eye open for some confirmation of Elaine's wishes.

Christmas Day began with Michael accompanying Colonel Archer, the Surgeon, Mister Robinson, and RSM Williams in looking over the men that had returned from Mafra. Satisfied that they were all fit enough for duty, Robinson was exchanged for Peers, the Veterinary Surgeon, and they adjourned to the stables. They examined the horses, with Lloyd watching from the background. Finally they were finished, and Archer turned to Michael.

"Excellent, Mister Roberts, you have done well. Now, there's two men from Ashworth's, I think, Sar'nt Major? Both with horses?"

"Yes, sir."

"Then they can go off with you tomorrow morning, Roberts. I'm sure Captain Ashworth will be pleased to have you all back." He pulled out his pocket watch and flipped open the cover. "We have a few hours before dinner, gentlemen. I'd be grateful if you all complete your duties before we enjoy the forthcoming feast." He smiled at everyone.

January passed in a continuous round of patrols and minor skirmishes. Cock's Squadron was sent north to Caldas in response to the arrival of French reinforcements at Leiria, and they were kept busy, countering French foraging parties, and frequently taking large numbers of prisoners, and Lieutenant Bishop making something of a name for himself as a bit of a firebrand. It was a little quieter at Anteporta as the position there was stronger, and more secure behind a river.

Michael took the opportunity of settled quarters to write to his grandfather. He told him about the diamonds, and asked him for his advice on what to do. He also told him about talking to Nascimento, and that he was prepared to consider his uncle's request, as and when he got back to Cornwall. Once more he found that a decision taken had lightened his mood, had removed a conflict.

The situation with the Regiment stationary in quarters had allowed the tailors to get on with their work, along with the tailors in the Regiment. By the end of the first week in January every man in the Regiment was properly fitted out in a new uniform. It cheered everyone up. Jorge and his colleagues were sent off back to Lisbon in company with a convoy of the Commissariat. Ashworth's Troop had been about the last to be completed, and Michael was able to say goodbye to his old friend, thanking him, and promising to meet him in Lisbon when he had the chance. He asked him to give his best wishes to all in Lisbon, and to make sure the Santiagos knew all was well.

Anteporta itself was a small village, and quarters were cramped, but all the men and horses were under cover. The village had been completely abandoned by its inhabitants, giving the dragoons free range for billets and stables. Francisco seemed most affected by the obvious impact of the fighting on the civilian population and he had become quieter, losing some of his cheerfulness. Lloyd spoke to Michael about it when they were out on a patrol. They had ridden well to the northeast, and seen no sign of French foragers. They were on their way home when Lloyd spoke.

"Begging your pardon, sir, but Francisco is out of sorts, sir."

Michael glanced across at him. "Yes. I've noticed that. I spoke to him back at Almoster. I tried to cheer him up." He grimaced. "It doesn't seem to have worked."

"No, sir, and I've had a chat with the lad as well, sir. To tell you the truth, sir, I think he's plain worn out by it all. It's been a lot for him, sir."

"So it has for all of us, Lloyd, and a lot of our dragoons are no older than him."

"No, sir, but they're not Portuguese, sir."

They rode on in silence for a while. "I can understand how that affects him, Lloyd, I don't like to see it either."

"No, sir."

"Do you think he needs a change of scenery?"

"It wouldn't hurt, I'm thinking, sir."

"Thank you, Lloyd. I shall consider it."

Lloyd was right, thought Michael. The young man had been through a lot, and seen a lot of suffering. Perhaps no more than others had, but he was young, intelligent, and obviously felt deeply about his experiences. He would talk to Roberta about it, as soon as he could.

That opportunity came at the end of January. Colonel Archer was visiting Anteporta, as he did regularly, and Michael was summoned to Ashworth's office. Ashworth looked a bit glum, and Archer got straight to the point.

"Mister Roberts, we have another job for you, which is why the Captain here looks so unhappy. He doesn't want to lose you again. However, we have been informed that there is a remount due to arrive in Belem for us. And the Lord knows, we need them. There are supposed to be two dozen, which is little enough between eight troops, we could do with twice that, however, I will take what we can get. You are to take one man from each troop, and Sar'nt Major Blood, and collect them. You will need to take a few days to get them fit after their voyage. With a bit of luck you should only be gone for two weeks, but it could be more, so best take Lloyd and your servants with you. The party will assemble at Sao Joao da Ribeiro tomorrow morning. There will billets at Belem, but I suppose you will stay at your house?"

"Yes, sir."

"Good, I'd like to see it myself some time. Mister Barra will have your papers ready for you tomorrow. Got that?"

"Yes, sir."

"Good." Archer paused for a moment. "Look, Roberts, I know you would rather be here with the Squadron, the Regiment, but the simple fact is that you are the best suited officer in the Regiment for this sort of thing, what with your Portuguese, and your contacts in Lisbon. To say nothing of Lloyd's skills with horses. With Blood with you as well you should have an easy time of it. Be back in no time, eh?"

Chapter 14

Senhor Venâncio's trip took ten days as expected. It was late when he got back to Lisbon, and he listened with interest to his wife's report about Catarina and Michael. "So, Lieutenant Roberts has designs on Catarina? Well, well. I wonder what she thinks of him?"

Senhora Venâncio smiled. "We can hope. And you have already made one or two subtly encouraging remarks to the Lieutenant, or so you told me."

"What? Oh, yes, I suppose I did. But I didn't expect anything to come of them. I spoke more in hope than expectation. I would have said the same to any eligible young man." He looked thoughtful. "It would be useful to have the girl taken off our hands."

The following morning Senhor Venâncio called on de Barcarena, and in the seclusion of his study, delivered a package he had received in Caldas from the French via a smuggler who acted as a courier. In return de Barcarena gave him a good supply of money, enough to support him and his household for a few weeks at least.

De Barcarena offered Venâncio coffee and while they were drinking he enquired about Senhora Venâncio's progress with cultivating Roberta.

"They are becoming good friends," replied Venâncio, "but we are far from sure that she will be of any use to us. My wife tells me she is not interested in politics, or the war, beyond wanting to know what has happened to Renard." De Barcarena grunted dismissively. "However," continued Venâncio, "it appears that her friend, Lieutenant Roberts, is interested in young Catarina."

"Now that is interesting." De Barcarena was suddenly energised. "You must encourage that, if you get the chance, and use it for you to get closer to the Lieutenant. Keep your ears open, who knows what you might discover." He gave a little, cynical chuckle. "And who knows, you might even get Catarina off your hands."

It was only three days later, late in the morning, that Michael and his party of dragoons arrived in Lisbon. They rode to Michael's home first, so that Blood and all the men would be able to find him if necessary. Michael smiled to himself as the men nudged each other at the sight of the stables and the back of the house. He could see that Bernardo had already made progress. Lloyd, Parra and Francisco set about unloading and caring for the horses and mules, while Michael took Blood in and introduced him to the Santiagos. Senhora Santiago was bustling around as she usually did when Michael suddenly appeared.

Leaving the organised chaos of the house behind, Michael rode on out to Belem with Blood and the rest. The remounts had not yet arrived, but he got the men settled into some decent billets, saw the horses were looked after, not that he needed to with Blood there. He told Blood he would return in the morning to see if there were any developments and finally got home with a couple of hours of daylight to spare.

Lloyd and Parra were sitting outside the stables with Bernardo when he rode in. Lloyd stood to attention and said "Everything is squared away nicely, sir. And Bernardo has been telling us that he's got on well in the garden, sir."

Michael dropped to the ground and handed his reins to Lloyd. "Then I had better have a look, come on, Bernardo, show me what you've done. And Lloyd?

"Yes, sir?"

"If all the unpacking is done, tell Francisco to cut along and see his sister, but I want him back tonight." He thought for a moment. "Tell him there's no message for Senhorita Roberta."

Lloyd's face was inscrutable as he replied, "Yes, sir."

Michael was surprised to find the garden looked bigger than he remembered, and said so to Bernardo.

"Ah, well, Senhor Miguel, that's because I have cut a lot back, opened up the paths and the view."

Michael turned to look at his friend. "Senhor Miguel?"

Bernardo shrugged. "We were friends when we were young, Bernardo and Miguel and Antonio and the others. Now I work for you, and I should call you what the Santiagos do, who have known you for even longer." He glanced sideways at Michael and grinned. "But perhaps Miguel when we have a drink together and you are not dressed up like that." He nodded at Michael's uniform with all its silver braid and buttons.

"That seems fair enough."

"Good, but there is something else I need to say. I am worried about the Santiagos. To be honest, I would have got more done in the garden, but I have been helping Senhor Santiago a lot with things around the house, maintenance that he hasn't been able to do. And the Senhora struggles at times, with anything a bit heavy."

They had reached the bottom of the garden and stood looking over the low drop down to the stables and paddock. "Thank you, Bernardo. I have been worried myself. I will see what I can do." After all, thought Michael, I can afford it.

Michael left Bernardo in the garden and walked back to the house. In the kitchen he asked Senhora for a cup of coffee, and waited while she made it, chatting inconsequentially about minor household matters. When it was ready he carried it upstairs to the sitting room himself. A fire was burning in the grate and Michael sat down close to it. From downstairs came the sound of voices, and then he heard light steps coming quickly up the stairs. He rose to his feet as Roberta came in.

"Hello, Michael, I hope you don't mind me showing myself up? I didn't like to put Senhor Santiago to the trouble." She stood, hesitantly just in the doorway.

"No, no, of course not, come in, sit down, would you like coffee? Senhora Santiago has just made some."

"Yes, please, if it's no trouble."

"I'll, err, I'll just go myself and fetch it."

A few minutes later he returned with a tray with coffee and all the accessories. In silence he served her, and then sat down, each of them on opposite sides of the fire. They sipped their coffee, both feeling unaccustomedly awkward with each other.

Michael spoke first. "How are you, Roberta?"

"Well, thank you. I still have Senhora Marcelino and her children with me."

Michael thought it would be a good idea to tell her about the diamonds. "Roberta," he began.

At the same moment Roberta spoke, "Michael."

They both stopped, then Michael said, "Go on, I insist."

"I am sorry to burst in on you uninvited and unannounced, but…"

"Roberta, you are welcome here whenever you like!"

"Am I, Michael?"

"Yes, of course you are. I do not wish to argue with you." He stared into the fire, avoiding her eyes. "I find I am a little," he struggled for the right words, "short tempered, feeling pulled every which way by everyone and everything." He tried to smile. "It's all very difficult. But you didn't come to see me to hear me complain? You were about to say?"

"It's the Venâncios," she began.

"Oh, God," Michael interrupted, his tone angry, "don't tell me they want you to matchmake between me and Catarina?"

"No, Michael, please, let me tell you."

As Michael listened and sipped his coffee Roberta told him everything that she learnt in the time that he had been away. Finally he asked, "And this fidalgo, who is he?"

"Baron Francisco de Barcarena."

"Damn it!" Michael swore. "Wait here a moment please." And he rushed from the room. He was back quickly and handed Roberta a piece of paper.

She scanned it quickly and gasped. "Our names and de Barcarena! Where did you get this, what is it?"

"It's a page from Renard's notebook. I took it when I killed him."

Roberta stared at him. "And the rest of it?"

"Destroyed. It was, err, appropriate at the time." Roberta raised her eyebrows quizzically at him. "It doesn't matter now, but he had drawings of the defences that are now holding off the French. If they had got to Massena…" He didn't finish the sentence. "I went through it, there was nothing else of interest."

"But this connects Renard to de Barcarena."

"Yes, it does, doesn't it. But it has our names as well. It could be argued de Barcarena's name is there as an enemy."

Silence fell as they both considered their shared information.

"And you say that de Silva can't do anything?" Michael asked.

"No, de Barcarena is far too well connected, to move against him would be dangerous."

Michael thought for a moment. "Then I suppose I had better go to someone who can do something." He looked at her. "I shall ride north tomorrow and tell Viscount Wellington."

At that moment Senhora Santiago appeared at the door. "Senhor Michael, I have put a little supper for you and the Senhorita in the dining room. I shall go and pour the wine." She disappeared.

Roberta said, "Oh, but I didn't mean to stay." Then she blushed at the double meaning in her words.

"Please, just a little supper, and I shall get Parra to see you safely home."

Some of the awkwardness that had passed as they had talked about the Venâncios and de Barcarena came back.

"Damn it, Roberta!" He paused and took a deep breath as Roberta looked shocked. "No, no, I am sorry, I didn't mean to snap at you." He looked into her eyes. "Please, are we still friends?"

"Yes, I do hope so, Michael." Roberta realised that she would have to tell Michael about da Rocha.

"Then, please," he gave a little wan smile, "Senhora Santiago will be disappointed if we don't do justice to her supper."

There were two places laid in the dining room, at the head of the table, and the seat to the right, where Roberta had sat before. There were plates of cold meats, cheeses and stored fruits. There was a bottle of very good wine. They were alone. Michael served Roberta before taking his own seat. They raised a glass to each other without speaking, and began to eat.

"How are things with you, Michael, really?"

"I am well, thank you." He saw the concern in her face. "Yes, I am." Inspiration struck and he sought to change the subject, to lighten the atmosphere. "But there is something you might be able help me with."

He told her about his concerns for the Santiagos, and taking on Bernardo to help. Roberta promised to ask around and see if she could find a suitable couple.

"There is one other thing that you should know, Michael, particularly if you might be taking an interest in the Venâncios."

"Oh?"

"Yes, and don't be cross, it's Catarina. She has asked after you several times. We have become quite good friends. I have also become a friend of Senhora Venâncio, but that is different. I genuinely like Catarina." Michael wondered for a moment if he should tell her what Father Nascimento had said about Elaine. Then Roberta went on, hesitantly.

"Michael, there is something else that I must tell you."

"Oh?"

"Yes, and it's about us, about our friendship."

Suddenly Michael knew exactly what Roberta was struggling to tell him, and found, to his surprise, that he was happy for her. He reached across the table and took her hand.

"It's da Rocha, isn't it?" He grinned, and Roberta blushed and nodded. "Roberta, I am happy for you. You have been a good friend, and, I hope, still will be." He stood up. "Come, let me hug you one last time."

Later that night, Roberta had departed, escorted by Parra, and Michael was in his room, a last glass of wine in his hand. He realised that he had still not told Roberta about the discovery of the diamonds. He had also meant to speak to her about Francisco, but both would keep for a while. He hadn't told her about Father Nascimento, and his view of Elaine's wishes. He knew Roberta would approve of what the priest had said. Would tell him it was what she had been trying to tell him. But he still wasn't sure. He looked at Elaine's picture on his bedside table, the lock of copper red hair shining in the candlelight.

"Elaine, I need to know, what you want. I need to know that your letter is what you want. Help me, please."

The following day dawned bright and still, with clear blue skies. Riding Duke, and accompanied by Lloyd on Rodrigo, he set out early for Belem. There he learnt that the horse transport had that morning crossed the bar and entered the Tagus. Unloading was expected to start when the tide was right in the middle of the afternoon. Michael sought out Blood.

"Sar'nt Major!"

Blood snapped to attention and they exchanged salutes. "Good morning, Mister Roberts."

"Morning, Blood. Have you heard the horses will be coming ashore this afternoon?"

"Yes, sir."

"Good, now, you may have to deal with it all without me. I have to go and find Viscount Wellington. It's err, something urgent that has come up in Lisbon."

"Ah, right you are, sir." Blood, along with the whole Regiment were aware that Michael was involved from time to time with what Stanhope had called Michael's special duties, frequently at the top of his voice and in the hearing of anyone who happened to be passing.

"Yes, well, I'll let you know what is happening, and you know where my house is if you need to track me down. But it's going to take me two days to get Wellington at Cartaxo and back."

"Yes, sir."

"Good, thank you, Blood."

Wellington's headquarters was in Cartaxo, some forty miles, and although Michael pushed the pace hard, the late start forced them to break the journey at Carregado. Starting off again just before first light, it was mid-morning when they found the headquarters. It was strangely quiet and deserted for the headquarters of the army. Michael was informed that Wellington was out, hunting, somewhere away to the west.

Frustrated, Michael set off with Lloyd, listening carefully for the sound of hounds in full cry. Within half an hour they were lucky. They met a rather sad looking infantry officer walking towards them, leading an obviously lame horse. He pointed them in the direction he had last seen the hunt.

Eventually Michael spotted the field, twenty or more horsemen spread around a small copse, and he could just make out the sound of hounds working through the small wood. He put a tired Duke into a canter, eager to catch Wellington before the hunt was off after another fox. He spotted him, sitting a little apart from the main field, keenly watching the working hounds. Lloyd hung back as Michael apprehensively approached.

A few yards away he spoke loudly, "My Lord?"

Wellington spun round to see who had dared to interrupt him. "What the devil do you mean, sir? Oh, Mister Roberts, isn't it?"

"Yes, sir."

"Well, I hope it's something damned important, we've hardly had any sport, but Crane is sure there's a fox in there." He grunted. "Can't say I'm so sure, but he's the huntsman. So, what is it, Mister Roberts?"

As succinctly as he could, Michael told Wellington about the communications with the French, and the suspected role of the Venâncios and, more importantly de Barcarena. He explained that de Silva felt unable to act against someone of such eminence.

Wellington sat on his horse, silently for a moment. He glanced towards the copse where his huntsman, Tom Crane, could be seen gathering up the hounds after an unsuccessful draw.

"Ha, see? I told you there was no damn fox in there." He stared at Michael, "But it seems we have some two-legged foxes in Lisbon, eh?"

"Yes, sir."

"And no Portuguese pack to run 'em down?"

"No, sir."

"Then you had better see to them, Mister Roberts. I know there has been communication with the French, and it's a damn nuisance. I want it stopped, d'ye understand?"

"Yes, sir."

"What are you doing in Lisbon?"

"Collecting remounts, sir."

"Got anyone who can do that for you?"

"Yes, sir."

"Good, tell him to do that, and you go and account for those foxes. I don't care how you do it, stop it for once and for all. D'ye understand me? Like you did the last one. And stay away from Mister Stuart, can't have the Ambassador involved in this, not diplomatic. Keep clear of de Silva as well, he's a good man, don't want to put him in a difficult position, or worse."

"Yes, sir."

"Good. I shall put things right with Colonel Archer. Come and tell me when you've done." He looked beyond Michael. "That your dragoon there?"

"Yes, sir."

"Damn fine looking animal he has. Very well, off you go Mister Roberts. I see Crane wants to try elsewhere."

On the way back to Lisbon, Michael spoke frankly to Lloyd. "Lloyd?"

"Sir."

"It seems I have another of those special jobs to do, and this one could be messy." He glanced across at Lloyd riding along next to him. "I would like you to stay with me. I don't know what you might do, I don't know how it might turn out. This isn't a French spy I'm after, it's some Portuguese. Important enough that General de Silva can't touch them."

Lloyd looked surprised. "Duw, sir, that's not good."

"No, Lloyd, it isn't." Michael paused to think, and decided that if he couldn't trust Lloyd then he couldn't trust anyone. "The thing is, Lloyd, there may well be killing, but not soldiering, if you take my meaning. I know I can do that, and I know you don't like that, but I won't ask you to do the same. If you would prefer you can go with Sar'nt Major Blood, I'm sure he would appreciate your help with the remounts."

They rode a long for a few moments in silence before Lloyd answered.

"The thing is, sir, if you remember the dockside in Oporto, sir, the thing is you offered me out then, and I made a choice, and we shook on it, sir. So I think I'll just come on along with you, sir." They rode on. "The thing is, sir, this is a nasty business, this war, here. Remember Sanchez's lancers when we took that French convoy near Ciudad Rodrigo? That was nasty, sir, but it's the only way, I'm thinking. It's that or let Buonaparte win, sir. And, begging your pardon, sir, you might need a covering file."

"Thank you, Emyr."

"Diolch, Mister Roberts, diolch yn fawr."

It was mid-evening and long since dark when Michael and Lloyd rode wearily in to the stables. He left Lloyd and Parra to deal with the two tired horses and walked up to the house. In the kitchen he found everyone else, and asked Senhora Santiago to prepare some supper for him, and Lloyd, and to have Francisco take it to the dining room for him, along with a bottle of something, but nothing too special, he was too tired.

As he ate and drank he considered what he was going to do. He would have to find out just how the Venâncios and de Barcarena were communicating with the French. How he asked himself, could he do that without the sort of manpower that de Silva had? He was going to need help, and more than just Lloyd. He was going to need at least some help from Roberta, but nothing that might put her, or de Silva into a difficult position. He wandered down to the kitchen and told Lloyd that he wanted them to ride out to Belem at first light, and told Francisco he wanted hot water to shave an hour before that. Beyond that he decided to sleep on it.

Michael found Troop Sergeant Major Blood looking over the two dozen horses that had been unloaded two days before. They were all mature horses that had spent from eighteen months to two years at the Regiment's depot. Apart from needing to recover from the voyage they were all good looking horses that only needed to acclimatise to the harsh conditions on campaign. Blood was not surprised when Michael informed him that he had been given orders by Viscount Wellington, and that he was going to have to deal with all the remounts and getting them back to the Regiment. He added that Wellington would be informing Colonel Archer of the change in plans.

Once back at home in Lisbon, Michael went to the study, his father's as he still thought of it, and wrote a note to Roberta, asking her to call later that afternoon. He sent Francisco off with it. He was going to need at least a little help from her. Then he changed into his civilian clothes and walked across Lisbon to see his lawyer, Senhor Furtado. It was a brief meeting. He told Furtado about the diamonds, about Quintela's offer, and his decision not to take it up. He then asked Furtado's advice on the best way to turn the diamonds into money in the bank. Furtado was blunt, take them to Rodrigues, he told Michael. After all, Quintela and his business was one of the biggest diamond traders, was undoubtedly trustworthy, and probably would have immediate access to the sort of money that would be involved. With regard to the Quinta, Michael had brought the deeds with him, and handed them to Furtado. The lawyer was somewhat taken aback.

"I knew nothing about this. But I do seem to recall your father saying something once about thinking of retiring to the country, or at least having somewhere out of Lisbon to go for peace and quiet. Although Mealhada seems a long way for that. It must be four days journey away." He took his glasses off, and absently polished them. "I will see what I can discover, but with the current situation, and the French." He shrugged helplessly.

"I understand only too well, Senhor. But do what you can, please?" And with that Michael was on his way.

Half an hour later, Rodrigues was rising from behind his desk to welcome Michael. "Michael, come in, sit down, would you like coffee? It's a pleasure to see you."

"Thank you, Senhor, but no coffee, thank you." Rodrigues waved away the porter who had brought Michael to his office, and the two were alone. Michael went on. "I have things to tell you, and something to ask of you."

"Go on, Michael, I am intrigued."

"First of all, I have recovered the missing diamonds."

"What? How? You have found Augusto? Who is he?"

Michael could not help but smile at Rodrigues' astonishment. "Not who, Senhor, but what." Michael briefly explained his discovery.

"That," said Rodrigues, "is quite remarkable. I shall have to tell the Baron. But can I also give him an answer to his offer?" He leaned forward, eagerly.

"You can Senhor, but I am afraid the answer is no."

"Oh, surely not, Michael, think of what you are giving up!"

"And that is exactly it, it is what I would be giving up if I accepted the offer, the army, my Regiment, my friends, my fight against Buonaparte. I hope you understand, and I hope the Baron will."

Rodrigues shrugged. "I cannot deny that I am disappointed. But let me guess at what you are going to ask? You want to sell the diamonds to us?"

Michael smiled and gave a simple "Yes."

"Please tell me that you do not have them with you?"

Michael laughed. "No, Senhor, they are safely secured."

"Very well." He smiled. "Give me three days, if you can?" Michael nodded. "Then come and see me, bring the diamonds, and, please, be careful. Do you have a bank in Lisbon?"

"Yes, Senhor Furtado has made arrangements."

"Excellent. Once we are agreed on a price, would you like me to finalise matters with him?"

"Of course, Senhor Rodrigues. That would be a great help. I am very busy, and may have to go away at any moment."

With all his business in the city finished, Michael went home to wait for Roberta. Out in the garden Bernardo was hard at work. Michael strolled down to see him.

"Bernardo! How is it all coming along?"

"Quite well, Senhor Miguel. I think you will be very pleased in the spring."

"Good. Now, there is something I would like you to do for me. Do you think you could find Antonio, and Carlos if he is around, and bring them to the stables tomorrow? Say at about ten o'clock?"

"Of course, Antonio will probably know if Carlos is around. I'll go now, if that is alright?"

"Yes, off you go, but not a word to anyone else, Bernardo."

Back in the house, Michael asked Senhora Santiago for coffee for two. "I am expecting Senhorita Roberta, and she seems to have an unfailing ability to turn up just as coffee is made. Francisco can bring it up."

To Michael's amusement, Francisco appeared with the coffee and Roberta, who had just arrived. He laughed, "Roberta, well timed as usual, the coffee is fresh!"

She gave him a smile, and for a moment the old magic between them was there again.

"So, Michael," she said once she was settled with her coffee, "what is this about? As if I can't guess, and you know I can't do anything."

"There is one thing, Roberta."

"What?"

"I need to be back in touch with Catarina. I need to get close to the Venâncios and she can help me do that."

"I don't like that idea at all, Michael."

"What? I thought you would approve?"

"I might, if I thought it was because of her, and not because you just want to use her, as a means to an end."

"But this is important, Roberta, you know it is. I wouldn't want to get involved with Catarina if it wasn't. You know my situation."

"Yes, I do, and you know my view on that. Oh, Michael, you could so easily hurt her, and she deserves better than that."

"What if I promise not to do that?"

"Promise, Michael? Another promise to a woman?"

Michael fell silent and cursed himself for saying that. They both knew that no good had come of previous promises.

"Very well, Michael. I do know how important this is. I am meeting Catarina tomorrow at twelve o'clock, in that little coffee house in the Praca do Carno. I suggest you happen by a little later. Give us a chance to get settled. Then it will all be up to you; I can do no more. But I will make a promise, Michael. I will promise you that if you hurt her that will be an end to our friendship!"

Chapter 15

At ten o'clock the following morning, Michael walked down to the stables with Lloyd. He had decided not to involve Francisco. He was concerned about the young man, and felt he would be better employed staying at home and helping the Santiagos. The weather was cold and damp, but inside it was dry and a little warmer. Waiting for him were Parra, Antonio, Bernardo, and, to his delight, the stocky figure of Carlos.

"Carlos!" Michael exclaimed. "It is good to see you, my friend." They shook hands warmly.

"Ah, Miguel, when Antonio and Bernardo found me, it sounded as if it might be like the old days, when we were really young." He laughed. "And I am currently without work." He smiled a broad smile. "The captain of my mule train did not like the way I got on with his wife. So, what is it that you want of me, and these two rogues?" He waved at Antonio and Bernardo.

" I have a great favour to ask of you all."

Much as he had done with Wellington, Michael explained the situation to everyone. There were frowns, and surprise at the mention of de Barcarena. "What I need to do is find out just how the communications are exchanged with the French. Then I have orders to stop it happening. This man, Venâncio, will need to be watched, and then we will have to follow him. Antonio, Carlos, I think you will be able to best help with following him if he leaves Lisbon, apparently he makes regular trips up to Caldas."

At the mention of Caldas, Antonio spoke out. "From Caldas it is easy enough to get across the mountains and come down near Torres Novas. It can be done in a day with a good horse or mule. If you know the way."

"Does that you mean you will help me?"

Antonio waved a dismissive hand. "Of course," he grinned at Michael, "if you feed me."

"That sounds fair to me," Carlos put in, "and perhaps you can help me find a new job afterwards?"

"I am in this as well," added Bernardo, "but I am paid by you already."

"That's true," said Michael, "I think would only be fair if you all get paid the same. Parra, you don't have to join us, I would be happy for you stay with Francisco and the Santiagos."

"Senhor, please, I cannot stay out of this, not if my friend Emyr is in it."

Lloyd chuckled, he had managed to follow the conversation, and now spoke, his Portuguese adequate, if his accent was a bit strange. "Jose, certainly I am in this, and gladly so."

"Then that is settled." Michael was relieved. He felt that with this help he might be able to do what Wellington had ordered. They quickly arranged that Antonio and Carlos would move in to the stables with Parra, so that everyone was immediately at hand. Michael left Lloyd to see to everything and set off to the Praca do Carno.

Michael was wearing his civilian clothes, and took post in plenty of time, just inside the entrance to a church, which gave him a clear view across the small square to the coffee shop. He had just checked his watch, when he saw Roberta cross the square form the direction of her home and enter the shop. Five minutes later he stepped further back into the dark entrance as he saw Catarina approaching. He decided to give them ten minutes before going in. He realised that he now had ten minutes to work out how to explain what he was doing there. As he stood there, feeling the damp air getting into his bones, he finally had an idea.

He crossed the square, pushed open the door, and walked in. He saw Roberta first, sitting at a table to the side of the room, facing the door. She looked up as he came in and smiled at him. "Why, Michael, what are you doing here?"

As he walked across to her he saw Catarina, sitting opposite Roberta, spin quickly round to look at him. "Looking for you, Senhorita. Ah, Senhorita Cardoso, how pleasant to see you."

Roberta waved to the waiter, "Another coffee, please," then turned back to Michael, "now, Michael, sit down and tell me why you are looking for me?"

Michael saw a glint in Roberta's eye and guessed that she was quietly enjoying putting him on the spot. "I am in Lisbon for a few days on Regimental business. Something has come up at home that I thought you might be able to help me with. I went to your house, and Francesca told me that you would be here." He smiled broadly at her, and sat down as the waiter brought another coffee.

"And what is it that I might be able to help you with?" Roberta asked him.

Briefly he told her about the Santiagos. "So, I was simply hoping that you might be able to help me find some more servants, I think a couple would be best. Younger, reliable."

"I shall give it some thought." Roberta told him.

"Thank you. Oh! There is one other thing, if you have time?" Roberta nodded. "I am getting worried about Francisco." He told her of his concerns, and she said she would speak to Constanca about it, see if he had said anything to her, and think about what might be done.

Michael thanked her, and then turned to Catarina. "I must apologise for monopolising your companion, Senhorita. Tell me, how are things with you? Well, I hope?" Michael thought he detected a slight flush at Catarina's neck, but the conversation became general and inconsequential.

Eventually, Roberta declared that she really must leave them, but that she would be in touch with Michael as soon as she had anything for him. She rose from the table, Michael standing too. She spoke to Catarina, "No need to leave with me, my dear, I am sure Mister Roberts will keep you company for a little while." With that she gave Michael a thin lipped smile, and swept out.

With Roberta gone, Michael sat down and asked, "Would you care for another coffee?" Catarina nodded, shyly.

The next hour passed pleasantly, as Michael made conversation with Catarina, and tried to draw her out a little. She was most relaxed and animated when the conversation turned to horses. Finally, she declared that she had to go, but that she had enjoyed talking. "

"Then we must do it again." Michael stated categorically. "Perhaps tomorrow? Here at the same time? I have nothing on hand tomorrow."

"I should like that very much." Catarina smiled, her eyes sparkling, and rising to leave at the same time.

The following day they met again, and continued their conversation where they had left off the previous day, talking about horses. Then, shyly, quietly, Catarina spoke. "Senhor Roberts, I have been invited to a small soiree, tomorrow evening. My sister-in-law and her husband will be there. However, the hostess has kindly said that she would be delighted if you too could attend."

Michael was, frankly, taken aback. It was what he had hoped to achieve, but had not expected this sort of success so quickly. He decided that perhaps Roberta was correct, and the girl did hold a candle for him. He would have to be careful if he wasn't to lose Roberta's friendship, he had no doubt that her promise would be kept.

The next morning Michael called Parra and Lloyd into the study. "I am taking the diamonds to Quintela's this morning, and I want you two along with me, just in case. Lloyd, you and I will be in uniform, with our sabres, Parra, can you wear a cloak and carry something?"

"Of course, Senhor."

"Then we will leave in half an hour."

From Michael's house to the Palacio Quintela was less than a brisk five minute stroll, and Michael was soon seated in Rodrigues' office, Lloyd and Parra outside with a porter.

"I had not thought to see these again, Michael." Rodrigues stared at the five little piles of uncut diamonds on his desk. With a pair of tweezers and an eye glass he carefully looked through them all. Then he consulted some papers he had to hand on his desk. He sat looking thoughtful for a moment. Michael was on tenterhooks.

"Very well. As you can imagine, trade with the Brazils has been affected by the war, and the French occupation was a blow to trade. Consequently, the supply of diamonds has not been what it was. Although with the French in the Netherlands, the demand from Amsterdam has dropped to nothing. Still, I have to be honest with you Michael," Michael's heart sank, here it comes, he thought, the value has halved or something, "the price of diamonds has gone up quite a bit. After all, in these difficult times they are an easily transportable form of wealth." He paused again to scratch some figures on a piece of paper. "In sterling, I can offer you twenty eight and half thousand pounds. I can make arrangements with Furtado and the bank for that to be credited to you in London. Is that acceptable?"

"Acceptable? My dear Rodrigues, it is quite splendid!"

Rodrigues laughed. "Ha, perhaps I should have offered less? But, no, I could not do that to the son of Edward

Roberts." He took a blank sheet of paper and started writing. "I shall give you a receipt for the diamonds, if you let Furtado have it, he and I will see to everything." He signed the paper with a flourish, and asked "Are you sure that you do not want to go into business with the Baron? Forgive me, I have to ask."

"That's quite alright, Senhor, but I am quite sure, thank you."

Still accompanied by Lloyd and Parra, Michael walked to Furtado's. The lawyer congratulated him on his wealth, and assured Michael he would take care of everything with Rodrigues, and also undertook to let Mister Rutherford know. Michael would have to decide what he wanted to do with the money.

Michael walked home with his mind in a whirl. It hadn't seemed real until now, but he to accept that he had gone from being financially comfortable, to being rather wealthy. He realised that he still had not said anything to Roberta about the diamonds. He thought he would wait to see how things were with her before telling her.

Michael was not entirely surprised to see Roberta at the soiree, with da Rocha. They seemed to be moving in the same social circle as the Venâncios. No doubt, he thought, with that quietly managed by Roberta. He felt it best to stay away from them. The soiree did bring a genuine surprise. There was a little dancing, and Michael danced with both Catarina and Senhora Venâncio. Then, in a quiet moment, he found himself standing with Senhor Venâncio watching both ladies dancing with other gentlemen. Venâncio addressed himself to Michael.

"Senhor Roberts, Catarina tells me that she has been enjoying a little of your company recently."

Michael feared the worst. "That is so, Senhor. First I met her by chance when she was having coffee with Senhorita Roberta de Silva. And then, just once, we had coffee together. I can assure that it was in a perfectly respectable establishment, Senhor."

"I am sure it was, and I mean no criticism. Catarina has clearly enjoyed your conversation, particularly about your horses. I remember that we saw them when we visited your delightful house." He took a sip of his wine. "I know, Senhor, that she misses her horses and riding. Perhaps you might invite her to ride with you? Senhora Venâncio and I would have no objection. I am sure that you are a man of honour and perhaps your man could also go with you? Simply for propriety. I do hope that I have not shocked you Senhor, but I study the modern liberal arts, I have little truck with old fashioned punctilios."

Michael gave him a brief bow of his head in acknowledgment of his statement. "Then, Senhor, with your permission, I should be honoured to take the Senhorita riding." The dance came to an end. "If you will excuse me, I shall speak to her now." The two men parted, both equally pleased with the conversation and its outcome.

Michael approached Catarina where she was taking a little refreshment. "Senhorita Cardoso, I wonder, if you would care to go riding with me one day?" Her eyes opened wide in shock. "I can tell you that Senhor Venâncio does not only approve, but it was he who suggested it." Catarina's eyes widened further, and a slight flush appeared at her neck.

"Why, yes, that would be wonderful." She regained some composure. "Thank you, Senhor, I am most grateful. Perhaps the day after tomorrow? I would need to make some, err, arrangements." She hesitated again. "I think I must speak with my sister-in-law, err, there are things… Excuse me please?" And she almost fled across the room.

Michael was suddenly aware that Roberta was at his elbow. "Michael," her voice was stern, "what did you say to her?"

"It's alright, Roberta. Senhor Venâncio simply suggested I invite Senhorita Catarina to go riding with me. She seemed rather surprised. But I think she agreed."

"Oh!" Roberta tapped Michael with her fan. "Be careful, Michael, that is rather a surprise and it might just be that Venâncio is playing his own game with you for some reason."

"Ah, that had not occurred to me."

"Then think about it now, and be careful, Michael. Now, while I have your attention, I have an invitation for you, you will receive a proper one shortly, but Senhor da Rocha, Alexandre," she smiled, "is holding a ball, and you are invited. As are the Venâncios, Senhorita Cardoso and half of Lisbon society, so far as I can tell. He has asked me to act as his hostess for the evening." She blushed and covered her face with her fan. "I shall expect you to attend, Michael, please."

"Of course, Roberta, you may count on it."

Parra spent a busy day, he started at Juan Moreno's stables where he managed to borrow a side-saddle that would fit Harry. Then he was hard at work washing and grooming the horses so they were fit for royalty. Michael had decided that he and Catarina would be accompanied by him and Lloyd. Lloyd was busy ensuring that Michael's accoutrements were in the very best condition, his own as well. Full dress uniforms was what Michael had ordered. And Michael's uniform was undergoing a clean by Francisco. Senhora Santiago was busy with Parra's best clothes.

To Michael's great relief the day of the ride was still, clear blue skies and a sharp feel to the air. It was perfect for riding. Michael rode Johnny, Lloyd was on Rodrigo, and Parra on Duke, leading Harry as they rode up to where the Venâncios were staying. As they approached the door of the house opened, and there stood Catarina, in a stunning riding habit of deep green velvet, trimmed with black, and a very fetching, and matching, hat with a veil. Michael was impressed.

He was even more impressed at the ease with which she managed Harry. He was not a particularly challenging ride, but it quickly became apparent that Catarina was an excellent horsewoman. They rode to the north west, out of Lisbon and into the rolling countryside.

They were out for some four hours before Michael returned her home, tired, but happy. They were also now Michael and Catarina to each other. Michael jumped down from Johnny, and helped Catarina down from Harry. As he did so the door opened and the Venâncios were there, their footman behind, holding the door. Michael saw Catarina's face as she saw them, saw some of the light go out of it.

At the door Catarina turned to Michael. "Thank you, Senhor," she had become formal in the presence of the Venâncios, "for a most enjoyable day." She smiled briefly and slipped in through the door.

"Senhor Roberts, thank you for your kindness to Catarina." It was Senhor Venâncio who spoke. "I believe that we shall see you at da Rocha's ball? We shall look forward to it."

Da Rocha's ball was two days later, two long days during which Michael could do nothing to further his investigations of the Venâncios. He was beginning to feel the strain, it was making him snappy although he did his best to stay positive. He thought a lot about his circumstances, too much at times, he felt. He needed something to happen to release the tension.

The ball was held in a fashionable hotel in the new part of Lisbon, rebuilt after the earthquake of '55. It was a glorious occasion as befitted the host and hostess and the modern hotel. Michael had to admit to himself that Catarina, while perhaps not classically beautiful, cut a very fine figure indeed in a new ball gown. He danced twice with her before supper, once with Senhora Lourenco who was there, and even once with Senhora Venâncio. Roberta was almost completely monopolised by da Rocha. Michael contrived to dance with Catarina for the last dance before supper, and his reward to take her in to the dining room. Supper was a loud and boisterous affair with little chance for any quiet conversation. He did notice that General de Silva and his wife were present, perhaps hardly surprising with Roberta the hostess.

After supper Catarina was stolen away by one of the young Portuguese gentleman who seemed in abundant supply. As he watched her, he heard a quiet voice next to him. "Senhor Roberts," it was da Rocha, "I wonder if I might have a word with you?"

"Of course, Senhor," Michael replied and followed da Rocha out of the ballroom and into a quiet side room. As they went Michael saw Roberta, caught her eye, saw her fan cover her face and her eyes drop. Once in the room, da Rocha closed the door and they were alone.

Da Rocha looked uncomfortable. "Senhor Roberts, I find that I must speak to you on a very delicate matter." Michael kept quiet. "It is a simple matter, but one best dealt with promptly." He took a deep breath. "I know that you and Roberta are friends of a very long standing. She has made it clear to me that you are her dearest friend. She has also made it clear that she hopes that you and I may also become good friends, because it is our intention to marry." He paused to gauge Michael's response. Michael was speechless. Da Rocha went on. "I am also aware that you and Roberta have been more than just friends. She has explained to me the nature of your friendship."

"Senhor," Michael began but got no further.

"Please, Senhor, this is difficult, please hear me out." Michael subsided with a nod. "She tells me that she loves you, and you her, as friends sometimes can. She does not want marriage to me to come between you." Da Rocha took another deep breath. "Senhor, Roberta tells me, and I believe her, that you can surrender your position as a lover, and yet remain a loving friend. That being the case, Senhor, I wish to offer you my hand and my most sincere friendship." He held out his hand to Michael.

"Senhor," Michael walked to da Rocha and took his proffered hand in his, "my friendship with Roberta, in all its aspects, is a thing most precious. We both knew something like this could, indeed would, happen. We have always understood that neither of us would stand in the way of the other. Senhor, I am proud to be your friend."

The two men stood for a moment, eye to eye, hands clasped, and both saw only sincerity. Side by side they walked back to the ballroom. Roberta waited just inside. They both smiled at her, and were rewarded with a smile that lit up her face. She knew that all would be well.

Towards the end of the evening, Michael was again approached, this time by Senhor Venâncio. "Senhor Roberts, I wonder, would you care to dine with us tomorrow?"

Michael dragged his gaze away from where Roberta was dancing with da Rocha, her happiness plain to see. "Of course, Senhor, thank you, it will be a pleasure."

"Excellent, shall we say five o'clock?"

Michael had much to think about that night. He had always known that love for someone else could come between him and Roberta. He had never thought that it would be

Roberta who found that love. He chided himself for his egocentricity, it reminded him of what Nascimento had said about Elaine's wishes, and his selfishness. It would take him a little time to reconcile himself to the loss of his lover, but at least he had kept a friend, a very good friend, and it seemed, gained another. Da Rocha's behaviour had impressed him, he doubted if there were many men who could have behaved as he did, but then he doubted if there were many men who could win Roberta's love as a wife.

As for Venâncios invitation, that seemed to him to offer opportunities, but quite how to take advantage eluded him. He knew he needed to prompt Venâncio to action so that he could see how he communicated with the French, see how de Barcarena was involved, but how to do that was the question. Eventually he fell asleep.

Somehow, by the morning, he knew what to do. First, he went down to the stables, where he found Lloyd, Parra, Bernardo, Antonio and Carlos. He told them that he would be dining with the Venâncios that evening, and he wanted to know if Venâncio went anywhere afterwards. It would be necessary to keep a watch, possibly for several days. He wanted to keep Lloyd on hand, and they agreed that the other four would stand watch and watch about in pairs, eight hours at a time. Hopefully it wouldn't be for long. Next, Michael shut himself away in the study and started to compose a letter to his grandfather, one that he had no intention of ever sending.

Michael arrived at the Venâncios' promptly at five o'clock. Parra and Antonio would be taking up their watch an hour later. Inside he was warmly welcomed by the Venâncios, and Catarina looked pleased, but greeted him a little shyly. Dinner was a small, intimate affair, the food was good and Michael learnt that they had a cook, a footman and a maid who was shared by the senhora and Catarina.

"It is a small establishment," explained Senhor Venâncio, "in Coimbra there were more, and hopefully there will be again, but this accommodation is too small for more."

The conversation flowed fairly easily, as did the wine, which was very good and that suited Michael. He drank a lot of it, and his speech became a little slurred, which would have surprised his fellow subalterns, who all had pretty hard heads when it came to wine. Eventually the table cleared and Senhora Venâncio and Catarina retired to refresh themselves, leaving Michael alone with Venâncio and a bottle of port.

Venâncio poured Michael a generous measure, and said "If I may ask Senhor, how is the war going? We get little reliable news, and are still afraid of the French taking Lisbon."

It was the opening Michael had been waiting for. "You need be afraid, Senhor. I have seen what Wellington has done to my beloved Portugal!"

"Wellington?" Venâncio was surprised.

"Yes, Wellington. He ordered the countryside stripped as he retreated before the French. And what for? Nothing, Senhor, I tell you, nothing." He leant forward conspiratorially. "Let me tell you," he slurred, "I have seen the fortifications out at São Julião da Barra. It is an embarkation point so that we can slink away with our tails between our legs when the time comes."

"And will that time come?"

"Oh, yes. If Massena attacks. And he doesn't even have to do that. You know our King is ill, mad?" Venâncio nodded. "Well, there's going to be a Regency, very soon, perhaps even as we speak, and everyone knows that when the Prince of Wales becomes Regent there will be a change of government. He will bring in the Whigs, and they are against the war. There will be a peace made with

Napoleon." He paused to take a sip of wine; he left that statement hanging in the air for a moment. "Then, perhaps, I can come home to Portugal, live here again, perhaps marry a Portuguese girl." He saw Venâncio's eyebrows rise in surprise. "Perhaps someone I already know. But I tell you this, Senhor, I know what I am speaking about. I am on Sir Stapleton Cotton's staff, often close to Wellington. I know what I hear." He took another, very small drink, and watched Venâncio thinking.

"That is very interesting Senhor, but perhaps we should join the ladies for coffee?"

More small talk followed, until Senhora Venâncio yawned, pointedly, albeit behind her fan, and Michael announced that he should be going. As he rose from his chair he casually asked, "Senhor, I have enjoyed our conversation, perhaps we might meet for coffee soon, and talk some more? I am usually in that rather nice coffee house in Praca do Carno about noon." He hoped Catarina was taking note, he thought that out of the corner of his eye he saw her give an almost imperceptible nod.

"That is an excellent proposal, Senhor, I shall certainly do my best to drop by there soon."

"Of course, Senhor. Senhora Venâncio, Senhorita Cardoso, my sincere thanks for a delightful evening, and I hope that soon I may return the favour and invite you to dine with me?"

With a slight bow, he followed Venâncio out into the hall. There, as he threw a cloak over his shoulders, pulled on his gloves, and took up his hat and cane, he managed to surreptitiously drop the unfinished letter to his grandfather. The letter that, in addition to some inconsequential chatter, repeated his opinion about the withdrawal from Portugal being inevitable and only a matter of time.

A little way down the street he paused at a dark entry. Antonio, Para and Lloyd were there. "Good evening, sir, are you alright?" Lloyd had noticed a slight sway as Michael had come down the street.

"Yes, thank you, Lloyd, been a lot worse. I think that all went off very well. We shall soon see if we can flush out the quarry. Antonio, Parra, are you both set for the night?" They nodded. "Excellent, then, Lloyd, home and some of Senhora Santiago's strongest coffee is in order."

Michael and Lloyd walked side by side through the dark and quiet streets. Lloyd spoke. "I know this has to be done, sir, and I don't like traitors at all, sir, but it's a dirty business we are about, sir."

"It is, Lloyd, indeed it is. But let us do our best to do it cleanly, eh?"

"Yes, sir."

Chapter 16

Senhor Venâncio left home shortly after daybreak, and set off walking briskly along the street in the early morning chill. He failed to notice the two men who followed him at a discreet distance. Twenty minutes later he arrived at de Barcarena's fine house, knocked on the door and was immediately admitted. De Barcarena was surprised at the early call, and received Venâncio still in his nightshirt and banyan.

"This had better be important, Venâncio."

"Oh, but it is, Baron. Lieutenant Roberts came to dinner last night. As you suggested, we are using Catarina to get close to him. He drank a little too much wine, and he was rather indiscreet. Then as he was leaving he dropped this. It is a letter, to his grandfather, I think. It repeats what he said at dinner."

De Barcarena read the letter, twice, his surprise showing clearly on his face. "Venâncio, this is important. It must go to Massena at once. Can you leave tomorrow morning?"

"Of course, Baron."

"Then call back here this afternoon, and I will give you a package to take. There will, of course, be the usual remuneration."

"Please, Baron, that is not why I do this!"

"Perhaps not, but we need to keep you in a certain style, do we not?"

Antonio and Parra were watching from an alleyway opposite. They followed Venâncio back to his home, and then Parra was on his way to inform Michael, leaving Antonio to watch.

Michael was pleased by the reports of Venâncio's early morning visit. He hoped it meant that the bait had been taken. Michael set off in good time to be at the coffee house before noon. He had not been settled for long, when the door opened and Catarina came in. He stood and waved at her. Catarina smiled at the sight of him and came across to join him.

"Catarina, this is a pleasant surprise."

"Oh, really? That wasn't a hint last night when you mentioned this little place?"

Michael shrugged and smiled. "Perhaps."

"Then, we are to be conspirators, Michael. That is rather exciting."

Michael chuckled "Indeed we are, Catarina" he said, and thought "how little you know young woman".

They talked about the dinner the night before, Michael working towards the subject he wanted to discuss. "How are Senhor and Senhora Venâncio this morning? It was a good dinner last night."

"The Senhora was still in bed when I left, but Senor Venâncio was up and out very early. And when he returned he promptly announced that he has to go away on a short trip! He is leaving first thing tomorrow."

"Oh? Did he say where he was going?"

Catarina put her cup down. "Caldas, I think. I don't for the life of me know why, or what business he has there, he doesn't talk to me about that sort of thing, tells me not to bother my pretty little head about it. The man is unbearable at times." She blushed. "But I shouldn't talk like that, please, forgive me."

"There is nothing to forgive, Catarina."

"Then, I wonder, do you think we might go riding again?"

"Certainly, but not soon, I am afraid." Catarina looked disappointed. "I have to be out of Lisbon for a while on army business. I simply do not know when I will be back.

Perhaps a week, perhaps longer, months even. It is the lot of the soldier." He had what he wanted, and as much as he liked Catarina he did not wish to become involved with her, at least not romantically. He could now gently drop her, and keep Roberta happy. He managed to keep the conversation going a little longer, and then made his excuses. "I am sorry, Catarina, I would like to sit here talking with you, but I am afraid that duty calls. I do have to go."

Catarina gave a little pout. "Will you come to see me when you return?"

"Yes, of course."

The reports from Parra and Antonio and the information from Catarina were just what Michael had hoped for. He gathered everyone together again in the stables. "From what we know it looks as if Venâncio will be leaving tomorrow. We must be ready to follow him, that means myself, Lloyd and Antonio being near Venâncio's house with our horses well before dawn. He will have to get a mount from somewhere, so we will have to be careful how we follow him. Bernardo, I want you to stay here, I have to think about the Santiagos, they need your help. Carlos, I think you had better be with us in the morning, until we are on our way. Then come back here, stay here for the moment, please?"

Carlos nodded, but added, "Typical, Antonio gets all the fun."

"Perhaps you can learn something about horses from Parra," Michael teased.

Long before daybreak Michael was waiting with Lloyd and Antonio in a little square near the Venâncios' house. They were in old, Portuguese clothes, and holding the reins of Johnny, Duke and Rodrigo, who were in civilian tack, old leather valises behind the saddles. It was cold and damp, and periodically they walked up and down with the horses in a futile attempt to get warm. A hint of grey was just beginning to appear in the eastern sky when Parra appeared.

"Senhor, Venâncio has left the house, walking north, Carlos is following him."

"Good, let's get after him."

They hurried to follow Carlos, keeping out of sight of Venâncio, Parra just ahead of them. Suddenly Parra waved at them to stop, and a few minutes later Carlos appeared. They gathered together near a corner. Carlos gestured. "There is a stable just a little way up there, I walked quietly past and took a look in. Venâncio is hiring a mule."

"Very well, we will wait here, you and Parra watch to see where he goes, but if he takes the Caldas road we should have no difficulty following him."

Venâncio did ride off on the direction of Caldas, and the three men mounted, said goodbye to Carlos and Parra, and followed at a discreet distance. They took it in turns to follow him, the other two hanging back, out of sight of Venâncio, but keeping their leader in view. Every half hour they changed over, just in case Venâncio looked back and saw the same riders behind him all the time.

After one turn, Lloyd dropped back to join Michael. " Duw, sir, I reckon we could follow him with a full squadron right behind him, and he'd never notice."

Michael laughed. "Yes, I think we could, but I don't want to take any chances."

They passed through the defensive lines, now not needed, at Sobral, and rode along past the spot where Michael had killed Renard. Unsurprisingly there was nothing to indicate that anything had happened there. Michael rode on without comment.

Late in the afternoon, with the grey day darkening even further, Venâncio rode into a small village and stopped at the only inn. The village looked to be still mostly abandoned, but there were signs that the inhabitants had returned after the departure of the French and were gradually rebuilding their lives and their homes, the inn amongst them. The three men carefully rode around the village and went a mile or so beyond before they stopped at an abandoned barn, a little off the road.

"No fire tonight. We are getting close to the front of the army, and a danger of running into French foragers and marauders. We will take it in turns to keep a watch, and be ready to leave before dawn. We will also have to be careful of our own dragoons. I know that Captain Cocks is in Caldas with his Squadron. We don't want any unfortunate incidents."

They passed a cold night, but the barn protected men and horses from the occasional shower, and kept the wind off. They had all passed less comfortable nights.

A little after it got light they watched an unsuspecting Venâncio ride pass on his mule a mere hundred yards away. Five minutes later Antonio followed him, and then Michael and Lloyd. Ten miles or so short of Caldas they reached the small village of Columbeira. Michael was in front, but waved the other two up to join him.

"Antonio, you follow him in. We will take a chance on what he is doing and Lloyd and I will ride around the village and wait on the Caldas road on the other side." Antonio nodded, pushing Duke on towards the village while Michael and Lloyd swung to the east to get to the Caldas road. They had barely taken up a position in a small copse when they saw Venâncio appear, but no longer alone. Another man was riding with him, also on a mule, and the two were deep in conversation. They waited patiently and soon Antonio appeared. Quietly they walked their horses out onto the road and joined Antonio.

"What happened, Antonio?" Michael asked.

"Not much, he rode into the town, that man was sitting in the square, there is a small fountain. They greeted each other, and rode on together. He was clearly waiting for Venâncio."

They continued to follow the two men as before. So far the countryside had been rolling hills and woods, the road full of twists and turns, all of which made following easier. The road took them past Obidos on its west side. Michael found the sight of the town overlooking the surrounding countryside brought back memories of the recent events around that town. Memories, but no regrets, none at all.

As they neared Caldas, Michael began to worry about the presence of Cocks' dragoons. Antonio was again in front and had just disappeared around a bend. Moments later Michael and Lloyd rounded it, and Michael thought his worse fear was about to be realised. Antonio was in the middle of the road, surrounded by half a dozen dragoons of the Sixteenth. There was no sign of Venâncio.

"Damn it all! Come on Lloyd, we are going to have to talk our way through this and see Cocks. I hope we can do it without scaring Venâncio off."

As they rode closer Michael was relieved to see a sergeant and corporal that he knew. "Sergeant Nichols, a word, if you please."

Nichols' face was a picture and he stared at the scruffy, unshaved Portuguese rider. "Ere, who the 'ell are you? That's Mister Roberts' 'orse!" and then "Bloody 'ell, beg your pardon, Mister Roberts, sir, I didn't recognise you."

Michael couldn't help but laugh. "That's quite alright Sergeant, and that gentleman there," he pointed at Antonio, "is with me. But, quick now, you just let two gentleman on mules go by?"

"Yes, sir, they've been by before, sir, known to us as it were, they always puts up for a few nights at the best inn in town, sir."

"Does they, by God. Good, now where can I find Captain Cocks?"

"'E's out on a patrol, sir, but Mister Tomkinson is in town, sir, big, white washed place, sir, in the main square, just by the front of the church, sir."

"That will do. And Sergeant, all of you, not a word of this, if you please." He looked around. "I am on one of my 'special duties' you have all no doubt heard about. And now you know more than most." One or two of the dragoons grinned. "So I am sure that I can rely on you." A round of nods reassured him somewhat. At that he rode on, and glanced to his side just in time to catch Lloyd giving Nichols a grin and a wink.

In Caldas a couple of unsuspecting dragoons were told in short order to get their horses out of sight, and then Michael led the way into the large house. A sentry on the door, quick on the uptake, snapped off a salute, that was spoilt by his attempt not to grin.

Tomkinson was completely bemused. "Roberts? Is that you man? And Lloyd? What's going on?"

Michael explained the situation to Tomkinson, who listened in amazement. "So this is what you get up to when you disappear from us?"

"Not always, Tomkinson. Just this time."

"Well what do you want me to do."

"I want you to put us up here, out of sight of everyone. Now, Nichols told me that this Venâncio is a regular visitor, always stays in the best inn. I want to know where that is so that my friend Antonio, here, can wander in and see what is going on."

An hour later as Michael took a late dinner with Tomkinson, Antonio returned, with news.

"Senhor Miguel, the man with Venâncio is a Senhor Joaquim Caetano, who is from Columbeira. They have met a man I know, a smuggler, Senhor. They talked for a while, shook hands, and the smuggler left. Venâncio and Caetano are having dinner."

"I say," said Tomkinson, "how did you manage to discover all that?"

"Senhor, women who work in inns are my friends, after a little silver changes hands."

Michael asked, "If you know this man, do you know where he lives?"

"Of course, Senhor."

"Then I think we need to pay him a visit. Have you eaten?"

"Yes, I got a lot for my silver."

"Then, if you will excuse us, Tomkinson, we will be back later. Lloyd," he called out, "where are you?"

As Antonio led the way through narrow back alleys he told Michael that the man was called Tobias Sequeira, and that Antonio had made a few trips with him across the mountains to Spain. Arriving at an anonymous door, Michael and Lloyd stayed in the dark to either side of it, and Antonio hammered on the door.

"Tobias, it's Antonio, Antonio Carvalho. Open up, I need to speak to you!"

A moment later the door opened a crack, and a voice asked "Antonio? Is that you? What do you want?" Then Michael threw his weight against the door and burst in, closely followed by Antonio, and Lloyd, who closed the door firmly behind him.

The man had retreated across the dim, ill-furnished room, and seized a knife that he waved threateningly. "Antonio, what the Hell is this?"

Michael answered him. "You had a meeting earlier, with a Senhor Venâncio from Lisbon, and Senhor Caetano from Columbeira." The man's eyes widened in surprise. "You came to an agreement; you shook on it. You will tell me what you agreed."

"Why, why should I tell you anything? Antonio, what is this?"

Antonio merely shrugged and remained silent. Michael went on. "I am a British officer, you are a smuggler, those two men are traitors to Portugal. You will tell me because you value your life."

Sequeira looked at Michael and saw only cold cruelty in his eyes. He hesitated, and Michael took out his knife and opened it, locking the blade. "Senhor, you will tell me everything, or you will die, slowly and painfully." Antonio shot a glance at Michael and saw a look on his friend's face he had never seen before.

"Miguel…"

"No, Antonio, it is Senhor Sequeira's decision to make." Antonio looked at Lloyd, who gave him the slightest of a shake of his head.

"Tell him, Tobias, please."

Sequeira looked at Antonio, and then back to Michael, who stood, impassive, waiting. He put his knife on a table. "And that is all you want?"

"Perhaps. Do you want your life?"

Sequeira sagged, and sat down in a rickety old chair. "Very well, Senhor." He took a deep breath. "He wants me to take a small package to Pedrogao, and deliver it to his son who lives there. It means passing through both British and French lines, but it is not the first time, and it is not so difficult." Michael wondered what Cocks would think about that. "And then I bring a package back, Senhor. That is all."

There was silence in the room for a moment, then Michael spoke. "Very good, Senhor, I believe you. And you will take the package, and also myself and Antonio."

Sequeira looked up in surprise. "And then, Senhor?"

"You will bring the other package and us back, and deliver the package to Caetano. You may then resume your usual activities. We will not say anything to anyone. But my friend here," he pointed to Lloyd, "will stay behind, and if we do not return, he will hunt you down and kill you. Do you understand?"

"Yes, Senhor."

At daybreak the three men were waiting just to the east of Caldas. Lloyd had reluctantly accepted that he had to stay behind, but he had a part to play. Cocks had returned later that evening, and it had been arranged that he would be at the picket they needed to pass, to make sure there were no mistakes. Then Lloyd would remain there to ensure they got back safely through the picket on their return. Michael's main concern was Sequeira, for the moment he was out of sight and calling on Venâncio and Caetano. It was a risk, but they could do nothing else. It was going to be a three day ride, bivouacking at night without fires. They had plenty of cold food, and wineskins of water. Each man sat lost in his own thoughts, Michael's were fixated on silencing the Caetanos and Venâncios. They were traitors, he had been told to deal with them, and he would, without a qualm.

Almost an hour passed, it was clear daylight, and then Sequeira appeared. He rode up to them on a sturdy looking mule. "Senhor, I have the package." He held it up for Michael's inspection. It was small, no more than a letter.

"Then let us go."

They found Captain Cocks waiting for them at the picket. He pointed out where they believed the French pickets were. To his surprise Sequeira agreed, and also told Cocks where his other pickets were. Michael suppressed a smile. He was sure that by the time they returned they would all have been moved, save this one, and that would move as soon as they were back. Watched by a dozen curious dragoons, Captain Cocks, and Lloyd, they rode their horses towards a gap in the hills and were soon lost from view in thick woods.

Sequeira led the way, twisting and turning along barely discernible tracks. The climb up into the mountains was steep and hard going, but once they reached the tops the going was easier as they followed the contours of the land. Thick woodland covered the landscape only allowing occasional glimpses of stunning views across miles of mountains. Sequeira led the way confidently, and they saw no sign at all of the French pickets.

That night they bivouacked in the lee of a hill above the village of Minde, according to Sequeira, where they could see lights burning hundreds of feet below them. It was a cold night, but the rain kept off, and the trees gave them some shelter. They were on the move at first light, glad of the warmth that the exercise brought them.

Another steep climb brought them to the summit of the mountains overlooking Pedrogao. There they took a rest and hungrily ate some of their cold rations. Michael looked thoughtfully down on the small village. "Are there any French there?" he asked Sequeira.

"Not that I am aware of, Senhor. They are all further to the south, around Torres Novas and beyond. They do send patrols. Caetano told me that they come to see him every few days in case there is anything for them."

"How close to Caetano's house can we get without being seen?"

"Fortunately his house is on this side of the village, Senhor, there is a thick wood only a few hundred paces from his back door."

"Very good. Antonio, you will stay in the wood with the horses. Sequeira, you and I will go to the house. I will wait outside while you conduct your business. When you come out, I will go in and have a word with Senhor Caetano. Then we will all ride quietly back to Caldas."

It was just as Sequeira had said, and two hours later, after a slow and cautious approach, Michael was standing with him, just behind a small outbuilding behind Caetano's house.

"Off you go, Senhor Sequeira, and be careful. If you warn him, I shall kill you."

Sequeira nodded, grim faced, and walked across the few yards of open ground to the back door. Michael watched as he knocked, waited for a moment, and then was admitted. Michael was taking no chances, the moment the door closed he was off, running across to flatten himself against the wall of the house. He pulled out his knife, locked the blade, and moved to the door. He tried the handle, and the door opened. Carefully, he slipped into what was the kitchen of the house. Across the room a door stood ajar and he could hear voices, Sequeira's and another. He listened carefully for a moment, there were no other voices, he pushed the door open and walked in.

"Senhor Caetano, I believe." He wasn't sure who looked more shocked. "No, don't get up." He waved his knife at Caetano who was siting opposite Sequeira at a small table. "Sequeira, do you have the package to take back?" Sequeira nodded. "Good, give it to me. Now, find some cord, and tie Senhor Caetano to his chair." It was the work of a few minutes, and then Caetano was secured. "Thank you, Senhor Sequeira, you can go now." Sequeira left quickly.

The package that Sequeira had delivered was on the table, unopened. Michael picked it up and slipped it in his coat. "I think I had better take that. Now, Senhor Caetano, you are a traitor." Michael walked around to stand behind him. "Tell me quickly, who do you correspond with in Lisbon?"

"Senhor," said Caetano, "You should go now. I am expecting friends, French friends, if you are quick, you may escape."

Michael seized the man's hair, pulled his head back and laid the blade of his knife on his throat. "A name, Senhor, then I will go."

Caetano almost shouted in his panic, "De Barcarena, he's a friend of General Pamplona, Pamplona's in Torres Novas!"

"Thank you," said Michael, and cut his throat.

Michael left the way he had come, and quickly joined Antonio and Sequeira at the edge of the woods. "That's that, let's get back to Caldas."

Antonio and Sequeira both looked questioningly at Michael. "What?" he demanded, querulously.

"Nothing, Miguel, nothing," answered Antonio, "let's go home, eh?"

The trip back to Caldas was as uneventful and unpleasant as the trip out. They found the picket of the Sixteenth with Lloyd waiting impatiently. "Duw, sir, I'm glad to see you. I've had three days of funny looks and questions from every sergeant who's come out with the picket. Baxter and Liddle, sir. Wanting to know why I'm not in uniform, and what you might be doing, going behind the French lines, sir."

Michael laughed. "Never mind Lloyd, we are almost finished here, then it's back to Lisbon."

"Did it go well, sir, begging your pardon for asking?"

"It did indeed, Lloyd, very well."

There was a grim tone in Michael's answer that told Lloyd not to ask any more questions.

Sequeira had decided for himself that Lieutenant Roberts was not a man to cross. When they got back to Caldas as night was falling, and Michael told him to deliver the package from the younger Caetano to the elder Caetano and Venâncio, he did exactly that. On his return to where Michael waited, on the outskirts of the town, he was able to report that Venâncio had said they would set off for Lisbon in the morning.

Michael listened carefully, then said, "Thank you, Senhor Sequeira, you have been of great assistance. I don't think we need detain you any longer, but I would suggest that you make no more trips to Pedrogao until the French have gone."

Sequeira replied with a brief, "Thank you, Senhor," and was gone.

Michael turned to Lloyd and Antonio. "I think we can be pretty sure of where Venâncio is going, and Caetano will, presumably, return to his home in Columbeira." He smiled humourlessly, "Tomorrow we will be off early, again, I am afraid. I want to be ahead of them, let them pass, and then follow them again. For tonight we just need to stay out of sight."

Michael was able to report to Cocks that his trip had been successful, and enjoyed a supper with him and Tomkinson, while Lloyd and Antonio ate with Cocks' servant and orderly. Dawn found them huddled up against the cold, waiting near the Sixteenth's picket on the road south. Eventually they saw two riders come down the road, pause briefly at the picket, and then pass on. A dragoon broke from the picket and trotted his horse over.

"Them's your travellers, Mister Roberts, sir."

"Thank you. Lloyd, Antonio, a gentle pace, I think." The three men rode quietly out onto the road and followed the two figures in the distance.

A couple hours or so later they were nearing Columbeira, and the rain had started to fall again, heavily, drenching everyone. Michael halted their little party. "Antonio, you ride on into the village, I want to know where Caetano lives. Lloyd and I will circle around the village and wait for you on the other side." Antonio nodded his consent and pushed Duke on into a fast walk, and then a trot to close the gap with the two distant riders. Michael and Lloyd swung off the road to ride due south.

It wasn't long before they saw Venâncio pass unsuspectingly by. To Lloyd's surprise, Michael said, "Let's go and find Antonio. I want to pay Senhor Caetano a visit, and we know where Venâncio is going, we can catch up with him later."

They met Antonio on the edge of the village. Michael waved them all off the road into an olive grove that skirted the village. "Lloyd, you wait here with the horses. Antonio, show me Caetano's house, and can we get there unobserved, do you think?"

"In this rain, Senhor? I think so, there is no one about in the village. I think a lot of people are still in hiding from the French."

Wrapped in their cloaks, their broad brimmed hats pulled low against the weather, Michael was confident they would not be identifiable. "Then let's go."

Down a narrow side street Antonio came to halt. "The next house on the right, Senhor, with the green door."

"Stay here, Antonio. I won't be long."

Antonio watched Michael walk to the door, and bang on it with his fist. He thought he caught a flash of steel in Michael's hand, but in the rain it was difficult to be sure. Then he saw Michael throw his weight at the door and crash inside the house. For a minute or two there was no movement, no sound save the falling rain. Then Michael emerged from the house and walked to Antonio.

"That's that taken care of. Let's get back to Lloyd."

It didn't take long to catch up with Venâncio, the road was reasonable and the horses in good condition. A dry night and good feed in Caldas had kept them in good shape. They slipped easily back into the routine of one following ahead of the other two and changing around every half hour. In the rain Venâncio stayed huddled on his mule and didn't look round once. He stopped for the night in the same inn, and Michael kept them moving on until they found an abandoned building just of the road that gave them cover for the night and a view of the road. They even managed to light a small fire, and passed a reasonable night.

The next day, they let Venâncio pass them by, and then followed him still undetected, all the way into Lisbon. They saw him return his hired mule, and walk home. It was just dark when they rode up to the stables at Michael's house.

Chapter 17

Michael sat in his dining room, a fire warming him, the remains of his breakfast before him, a cup of coffee to hand, and deep in thought. He had dealt with the cross border communication; it had been easier to get in and out behind the French lines than he had imagined it would be. He also knew for certain that Venâncio and de Barcarena were the Lisbon end of the supply of information to the French. That would have to be dealt with. He wondered for a moment about Catarina. He realised that he rather liked her. He knew she liked him, and that was unfortunate, and doomed to disappointment while he was still bound to Elaine. He wondered how he would react if Nascimento was right, and he did get a sign from Elaine that he was a free man, that she truly wanted him to love again. He dismissed the thought.

He turned his thoughts back to the problem in hand. Although he knew about Venâncio and de Barcarena, he had no concrete proof. Without something solid and incontrovertible de Silva was powerless, unable to act against a man with such powerful friends and allies. They would prefer not to believe they had supported a traitor; it would take something very substantial to remove that support. The Venâncios, however, were a different matter, and the proof against de Barcarena that Michael needed might be found there. If he was going to take any action against them, he would need to get Catarina out of the way, and deal with their servants as well. It wouldn't be easy. He couldn't ask Roberta for help, and he certainly couldn't go to de Silva.

At that moment Francisco appeared to clear away the breakfast things. A thought struck Michael. "Francisco?"

"Yes, Senhor?"

"Have you seen your sister while I have been away?"

"Yes, Senhor, only yesterday before you got back."

"And how are things at Senhorita Roberta's?"

"Oh, quite well, Senhor. My sister was busy yesterday, and will be today, the Senhorita has invited some ladies to a little soiree." He shrugged. "No men, Senhor, none at all."

"Really? And do you know who is going?"

"Yes, Senhor. Err…" Francisco hesitated.

"Come on Francisco, tell me."

"Senhorita Catarina will be there, Senhor, and Senhora Venâncio." He shrugged again "I do not understand it, Senhor, just ladies."

Michael chuckled, and replied, "Don't worry about it, Francisco." But his mind was already racing with ideas. "Did you say you might see Constanca today?"

"No, Senhor, because she said she will be busy, and I thought you might be back."

"Do you know where Senhor Lloyd is?"

"Down at the stables, Senhor, with Parra and your friends, Senhor."

Michel sat, deep in thought as Francisco cleared the table, and left him alone. After a while he rose slowly from the table, and still deep in thought, made his way down and out to the back of the house. Bernardo was hard at work on the garden. He saw Lloyd walking towards him from the stables. He was wearing his scruffy civilian clothes, as was becoming a habit when in Lisbon, for both of them. Michael thought he was looking more and more Portuguese every day.

Lloyd saw him and greeted him. "Bore da, sir, Duw, but it's a chill one. Still, it's dry, sir."

"Morning, Lloyd." He glanced towards Bernardo, and saw he was well out of earshot. "Lloyd, I'm afraid that this business isn't finished."

"No, sir, I didn't think it was." Lloyd, took a deep breath of the chill morning air. "What are we going to do then, sir?"

Early evening found Michael and Lloyd still in their civilian clothes, wrapped up on cloaks, scarves pulled up over their lower faces, hat brims pulled low, and lurking in a familiar alleyway opposite the Venâncios house. Under their cloaks both men had a pair of pistols. The plan was simple. They would wait until they saw Catarina and Senhora Venâncio leave, then they would go to the rear of the house, surprise the servants at pistol point, tie them up, and then Michael would go after Senhor Venâncio. He planned to tie him up as well, and then search for the evidence he felt sure was to be found in Venâncio's study. Once he had that, they could take Venâncio to de Silva. Hopefully they would also find evidence to prove de Barcarena's treason.

Things started to go wrong immediately. The front door opened and Catarina came out with the Venâncio's footman. There was no sign of Senhora Venâncio. Michael cursed under his breath.

"Now what, sir?" Lloyd muttered quietly.

Michael hesitated for a moment. "We will carry on Lloyd, we might not get another chance like this, with Senhorita Cardoso out of the way."

They waited until Catarina and the footman vanished around a corner, then slipped quietly across the road and down a nearby alleyway. It was even darker than in the street, and they moved forward cautiously. Around a corner, down another alleyway, Michael counted his paces, and halted at a stout looking wooden door set in a wall.

"This should be it," Michael whispered. This was where they really needed some luck. He gently pushed at the latch of the door, it lifted, and the door swung open.

Michael let out his breath that he realised he had been holding. Inside there was a small courtyard, lit by the light from a window, with another door next to it. They moved slowly and silently forward. Michael could see that the window gave a view of the kitchen, with two women sitting at a table, one sewing.

Michael and Lloyd moved to the door. They drew out their pistols, cocked them, the clicks sounding loud in the quiet of the night, and pulled their scarves well up. The last thing Michael wanted was any witness seeing his scar. He nodded to Lloyd, who had both his pistols in one hand, the other on the doorknob. Lloyd twisted the knob and pushed the door open. Michael stepped into the room.

"Good evening ladies, please remain quiet and no harm will come to you. Ah! No!" This last, sharply, as the younger woman gathered herself to scream. She subsided in silence. "Thank you, Senhorita." Lloyd had followed him in and quickly tied the two women to their chairs.

"Please, Senhoras, just sit quietly and no harm will come to you. My friend here will keep you company for a little while. Not a word from you, please." Wide eyed, both women simply nodded.

Leaving Lloyd in the kitchen, Michael moved cautiously through the house. He knew from his previous visits that Venâncio's study was on the ground floor. The door stood slightly ajar, and light spilled through the gap. He pushed it gently with his foot, and it swung open. Venâncio was sitting at his desk, and did not immediately see Michael until he had taken a few steps into the room.

"What! Who the hell are you?" Venâncio barked.

"Never mind," replied Michael, "sit still and keep your voice down. Where is your wife?"

"Why? What do you want with her? The only money we have is here, in that box." He gestured to a strong box sitting in the corner of the room.

"Senhor," Michael pointedly waved a pistol at him, "I need to know where your wife is. If you want to keep her safe, you will tell me."

That was the moment when the plan finally went completely wrong. Michael saw the flicker of movement in Venâncio's eyes as he glanced behind him. He spun around to see Senhora Venâncio coming at him, a large candlestick raised above her head. He stepped towards her, raised his left arm to block the blow, and hit her hard on the side of her head with the pistol in his right hand. She staggered, fell, her head hit the corner of the strong box with a sickening crunch, and she fell to the floor, unmoving.

Michael turned back to Senhor Venâncio. He had pulled open a drawer in his desk, and now had a pistol in his hand. As he brought it to full cock, Michael fired. The ball struck Venâncio full in the centre of his chest, and he fell behind the desk, his pistol going off as he fell. Michael had no idea where the shot went, nor did he care. He ran full tilt back to the kitchen where Lloyd was standing, both pistols aimed at him. He raised the muzzles as Michael burst in.

"Go!" Michael shouted, remembering to use Portuguese. He saw Lloyd hesitate at the short, shouted word. He shouted again and waved towards the open door to the yard. Lloyd understood, and to Michael's relief he didn't respond with a "Yes, sir." He just turned and ran, Michael at his heels. In the alleyway, Michael called out, "This way," and took the lead. They ran for ten minutes or more, keeping to back alleyways and lesser streets, before Michael pulled up, panting heavily.

"Not according to plan, damn it, but it will have to do."

Lloyd noticed that one of Michael's pistols was still at full cock. He gestured at it, "I heard two shots, sir?"

"You did, Lloyd, you did. Venâncio wasn't quite quick enough, and missed." He took a few more deep breaths. "Now, let's go home and have a drink, eh?"

"I think that is a very good idea, sir."

It was unconventional, but Michael shared a bottle of port with Lloyd in the sitting room. They talked about horses until the bottle was empty.

Michael slept well and in the morning felt remarkably clear headed. He took his coffee and strolled from the dining room, into the ballroom, and across to one of the windows overlooking the broad reach of the Tagus. He could see the ships of the royal Navy that guarded the river, and the many merchant ships that were bringing much needed supplies in to feed Lisbon's swollen population. He felt entirely at ease, and was aware that he enjoyed the dirty war, as he had called it. He enjoyed the freedom of action it gave him, and the sense of satisfaction that came with knowing his actions had made a real difference to the prosecution of the war against Buonaparte.

He was also fully aware that if he was to continue fighting that war, he would have to stay and fight the more conventional war as well, but staying in the Sixteenth was no hardship. He was well aware that he was acquiring something of a reputation, perhaps not a very wholesome one, but that couldn't be helped, he acted as he saw fit. Recent events wouldn't help. News of his disappearing behind the French lines in civilian clothes, combined with Lloyd's refusal to say anything, would be all through the Regiment like wildfire. That couldn't be helped either. He just hoped that he could get back to the Regiment and the proper soldiering he enjoyed as much as fighting the dirty war.

From the dining room came sounds of clattering dishes as Francisco cleared the table. He would have to do something about him soon. The sights of war had deeply troubled the young man, as they had Michael. He thought back to the desolation of what had been the village of Almoster. He was glad that Francisco hadn't seen the dead at the quinta. He felt his anger beginning to rise at the thought of what the French had done to his beloved Portugal and its people. He felt the slightly detached, cold, calm that came with his anger. He thought of the Venâncios, and the Caetanos, and was glad.

The sound of voices broke in on his reverie. Footsteps came running up the stairs, and Roberta burst in on him.

"Michael, have you heard? The Venâncios are dead!"

He knew he couldn't hide the truth from Roberta, she knew him too well. "Yes, I know."

Roberta stared hard at him. "Michael, was it…" She could not finish the question.

Michael shrugged. "Does it matter?"

She stood silent for a moment. "I got a message from the General. He went to see for himself. Catarina found the bodies when she returned from my soiree last night. The story is that two brigands broke in, tied up the servants and then killed the Venâncio's. There were shots fired, and they fled without taking anything."

"That sounds correct."

"It was you, wasn't it."

"Yes, I was hoping to find evidence linking them to de Barcarena. Unfortunately things went awry. Venâncio tried to shoot me. He wasn't quick enough."

"And the Senhora?"

"She tried to club me with a candlestick. Would you like some coffee?"

"Coffee? You have killed two people, Catarina is in a terrible state, and you ask me if I want coffee?" Roberta voice rose until she was shouting.

"Roberta, it was necessary, and you know it was."

Roberta's shoulders sagged and she looked out at the Tagus. "Yes. Yes, I know." She turned her gaze back to Michael. "But you. What has happened to you, Michael, that you can stand there so calmly and offer me coffee?" She turned to leave. "But just in case there is any humanity left in you, you might call on Catarina. I think she will be pleased to see you, although God knows why." And with that she was gone.

Michael gazed at the river. He would go and see Catarina, then he would go and see Roberta, try to make things up with her. He had no wish to lose her as a friend, and he was happy for her and da Rocha, even though he would miss her as a lover.

In the mid-afternoon, out of uniform, he called at the house that he now had to think of as Catarina's. A rather pale footman answered the door, and showed him into a small sitting room. He noticed that the door to the study was firmly closed. He had barely waited five minutes when the door opened, and a white faced Catarina entered, her colour accentuated by the black dress she was wearing. He rose to his feet.

"Michael, thank you for coming to see me. I didn't even know you were back in Lisbon."

"I got back the day before yesterday. I had intended to call today anyway, but Roberta called on me earlier. How are you, Catarina? Or is that a ridiculous question?"

The door opened and a woman Michael recognised came in with a tray with cups and coffee. She put the tray on a small table, glancing at Michael as she did. Michael saw not a hint of recognition, then she was gone.

"No, Michael, it is not a ridiculous question. To tell you the truth, I am not sure how I am." She poured two coffees and handed one to Michael. "Forgive me, please, sit down." They settled in chairs opposite each other. "It was a shock. Tomás, he's the footman," Michael nodded, "he unlocked the front door, and I went in first. The study door was wide open, which was unusual, I looked in." She pulled a white lace handkerchief from her sleeve and dabbed her eyes while she gathered herself. "I saw the Senhora first, and then just the Senhor's feet, sticking out from behind his desk." She smiled wanly at Michael. "I am afraid that I screamed. Then Tomás went for help."

Michael spoke to give her time. "Roberta said that shots were fired, did no one hear them?"

"Apparently one neighbour thought he heard something, he looked out, but could see nothing untoward, and there were no further noises. No passers-by have come forward. General de Silva came, although it was the middle of the night. His men went around everywhere, asking questions. The general himself searched the study, although I do not know why. I suppose he had his reasons."

Michael was relieved by her account, and asked, "But how are you? Is there anything I can do?"

"I will be alright, Michael. It is just the shock. The shock of finding them, and the shock of what it means."

"What does it mean?"

She brightened up and smiled at him. "It means I am a wealthy and independent woman, Michael."

"What?" Michael's surprise was genuine.

"You see, Senhor Venâncio had no family. My brother had left everything to his wife, but with the proviso that if she had no children, then everything will be mine." She smiled again, "Michael, once everything is settled, I will be a wealthy woman and I can do what I like."

Michael sat speechless. Catarina looked shyly at him over the top of her coffee cup as she took a drink.

"Michael, I know I should wait, but it occurs to me that you could be called away on duty at any moment for who knows how long." She took another sip of coffee as Michael had a sudden premonition. "I need to tell you, Michael, that I have become very…" she struggled for the right word, "attracted to you, with all your attention to me recently. I wonder, I hope, that was because you feel the same way about me." She blushed scarlet as she spoke.

Michael was stunned. He was at a complete loss at what to do or say. He just knew that he had to get away. "Catarina…" He dried up. "Catarina," he tried again. "I do think you are a most attractive young woman, and I find you are very good company. But this, this is very sudden. Forgive me, you have me completely at a disadvantage." His eyes had been everywhere except on Catarina's face. He forced himself to look at her, to meet her gaze that was full of hope. "I do not know, Catarina." He saw the disappointment. "I, err, I," inspiration came. "I was going to tell you that I must go away for a few days, I am called to headquarters," he lied, but he was damn sure that was where he was going, first thing tomorrow. "I will come to see you again when I get back. We can talk more, I can begin to get used to your new circumstances, we can get to know each other better." Another thought struck him. "You are in mourning, you must observe the formalities, I know what Lisbon society can be like. And we should be careful to make sure we are sure," he finished rather lamely.

Catarina managed not to look too disappointed. "You are right, Michael, I should not be so hasty." She managed a small smile. "You will come and see me when you get back?"

"Yes, of course."

On his return home he gave his instructions. "Lloyd, Francisco, pack everything for a return to the Regiment. And let Parra know. I want to be away at first light, I want to be at Cartaxo tomorrow evening and it's forty miles." The horses were in excellent condition, even after their recent trip over the mountains. He knew forty miles was a very good distance, but they had done it before, and, once back with the Regiment, if he could achieve that, the demands would be much less.

He paid Antonio and Carlos as agreed, he also gave them each a letter of introduction to the Commissary at Belem. "I don't know if these will help, but the man seems keen to help me, I think he thinks I have more important friends than is actually the case."

"It has been a pleasure, Miguel," Antonio said and shook Michael by the hand.

"Thank you," said Carlos, "perhaps I can find a mule captain with a less attractive wife." He too shook hands, and then the two men went off.

Once everything was in hand, he walked over to see Roberta. He was not sure how things now stood between them, But he had to go, he had to try, he had to apologise. Constanca showed him into Roberta's sitting room with none of her usual gaiety. Roberta sat in her usual, comfortable chair, and looked coldly at him.

Michael launched straight into what he had come to say. "Roberta, I am sorry about my behaviour towards you this morning. It was unnecessary. I have lost a lover, and I can accept that because your happiness is important to me. I do not want to lose a friend. I hope you can believe that. I have been to see Catarina, we have talked. I have tried to be... tried not to hurt her. She clearly has developed feelings for me, and for that I take full responsibility, but you know why I did what I did. And you know why I cannot return her... her affections. No, Roberta, please do not pull that face at me. I will also tell you that you are right, something has happened to me. I am not sure what, and I certainly do not have an answer." He paused for breath. "You may find this difficult to believe, but at Mafra I spoke to a priest. Yes, really. He told me that I have brought things upon myself, that I have to find a way to accept that Elaine has released me. Then, he said, I might be free." Michael finally fell silent.

Roberta remained silent. Eventually she spoke. "I believe that you mean what you say. I have known you too well and for too long not to. I am relieved about how you feel about me and Alexandre, and I hope that we may remain friends for many, many years. And, if I might say, as a friend, I think your priest is correct. Only when you accept that Elaine set you free, that you can return the affections a of a woman without feeling guilty, only then will you be able to find happiness. Now, tell me what Catarina said to you?"

Michael told her, as well as he could remember, and Roberta asked him, "And what are you going to do now?"

Michael squirmed internally. "I have to go to Cartaxo, to report to Wellington."

"And then?" she was relentless.

"I don't know. I may well be told to return to the Regiment. It can't be helped."

"No, I don't suppose it can. I suppose Catarina may as well learn about the misery of loving a soldier now as later."

Michael still stood before Roberta. "I should go."

"Yes, I think we both need a little time for thought and reflection."

"Just one thing."

"Yes?"

"You said the General searched Venâncio's study himself. Did he find anything?"

"No, Michael, nothing at all."

It was a long day's ride to Cartaxo, but the rain held off, and the road was reasonable. On arrival he managed to obtain a billet for himself, his party and the horses and mules. Then he went in search of Wellington. At headquarters he was fortunate enough to run into Colonel De Lancey.

"Good Lord, Roberts, what are you doing here?"

"I beg your pardon, Colonel, I've just come from Lisbon, and I have information for Viscount Wellington."

De Lancey looked questioningly at Michael. "Intelligence matter, is it?"

"Yes, sir."

"Hmm, ye'd best come along with me. Wellington is about to dine, so be quick."

De Lancey led him into a small house, knocked at a door outside which stood a sentry, opened it, stuck his head in and said, "Lieutenant Roberts for you my Lord, says he has some information." He turned back to Roberts, "In you go."

Wellington was sitting at a small table covered with papers and maps. He was alone.

"Well, Mister Roberts, I hope you have come to report your foxes accounted for?"

"Yes, my Lord, all bar one that is." Wellington looked askance at Michael. "The line of communication is destroyed, my Lord, and the individuals concerned have been dealt with. Unfortunately de Barcarena is deemed too well connected to tackle without more than the word of myself on the matter. No hard evidence was found, my Lord."

"Does de Silva know this?"

"Yes, my Lord."

"Hmm. Very good, then we must leave it at that, for the moment. Good work, Mister Roberts. Tell me, is there any reason why you should return to Lisbon?"

"No, my Lord."

"Good. Colonel Archer has not been entirely happy about losing you, Roberts. You may rejoin your Regiment, with my compliments to the good Colonel. Good night, Roberts.

"Good night, my Lord."

The ride to Ribeira, where the Regiment's headquarters was, was a mere twelve miles or so, and Michael and his party arrived there in the late morning. Colonel Archer was sick and had gone to Lisbon, so it was Major Pelly that he reported to. Pelly was pleased to see him back, and they lunched together before Michael rode on the short distance to Anteporta. Captain Ashworth was extremely pleased to see him. They moved back into their old billets and began to settle in. It was not for long.

The following day it became clear that Massena and the French army were retreating towards Spain. The British and Portuguese army, the Sixteenth to the fore, went in pursuit.

Chapter 18

Michael was huddled up in his cloak, sitting uncomfortably on Duke. He was wet, he was cold, he was hungry, but most of all he was angry. He had been angry for some days now, and it burned in him, cold and hard, and almost undetectable, lying just below the surface of his usual cheerful demeanour. Waiting.

For a long week the Sixteenth had been following the Light Division as they led the pursuit of the retreating French army. A temporary change had brigaded them with the Fourteenth Light Dragons, and with Archer still sick in Lisbon and Major Pelly commanding the Regiment, the brigade was being commanded by Colonel Hawker of the Fourteenth. There were only three squadrons of the Sixteenth, Cock's Squadron was detached, and away to the west somewhere. Ahead, their old friends, the German Hussars, were leading the advance along with the Royal Dragoons.

Along the way they had marched through small villages and larger towns. Everywhere he saw the same sights. Houses plundered, burnt and defiled, dead and dying Portuguese civilians, men, women and children, victims of French cruelty and atrocities, surrounded by filth and corruption. There was the detritus of a fleeing army, dead French soldiers, dying French soldiers begging to be saved from vengeful Portuguese peasants, but left to their fate as the army marched on. Slaughtered baggage animals and smashed wagons lined the roads. The countryside had been stripped as the British and Portuguese army had retreated through it to safety of the lines. The following French had plundered it on their advance, and now they were desperately seeking any food left as they retreated, fleeing from starvation in front of the lines. The savagery of the French shocked everyone, in Michael it fuelled his hatred and fanned his anger to a white heat.

For the last two days they had been hard on the heels of the French rear-guard, with occasional skirmishes, but none that had involved the Sixteenth. They had marched through Leiria just after first light, and now, five hours later, were approaching Pombal on the road north to Coimbra. It had stopped raining, and the road had dried, but, like everyone else, Michael was cold and his uniform had still not dried out. With the lifting of the rain, the Light Division began to push the pace until they were closing fast on the small town of Pombal. The rapid advance came to a halt on high ground that gave a view of the town and the plain in front of it. From there it became apparent that the French had eight squadrons of dragoons formed up on the plain in front of the town. The Hussars and the Royals formed to attack, the Hussars in front. The Sixteenth, save for Cocks' squadron, were in a supporting role, at the back, along with the Fourteenth. Michael, as usual, on the extreme left of Ashworth's squadron, Lloyd beside him, Sergeant Taylor behind. He saw little of what followed, as the Hussars, unexpectedly joined by Cocks' squadron appearing from the west, charged and the French retreated.

Immediately the infantry of the Light Division advanced, and set a pattern that was going to be repeated over the next few days, as the French were driven up the valley of the Mondego towards Spain. The following day, after a miserable night in the open, they came up with the French rear-guard again, at the town of Redinha. It had rained all night, and every man was again soaked to the skin. Woods hid most of the action from Michael's view. His frustration at their inactivity did nothing to lessen his anger. The fight was taken on by the infantry as Wellington pitched four divisions against the French rear-guard, and forced them back across the narrow bridge over the Rio Anços.

The next day the Light Division again came up against the French rear-guard at Casal Novo. Early morning fog almost caused a disaster as General Erskine, commanding the Light Division while Crauford was in England, sent the Division blundering into a strongly held position. With help from the Third Division, the Light Division was finally successful and drove the French back some fourteen miles in the day. The ground was entirely unsuitable for cavalry, the closest the Sixteenth got to any fighting was when Captain Swetenham's Squadron was sent forward to support the Light Divisions artillery.

Fog delayed what became a day's long march, until as daylight was falling, the Light Division was again launched against the French rear-guard at Foz do Arouce. The same pattern was repeated as the Light Division attacked head on and two other Divisions worked their way around the French flanks. Hard fighting followed, but the victorious Light Division benefitted from the capture of a French camp, and all the food being cooked. They were the lucky ones, as the advance had by now outstripped the ability of the commissary to supply the troops.

A long day halted in the rain, waiting for the commissary supplies to catch up, did no one's humour any good. Michael was getting particularly concerned about Francisco. He was getting quieter by the day, clearly disturbed by the sights they saw and at times he seemed quite distracted. Lloyd and Parra seemed happy enough, but they were of a similar age, and always had horse matters to discuss.

Another long and wet day followed as they pushed on up the Mondego valley, following the trail of dead mules and baggage animals. Still there was no fighting for the cavalry. All they did was push out patrols and pickets at night. Then, finally, there came a chance.

The valley became open countryside, unhampered by woods or enclosures. General Slade was in command of the cavalry while Sir Stapleton was, like Anson and Crauford, on leave in England. He had to hand two brigades of British cavalry and two troops of horse artillery. He hesitated. Michael and his fellow cavalrymen champed at the bit; it was an ideal opportunity for them to take a lot of prisoners. At length, Slade sent forward just two squadrons, who took what prisoners they could, but it was generally felt to have been a chance wasted.

The same happened the following day. Slade spent half an hour watching a small French force march across an open plain. By the time he decided on a course of action, and sent for the cavalry and guns, it was too late. Slade's inaction was loudly criticised.

Michael gave vent to his feelings to Henry van Hagen. "It makes me mad, Henry. There are those bastard French, marching away under our noses, and Slade just sat there and watched. We could have taken the whole lot. He just wastes time being so damned indecisive."

"Yes, he's not very good, is he? It's a shame Sir Stapleton and Colonel Anson aren't here. But I hear that Slade was just the same when he was with Moore. Should have been at Sahagun, but managed to arrive late."

A week later and the slow, steady pursuit, hampered by supply shortages, bad weather and Slade's hesitation every time the French came in sight, caught up with the French at Sabugal. For the first time in four days it had stopped raining, and the Sixteenth were sent on a march to get around the French flank. They arrived too late to do anything. Once again the Light Division won the laurels.

At long last, however, the French were out of Portugal, and the pursuit ended. A few days later the Regiment found itself back in its old quarters at Gallegos. It was not the village they remembered. Half of the buildings had lost their roofs to the French demands for firewood, and more than half its inhabitants had been forced to leave. It was a sad sight.

By the end of April, the Sixteenth, the German Hussars and the Light Division were well settled back in their familiar role of pickets along the border, strung out over a thirty-five mile front. The rest of the army was to the rear in cantonments, except for one division blockading the fortress of Almeida, which was still in French hands. A proper siege was impossible as Wellington had no siege artillery to hand. Supplies for all were still short, with everything having to be transported the length of the Mondego valley. The horses in particular were suffering, the commissary was able only to supply half rations, and the rest was made up of green corn, beans and rye. One piece of good news was the return from England of Sir Stapleton Cotton. No one was sorry to see Slade return to command of his brigade.

Then, at the start of May, Massena and the French army advanced to try to relieve the blockade around Almeida. Michael was enjoying a frugal breakfast with van Hagen and Keating when they were alerted by shouts in the street calling everyone out and to form on the alarm place. Within minutes the Squadron was forming as sky slowly brightened with the dawn. He left Francisco and Parra hurriedly packing up all his baggage and loading the mules, and took his usual post on the left of the squadron, riding Johnny, Sergeant Taylor behind him, Lloyd to his right. Out in front Ashworth was sitting facing them. As soon as he was satisfied that the Squadron was formed , he wheeled his horse around and gave the order, "Squadron, walk!." This was almost immediately followed by "Squadron, trot!" and he led them quickly up the hill that overlooked the Azaba river, familiar ground to all of them.

The squadron crested the hill and halted, as the regiment formed in line, Ashworth's on the extreme right. To the right the Hussars were also formed and waiting. Very soon they saw the pickets of the German Hussars come galloping down to the bridge and up the hill towards them. They reported to Sir Stapleton and Arenschildt, who were also on the hill. The word was quickly passed along that two very large columns of French cavalry and infantry had left Ciudad Rodrigo, and were advancing on Gallegos and Carpio, which was some five miles to the south. General Erskine, still commanding the Light Division, joined Sir Stapleton and Arenschildt. After a quick conference, orders came for a withdrawal to the line of the small stream that ran behind Gallegos.

Once in position, the cavalry threw out skirmishers and dismounted to await the advance of the French. Along the edge of the stream the Light Division took up position, cavalry and infantry intermixed in mutual support. When the French cavalry appeared, it halted and began to send out its own skirmishers. For the rest of the day, Michael looked on as the cavalry skirmishers of both sides took pot shots and achieved very little. It became clear that the French cavalry were waiting for the French infantry to catch up with them, marching from Ciudad Rodrigo.

The Regimental baggage had already been sent to the rear, beyond the dos Casas river and the small village of Fuentes d'Onoro, Francisco and Parra with it. Michael would be riding Johnny for the foreseeable future. With nightfall the two sets of skirmishers fell away from each other, and the British established themselves along the stream, the main bodies getting what sleep they could a few hundred yards further back. It wasn't the first time that Michael had slept in his cloak, Johnny's reins in his hand, nor, he suspected, would it be the last.

Well before dawn, with sleep elusive, the Squadrons mounted and waited for the sun to rise. Over the course of the morning they slowly retired in the face of superior numbers of French cavalry, leap frogging other squadrons who turned to face the French and threaten to charge if they got too close. In amongst them the infantry of the Light Division marched, the rear most companies turning to face the French from time to time. It was nerve wracking work. Any mistake in positioning or timing could allow the French to charge them at a disadvantage. The countryside was covered with scattered woods, which gave cover for infantry skirmishers, but could also hide French squadrons from view. There were sporadic outbreaks of firing, but by midday they had reached the relative safety of the main position of the British and Portuguese army.

The cavalry and the Light Division parted company, for the moment. The cavalry, two brigades, four regiments in all, were strung out along a ridge behind and to the right of Fuentes d'Onoro. There they were pleased to have Anson rejoin and reassume command of the brigade from Arenschildt. Arenschildt was good, and respected, but Anson was one of their own, an officer of the Sixteenth. Slade's brigade of the Fourteenth Light Dragons and the Royal Dragoons was to the right. Anson's was formed with the Sixteenth as its right hand regiment.

The French cavalry that had been driving them across the countryside to Fuentes now halted, and French infantry came forward to launch a ferocious assault on the village itself. With the fall of the land and intervening trees, from Michael's position it was difficult to tell what was happening, but he could hear an almost continuous rattle of musketry and see clouds of smoke floating up from the village. The fighting raged all through the afternoon, but the British infantry held the village, and at dusk the fighting petered out. *vedettes*

That night Ashworth's provided the forward videttes and pickets on the right of the British position. The weather was mild and dry, and the night passed quietly. As was often the case, the British and French vedettes were within easy hailing distance of each other, and regularly called out to each other to avoid any unnecessary and unpleasant incidents.

Fortunately for Michael the following day passed almost without incident, and he was able to catch up on his sleep a little, lying next to Johnny, who also dozed on his feet. It was a long, slow day. They could see part of the French army, cavalry, infantry and artillery, and it didn't seem to be in a hurry to do anything. Occasionally, bodies of cavalry were seen riding off to the south, towards the extreme left of the British position. At the far right, Michael learnt, his friend Don Julian Sanchez was occupying a small village with his lancers and a single infantry battalion. Late in the afternoon the Regimental baggage appeared, and Michael at last got a reasonable meal, albeit cold, and exchanged Johnny for Duke.

A nervous, restless night followed. In the early hours they heard a division of infantry on the move, marching off to the right somewhere. Just before dawn both brigades of cavalry were roused and followed the infantry to the right, where they were scattered in squadrons over a three mile front. It did not engender a feeling of security.

Daylight revealed that the cavalry and the infantry, the new, raw 7th Division, was covering the right flank from Fuentes d'Onoro to the distant village of Poco Velho, itself nearly three miles from Nave de Haver and Don Sanchez's position. No sooner had this become apparent to all, but sporadic, light firing was heard from the direction of Nave de Haver. Michael couldn't see what was happening, but the sounds of fighting slowly got closer.

Sir Stapleton galloped up to Ashworth, spoke briefly, and then was off again. Ashworth gave his orders, "Threes, right, walk, trot," and the squadron was hurrying in the direction of the fighting, along with all the other cavalry. Forming rapidly to face to Nave de Haver on the slope above it, Michael could see that the British cavalry, some of which had already taken heavy casualties, were facing an overwhelming number of French dragoons. Then Michael heard the sound of heavy infantry fire from the village itself, before the defenders of the village were seen running to rest of the 7th Division, and large columns of French infantry started to appear from the woods around the village.

The infantry were saved by a desperate charge of two squadrons of the German Hussars. They reached the relative safety of the rest of the Division, which promptly began to retire towards Fuentes. The cavalry regiments formed in column of squadrons facing the French cavalry, and Ashworth's was at the head of the Sixteenth.

Ashworth turned to face the Squadron for a moment. "Keep close, keep your order, we must keep together." Then he turned to face the French and his orders rang clear, "Squadron, draw swords, walk," then "Squadron, trot." They began to move rapidly towards the nearest French squadron. "Squadron, gallop", the distance between was down to fifty yards, "Squadron, charge!"

To Michael's astonishment the French dragoons tried to turn away from them, and then they struck. Michael cut down the man in front of him, turned to see Lloyd taking another dragoon. He reined up and took breath. The French were not standing and making a fight of it. Lloyd rode up beside him.

"Duw, sir, will look at their horses, sir, they're half starved and in terrible condition."

It was true. The French mounts were no match for the British horses, who were better fed, in good condition, fitter and stronger. Michael heard Ashworth's voice through the din, "Threes, right, trot," and he led the Squadron around the side of the Regiment to the rear. Ten minutes later they were reformed at the back of the Regiment. Michael looked around, remarkably there was only one man missing. Michael just had time for a quick glance behind him, where he could see the 7th Division marching hard for high ground.

What attracted his attention more was the sight of Captain Belli's Squadron that had already been in action, out in front of the army. It had been Cocks' Squadron, but Belli had re-joined the Regiment three days ago and taken command, Cocks taking the wounded Murray's Squadron. There was no sign of Belli, Weyland, or Blake. Tomkinson was absent, sick, and Bishop sat in front of a very depleted squadron. It looked as if they had suffered badly. Michael turned his attention back to his own squadron.

Over the next half hour both of the other two squadrons still effective took their turns to charge at the advancing French cavalry. To either side the other three regiments were doing the same. Then it was Ashworth's turn to charge again. Michael rubbed Duke's neck, "Here we go, lad, steady now." Next to him Rodrigo tossed his head, and he heard Lloyd mutter something soothing in Welsh. Then the orders came again, and they were advancing. The few hundred yards to the French dragoons was covered in moments, and again the French seemed less than keen, trying to evade the Squadron as the well formed mass of men and horses bore down on them. They came in at a slight angle, and Michael found himself momentarily unopposed. He concentrated on keeping the Squadron together, yelling at the men to keep close, to keep together as they ploughed into the French, who turned and broke, then calling to them to halt, to reform.

Once contact was broken, they made their way quickly to the rear of the regiment before any supporting French squadrons could charge them. Reaching the rear, Michael saw something to gladden the heart of any dragoon. The Light Division now stood just behind them, its battalions formed into square, horse artillery guns supporting them. A few minutes later and all the cavalry had retired through the gaps between the squares, at the sight of which, the French cavalry halted.

Once again they faced the French, but then started to withdraw as the Light Division began to march back towards the main British position. Still at the rear of the Regiment, Michael could see, beyond the Light Division, the 7th Division forming in a new defensive position. The French rode towards the squares, which halted, and then drove them off with devastating volleys of musket and rifle fire. The cavalry advanced again, to take advantage of the chaos in the French ranks caused by the volleys, and to give the Light Division some time to continue their march.

Once more Ashworth led them forward. Michael and Duke crashed into the flank of a squadron of French dragoons. The man in front of him tried to turn away, then Michael saw another French dragoon coming at him, ready with a thrust. With a shock, he realised it was the French dragoon Colonel from the Mondego and Calhariz. He came straight at Michael, his face a mask of hate, teeth bared in a snarl. Michael started to turn Duke to meet the attack, readied himself to parry the thrust, but then the horse stumbled, started to fall. Michael saw blood spouting from Duke's neck, just behind his head. He missed the parry and the French Colonel's thrust missed as Duke went down. The Colonel's horse swerved right to avoid the falling Duke, and as the Colonel passed he made a wild swing to his left, and the end of his blade sliced into Michael's unprotected arm, and struck bone. Sharp pain like fire coursed through his arm, and Michael could not help the wild, high scream that came from him. His arm was suddenly useless, he lost his reins, Duke fell and rolled, somehow Michael was clear of the thrashing, screaming horse, losing his grip on his sabre and clutching at his arm.

Horses closed protectively around him, and then Lloyd was kneeling next to him.

"That Colonel…" Michael managed to gasp out.

"Yes, sir, the bastard got clear, I'm afraid, sir."

He swiftly untied Michael's black, silk neckcloth and pulled it from around his neck. Then he was trying to prise Michael's hand away from his arm, blood pouring over the gloved hand.

"Come on, sir, let go now and I can bind it up."

Michael pulled his hand away, and then yelled again as Lloyd wrapped the neckcloth over the wound and tied it tight. "Sorry, sir, looks like it's broken as well."

Lloyd stood and got an arm under Michael's right arm. "Now then, sir, let's get you up on Rodrigo."

Michael tried to look around, "Duke…" he began.

"He's dead, sir, sorry, sir, shot in the neck, must have hit his artery. Now, up on this horse, quick now, sir."

Michael heard Sergeant Taylor shouting, "Hurry up, Lloyd. Riley, watch your right, man."

Somehow, Lloyd managed to push and shove Michael up onto Rodrigo, Michael gasping and swearing at the pain. Michael's sword was hanging from his wrist, he clutched at his left arm, squeezing it with his right hand, trying to stop the pain. Lloyd started to lead them away towards safety. He heard Taylor again.

"Riley, you go with them, cover them. The rest of you, back to the Squadron."

Michael turned his head to the side and saw four dragoons riding away. Lloyd was walking quickly, sabre in hand, Riley on his horse on their left. He felt faint, and swayed, heard Riley.

"Come on, now, Mister Roberts, sir, hang on, sir."

Michael felt a hand on his shoulder, shaking him and the pain shot through his arm. He roused himself, gritted his teeth, and watched the blood oozing between his fingers. "That glove's ruined", he thought to himself.

Somewhere behind the lines of waiting British infantry they found a group of busy surgeons. Lloyd eased Michael down, freed his sword from his wrist and put it in the scabbard. Michael stood, shakily. He looked up at Riley.

"Thank you, Riley," he said, "and you, Lloyd." He paused, to take a deep breath. "I think I can manage now. You should get back to the Squadron." He tried to smile, but could only manage a grimace.

"Begging your pardon, sir, but I don't think that's a very good idea." Lloyd looked across the scene at the surgeons. "They look might busy, sir, and I can't see our surgeons."

"Very well, Lloyd." He gave in. "Riley, see if you can find our baggage, get Francisco and Parra over here, then you can go back to the Squadron. How's that, Lloyd."

"Chwarae teg, sir, that will be just fine," Lloyd looked grim, and Riley rode quickly away.

Lloyd finally prevailed on a much harassed surgeon to look at Michael. The man was brusque, quick and efficient. The neckcloth was cut away and the sleeves of Michael's jacket and shirt were unceremoniously sliced open. At the surgeon's direction Lloyd held the wound closed and he swiftly stitched up the wound with silk thread, every stitch a vicious stab. To no one in particular the Surgeon muttered, "It's a clean cut, it should heal well. Missed the artery, thank God." Then a roller bandage was wrapped around his arm and tied snugly.

With the wound closed the surgeon gently moved Michael's arm, causing him to wince and grit his teeth at the sharp pain. The arm was put in a sling. "I'm afraid your arm is broken as well, Lieutenant, but it's a clean break and should knit nicely if you keep your arm still for three months or so, and then another month to get full use of it back."

He then advised Michael to find his way to the hospital at Castanheira, twenty miles back into Portugal. With that he was gone.

It took Riley an hour, but he brought Francisco and Parra to where Michael was now resting, his back to a low stone wall. Lloyd and Parra helped Michael up into Johnny's saddle, his spare, civilian one. The Welshman mounted Rodrigo and, looking anxious, asked Michael, "Are you sure you will be alright, sir?"

Michael managed a smile. "Yes, of course. Now, both of you, back to the Squadron, Sergeant Taylor will be missing you." He watched for a moment as the two dragoons rode off in search of the Regiment. His arm hurt like the very devil, and just hung uselessly in the sling. He didn't like to think about it too much. Instead he turned to Francisco and Parra. "Let's go and find this hospital," he said, and urged Johnny forward.

Chapter 19

Three weeks later, Michael, Francisco and Parra rode wearily up to the stables of Michael's home in Lisbon. Michael's arm was still not strong enough to grip anything, but was slowly improving. The wound itself was healing, leaving a dull ache, and now he just had to be careful not to knock it against anything and let the bones knit. Even with his arm in a sling he could at least now manage to mount and dismount without help. Senhora Santiago fussed more than ever when she saw the sling.

Michael sent Francisco off, as usual, to see his sister, but asked him to return later that evening, as he needed help and Lloyd was with the Regiment. Two hours later he was back, with a not unexpected message from Roberta, she would call on him in the morning. He was a little disappointed that she hadn't come straight to see him, he assumed Francisco had told her why he was back in Lisbon, but then he had to remind himself that things were different between them now.

He rose early, and Francisco shaved him and helped him to dress in his civilian clothes. He arranged for Francisco to serve coffee when Roberta arrived, to save Senhora Santiago the climb up the stairs from kitchen to drawing room. He dispatched Bernardo to the tailor where Jorge worked. He needed a new dress jacket. He gently tried to move his fingers, to make a fist. It was slow, but he thought he could detect an improvement.

Roberta arrived, and looked different, and it took him a moment to realise what it was. She had a real sparkle in her eyes, and just seemed lighter of heart and spirit. He took her hand and kissed her cheek. "Da Rocha is good for you," he said, smiling with genuine delight.

"Oh, Michael, is it so obvious?"

"Yes, I'm afraid so."

She blushed, a little, and pointed to his arm. "But you, Michael, you don't look so good, how bad is it?"

Michael shrugged, and tried to make light of his wounded arm. "It aches, if I knock it, it hurts. I can't grip anything. It is slowly improving, but it's annoying."

"What do the surgeons say?"

"They say that I must give it time, that there is no reason why I shouldn't recover full use of it."

"How long will you be in Lisbon?"

"I don't know, two or three months, until I can ride with it again. A one armed dragoon isn't a lot of use." He took a sip of his coffee. "Err, I was wondering," he looked out of the window, avoiding Roberta's eyes, "how is Catarina?"

"Ha!" Michael heard the annoyance in her voice, and winced. "Yes, you need pull a face, Senhor Roberts. Well, you need have no fears on that score. She has gone back to Coimbra, back to her quinta, a wealthy and independent young woman." She paused, waiting for some reaction from Michael. She waited in vain. "She was a bitterly disappointed woman, Michael."

"I had to go; you know that."

"Oh, yes, of course." Her voice dripped sarcasm. "But you could have sent some word, anything."

Silence fell.

"I will not be cross with you, Michael. I know the story, I understand, even though I think that you are wrong. And I remember what you told me, about that priest, I just hope that what he said comes to pass, otherwise…" She left the rest unsaid.

They sat in silence and drank their coffee. Eventually Michael broke the silence. "How is Senhor da Rocha?"

Roberta smiled as she answered. "He is very well, thank you. And you are right, he is good for me. Oh, Michael, I haven't felt like this for a long, long time, it's..." She stopped. "I'm sorry, Michael, I shouldn't talk like this to you."

"Why not, we are friends, are we not?" He looked hard at her.

"Yes, Michael, of course we are."

"Then I am happy for you, Roberta." And he realised that he was. He decided that now was as good a time as any. "I have some good news."

"Oh?"

"Yes. I have recovered my father's diamonds."

"What! Oh, goodness. How? Where were they? Who had them? Who is Augusto?"

Michael laughed, gently, at her surprise and confusion, and then told her the tale.

"So," Roberta said, thoughtfully, "you are now quite a wealthy young man. Very eligible, in fact..."

"Roberta, no!"

She burst out laughing. "Oh, Michael, your face. But I am very happy for you, truly I am."

A companionable silence fell, then Roberta suddenly said, "And now, I have something else that I must tell you, you said you were worried about Francisco?" Michael nodded. "Well, you might not like this, but Alexandre's valet has left him, well, he got rid of him, actually, too fond of the bottle. Anyway, he's looking for a new valet, and I just thought..."

"Oh!" Michael thought for a moment. "That sounds good, and I suppose it would mean he would see more of

Constanca. But I still need him, Lloyd is with the Regiment."

Roberta, practical as ever had an answer. "Then we must find someone for you, and to help the Santiagos, I have not forgotten that either, and I might have an idea that will serve both purposes." She smiled.

Michael laughed. "You have all worked out already, don't you!"

"Of course. Constanca has an aunt, a sensible lady, who has a young son of twenty. He has a sense of adventure, but is also sensible like his mother. Her husband was killed in fighting last year. She was working for a family in Lisbon, but they have left for the south where they have property, and did not need her anymore. I can recommend her, Michael."

"What about you? Don't you need more help?"

"No, the Marcelinos have finally gone back to Coimbra, so I get by quite nicely with just Constanca. And Alexandre has servants as well."

"Ah, yes, of course." Michael grinned at her, and she waved her fan at him.

"Now, Michael, do not tease, it as bad as you sulking!" they both laughed. "As you have no duty to call upon your time, I shall send them to see you, shall we say tomorrow at ten o'clock?"

"Don't you think it might be an idea to speak to Francisco about this?"

"Oh, but I have, last night."

Michael simply shook his head and gave in to the inevitable.

By mid-June, Michael was beginning to see and feel a definite improvement in his arm. The cut had healed, leaving nasty looking scar. He was keen to get full use of it back, and quickly. Two regiments of dragoons had been reduced from four squadrons to three, and the excess officers sent home. Michael feared that the same could happen to the light dragoon regiments, and if he was still on the sick list, he would be among the first to be sent to England. Not that the Sixteenth had a lot of officers to lose, he had heard that Captain Belli had been taken prisoner, and Blake had died of wounds. Weyland had been wounded slightly, but was back with the Regiment. In the meantime he acquired a new dress jacket from Tavares, who had used the lace and buttons off the damaged one. He had also got a new valise, and ordered replacement horse furniture and appointments through Collyer, the Regimental Agent. Everything on Duke had been lost. He hadn't done anything about finding another horse. Then he received word that Colonel Archer was going home sick. He had not enjoyed good health and was handing command of the Regiment to Major Pelly. He wasn't sure of Archer's movements, but he rode out to Belem to see the officer responsible for billeting, and offered to accommodate the Colonel while he was waiting for a ship home.

In the event, Archer only needed one night in Lisbon, but gladly accepted Michael's hospitality. They dined together, just the two of them, and then sat with a good bottle of port. The evening was warm and a gentle breeze was coming through the open windows and into the house from the Tagus. Archer had brought Michael up to date with the Regiment, including the events of Fuentes that Michael had missed. He knew about Belli and poor Blake, but then Archer gave him some fresh news.

"Did you know that Sergeant Taylor was killed?" he asked.

"Damn, no, I didn't. He was a very good man. How is Mrs Taylor? What will happen about her?"

"She has taken it well. I suppose the wives are always half ready for it. Of course, we should ship her home, but, frankly, she's too useful, keeps the other wives in order. Williams got made up to Sergeant."

Michael nodded, "He should do well. Who got the corporal's stripes?"

"Ah, yes." Archer hesitated. "That would be Lloyd."

"What? Oh, I see."

"As you know he's been a corporal before, and now he seems to have overcome his fondness for the bottle, it seemed a good idea to give him another chance. It's a compliment to you, but it means you will need to find a new batman."

"Yes, sir, I will."

"I asked him if he would prefer to stay as your batman, I know he has been with you on a lot of your, err, special errands. But he said not." Archer paused. "Oh, yes, and there's the question of your horse, Lloyd is still riding it. Perhaps you could let Major Pelly know what you want to do about it?"

Michael thought for a moment. "Well, sir, we are always short of horses, and I don't exactly need it at the moment. I see no reason why Lloyd shouldn't continue with it, and look after it for me, until I can rejoin, if that's acceptable to you, sir."

"It's a trifle unconventional, but you are quite right about the shortage of horses, so I have no objection. Perhaps you can write to Pelly and tell him so, tell him I am in agreement."

"Of course, sir"

Archer sat quietly for a moment and Michael sensed some hesitation before he asked. "But tell me, how are you?"

Michael lifted his left arm and flexed his fingers a little. "It's slow, sir, but it is improving every day. I have seen one of the surgeons out at Belem, sir, and he said I should get full use back, in time. Another six weeks, less if I'm lucky. Then I will have to recover my strength in it."

"Good, good, I'm glad to hear it." He pulled out his watch. "I have an early start, Roberts, wouldn't do to miss my ship, so I shall bid you a good night, and thank you for your hospitality. I hope, one day, that I may be able to return it in England."

After Archer had gone, Michael poured himself one more glass of port, and took it up to his room. He sat in the late evening twilight, and felt sorry for himself. Separated from his Regiment, just when he had chosen it over wealth and commerce, Roberta lost to da Rocha, leaving him feeling abandoned, and Lloyd choosing stripes over their agreement, another abandonment. He looked at the portrait of Elaine, standing on the table by his bed. He thought of Catarina. Had he made a mistake there? He thought not, to pretend love when his heart was bound to another would have been wrong on so many counts.

In his dark mood Michael felt his anger, still potent, but lying quiet at the moment. He could, he thought, control it, use it as necessary. Use it against those who crossed him.

Archer left early, leaving Michael to take a solitary breakfast. It was brought up to him in the dining room by Senhora Pinheiro. She and her son, Frederico, had proved worthy of Roberta's recommendation, and there was a cheerful, active feel to the house, although he missed Francisco. He remembered something Senhora Santiago had said to him recently when he had said something to her about the difference Bernardo and the Pinheiros had made.

"Ah, Michael," she still called him Michael when they were alone, otherwise it was Senhor Michael, "it is much better now. All that is missing is a Mistress of the house." Only his Baba would have dared to say that to him. She had quickly added, "Now that we have the Pinheiros perhaps you should think of entertaining more." He had just laughed the whole episode off. Now he gave it a little thought, and then wandered down to the kitchen.

He found Senhora Santiago and Senhora Pinheiro busy, and the sole occupants. "Senhora Santiago," he began, "I have been thinking. Do you think we might manage a small gathering one evening? A small soiree?"

Had Michael realised the consequences of that simple question, he might have kept quiet. He had no idea of what he was about to unleash. Senhora Santiago had positively beamed at him, and then the work had started. To be fair, his role was pretty much limited to arranging the guests, and, he realised, agreeing to Senhora Santiago's suggestions, and paying the bills. For five days the house was in turmoil, and then the evening arrived. Michael had spent most of the day out of the way in the stables with Parra. Ostensibly he was going over the new saddle and horse appointments that had arrived from England a few days earlier. It was entirely unnecessary, and Frederico kept appearing with questions from Senhora Santiago, the final one being, "Beg your pardon, Senhor, but Senhora Santiago says isn't it time for you to get ready, and there is hot water for you to shave, sorry, Senhor."

Roberta and da Rocha were the first to arrive, she had promised she would be, to help greet the guests, many of whom she had suggested. General Peacocke was punctual, and arrived with Commissary Dunmore. Shortly after them came General and Senhora de Silva. Senhora Lourenco, Senhor and Senhora Rodrigues, Senhor Furtado joined the gathering, along with half a dozen couples Michel didn't really know, but had met on various social occasions. As Roberta had advised, "if you want to receive invitations, you must also issue them".

The evening proceeded with much laughter, a little dancing in the ballroom to a string quartet that had appeared, there was good food and plenty to drink. The view across the Tagus was much admired. De Silva and his wife were standing in one window, looking out at the broad reach of the river where the fleet lay. Michael joined them.

"Senhor Roberts, this is a splendid view," the General observed, "But, tell me, what is that building I can see?"

"Oh, just the stables," Michael replied.

"Really? Do you think we might steal away for a few minutes. I would like to see them." He turned to his wife. "Forgive me, my dear, I promise not to be long." She gave him a little, knowing smile.

Michael was a bit taken aback. "Yes, certainly, General. This way." And led him out of the ballroom and downstairs.

The General followed Michael until they were approaching the stables, then he put a hand on Michael's arm. "I think this will do."

"General?"

"Forgive me, please, Mister Roberts, but it is necessary that I have a few words with you in private." He waved his arm around. "Here there is no risk that we might be overheard, and if we are quick, our absence will barely be noticed. I am afraid that I have serious news. Someone in my organisation has been passing information to de Barcarena. They have been dealt with, but we have an idea that some of what he passed on concerns you."

"Me?"

"Yes, I am afraid so. To be brief, it is possible, even probable that de Barcarena knows about your involvement in breaking Renard's spy network." He paused, taking a deep breath. "It is also possible that he knows Renard is dead and that you killed him."

"Damn!" Michael swore.

"I am afraid that it gets worse. It is highly likely that he has passed this information to the French."

"What, but I put an end to that back in February!"

"Ah, so that was you!"

"Oh, err…"

"Do not concern yourself with that. No one will learn of it from me. In fact I think it was rather well done. However, the death of the Venâncios made him suspicious. He started asking questions. One of my men was rather overwhelmed to be courted by such figure in Portuguese society, and told him too much. He tried to get confirmation from another, who, fortunately, came to me." De Silva shrugged. "He won't be learning anything more, but I fear the damage has been done. He also knows about Roberta; she is now under a discreet guard. Da Rocha knows nothing. She is, understandably, giving up her work for me, although she has promised to keep me apprised of any interesting gossip. It is ironic that she should be revealed just now. Anyway, de Barcarena knows that Roberta introduced you to the Venâncios through Catarina Cardoso, so he may also suspect you of having a hand in their demise."

"But what can we do?"

"I can do nothing, Senhor, I have put a discreet watch on de Barcarena, but I can't keep it up for much longer, and it has to be intermittent to avoid detection. He is a man with powerful friends who would require some very, very convincing evidence to turn against him. Unfortunately that has not been forthcoming." He looked around, and then went on. "What I can tell you is that twice a week he visits a lady friend, as regular as clock work. So regularly that we do not bother to watch him on those nights. He has bodyguards, but he always leaves them in the street, and they go off to the nearest tavern for an hour. The lady has rooms on the Praça das Flores, above a seamstress' shop, on the south side. He arrives at seven o'clock. But, Senhor, there is nothing that I can do." De Silva emphasised the "I".

Michael nodded, thoughtfully.

"His next visit will be tomorrow night. Now, I think we should get back in before we are missed."

Back inside it seemed they had not been missed, and the two men quietly joined a small group of Roberta, da Rocha and Senhora de Silva. The Senhora turned as they approached.

"Ah, there you are, Lucas, I was telling Roberta and Senhor da Rocha about the performance at the Opera. I have taken the liberty of inviting them to join us in our box." She turned a smile on Michael. "Senhor Roberts, perhaps you would care to join us as well. It is the day after tomorrow. Do say you will come."

Michael gave her a little bow. "I will be delighted, Senhora."

The following evening Michael was in Praça das Flores, just as the church bells struck the half hour. He strolled casually around the square, no one took any notice of the scruffy looking individual sloping around in a disreputable looking cloak, that hid the sling supporting his left arm. A door next to the seamstress opened into a gloomy hallway, and Michael could just make out a stairway. He pulled up a scarf over his face, drew a pistol from inside his sling and climbed slowly and quietly up the stairs. To the front of the building was the dim outline of a door, visible in the little light that penetrated that far. He tapped gently.

He heard light footsteps, and then the door was pulled wide open and an attractive, but scantily dressed woman started to say "Francisco, you are…" Michael thrust her back into the room, kicking the door closed behind him, and pointed the pistol in her face.

"Senhorita, if you value your life, not a sound." Wide eyed, she nodded. "Where is your bedroom?" She pointed, and he pushed her into the room and shoved her face down on the bed. Carefully he secured her arms behind her back with a cord he had brought with him, wincing as his arm complained of the treatment. Then he gagged her with a silk stocking that had been lying on the floor.

"Now, Senhorita, all you have to do is lie there quietly for a little while, and you will come to no harm. Please, do not be difficult, or try anything rash." She nodded.

Michael left her lying there and went back into the main room. The door from the stairs opened directly into it. He placed a chair where he could see the woman and watch the door, but would not be immediately visible to anyone entering. Then he realised that the woman had thought he was de Barcarena, and he had knocked, but that would not be a problem. He rested the pistol on his lap, brought it to full cock and settled to wait.

Some five minutes passed, then Michael thought he heard a door close downstairs. Sure enough, a tap at the door came moments later. He rose silently from the chair and crossed the room to the door, holding the pistol in his left hand by the barrel. With his right hand he pulled the door open, keeping behind it.

"What are you doing, Mariana?" Curious and unsuspecting de Barcarena walked into the room, and Michael pushed the door shut with his body, taking hold of his pistol in his right hand and raising it to point at the man's face.

Stunned, De Barcarena took a couple of steps back and said, "Do you know who I am?"

"Baron Francisco de Barcarena."

"Yes, I am, and you…"

He got no further, Michael pulled the trigger, and shot de Barcarena square in the chest. Then he spun round, ran for the stairs, and in seconds was out in the square. He could hear a few shouts of enquiry about the noise, and quietly and calmly walked away.

The following evening Michael joined the de Silvas, Roberta and da Rocha at the opera at Sao Carlos. The occasion was a performance by Angelica Catalani of La Morte di Semiramide. There was no doubting the quality and skill of Catalani, and although no great lover of the opera, Michael realised he was witnessing something special.

At the interval they all went to the refreshment room, and the glasses of ice cold white wine were welcome. The General led Michael aside while the others were chatting with acquaintances.

"Lieutenant, have you heard the news, all Lisbon is full of it?"

"What news is that, General?" Michael's face was expressionless.

"Last night, de Barcarena was visiting his mistress, and someone shot him. He's dead."

"What? Really? That's, err, a surprise?"

"I don't know about a surprise, Lieutenant, but it did provide an excuse to search de Barcarena's home, looking for anything that might to point to someone who had a reason to kill him."

"And did you find anything?"

"No, nothing like that, but we did find compelling evidence that he was engaged in correspondence with the French."

"Oh!"

"Yes, oh. Some of it was very interesting. Unfortunately it confirmed my suspicions that he had passed on information about you. Strangely that particular evidence cannot now be found."

"Ah, thank you, General. Do you have any idea who might have killed him?"

"Not the slightest. We are working on the possibility of a jealous lover. Shall we rejoin our company?"

Half listening to the conversation, Michael happened to glance out of one of the tall windows that pierced the upper façade of the building.

In the fading, evening light, a woman was standing in the square outside the Opera House, wearing a dark, hooded cloak, her back to him. Suddenly she threw back the hood, and her copper red hair flashed. Her head turned slightly for a split second, and he caught a fleeting glimpse of a profile. It was impossible. Then her head tipped to one side for a moment. His companions were left bemused as Michael suddenly broke from them, striding across the room, pushing his way through the crowd with barely an 'excuse me' or apology. He got to the doors, crashed through and on to the stairs down to the theatre's lobby. He ran across the almost empty lobby to the theatre doors and through them. In the square a barouche, its hood down, had drawn up, and a man was handing the woman into it. He closed the door even as Michael strode forward, then she turned, and looked straight at him, the late light of the setting sun falling full on her face, framed by her red hair. Michael stopped dead; she was a complete stranger. The door on the other side of the carriage slammed, and it immediately moved off. The square outside the theatre was empty. Stunned, confused, Michael stood there, looking all around. There was no one there. Then the realisation came to him, that was the very point, the truth that he had to accept. There was no one there, she had gone.

A feeling of almost overwhelming loss swept over him, along with a sense of release, of freedom, freedom because he was alone, there really was no one who he was bound to, but the sense of freedom quickly gave way to a feeling of utter loneliness and abandonment. His love for Elaine was a beautiful memory, and like all memories, it was in the past. It was gone, she was gone, forever. He stood for a few minutes, tears rolling down his face. Then it came to him that this was what she had wanted for him, for him to be free. Father Nascimento was right, he had to let her go, and with that revelation he felt a great weight lift from his soul. He would hold the precious memories, but they would not hold him. He composed himself, blew his nose, and turned to walk back into the theatre, back to his friends, and towards the future.

BRINDLE BOOKS

Brindle Books Ltd

We hope that you have enjoyed this book. To find out more about Brindle Books Ltd, including news of new releases, please visit our website:

http://www.brindlebooks.co.uk

There is a contact page on the website, should you have any queries, and you can let us know if you would like email updates of news and new releases. We promise that we won't spam you with lots of sales emails, and we will never sell or give your contact details to any third party.

If you purchased this book online, please consider leaving an honest review on the site from which you purchased it. Your feedback is important to us, and may influence future releases from our company.

Also by

David J Blackmore

Published by Brindle Books Ltd.

To The Douro

Wellington's Dragoon; Book One

A young man's decision to fight leads to a war within a war...

To love...

To loss...

...and a quest for vengeance, as he plays a vital role for the future Duke of Wellington.

To by this book from Amazon, you can scan the QR code below.

Also by

David J Blackmore

Published by Brindle Books Ltd.

Secret Lines

Wellington's Dragoon; Book Two

From the battlefield of Talavera,
by way of the guerrilla's merciless war,
to the back streets of Lisbon,
our hero fights to keep Wellington's great secret.
Can Michael gain the revenge he seeks and protect
the Secret Lines?

To by this book from Amazon, you can scan the QR
code below.

Printed in Great Britain
by Amazon